MW01611953

Heaven's Blue

Inspirational Romance

by
Penelope Marzec

Copyright 2004

ISBN: 1-58749-446-9

Earthling Press ~ United States of America

Dedication

For my cousin, Sandy Karchella, and all the other lost children. May the Lord find them and bring them home.

See that you do not despise one of these little ones, for I say to you that their angels in heaven always look upon the face of my heavenly Father...it is not the will of your heavenly Father that one of these little ones be lost.
Matthew 18:10 & 14

Chapter One

From the top step at the entrance to Holy Redeemer Church, Samantha Lyons searched far out past the edge of town. The tiny gray speck on the horizon that was Field Station Number Thirty-Seven sat in the endless green of salt hay. Sighing, she fixed her gaze on her tiny home, a spot easy to miss unless one knew where to look for it. Despite the lack of conveniences, she had come to love the modest dwelling.

For two years Samantha had studied the effects of a new pesticide on the salt marsh mosquito as the final application of her doctoral thesis. The very real possibility that she would not finish her work was bad enough, but the idea of leaving her first real home tore at her. Sorrow welled up in her throat, threatening to choke her.

Shading her eyes, she glanced up and down the main street of Clam Creek, New Jersey. She doubted that she would catch a glimpse of the college junior who had signed on to be her assistant. Ginger Blaine had decided that the lonely life of a research scientist on a salt marsh was no way to live and had driven away, vowing never to return.

Lowering her hand, Samantha ambled slowly down the church steps, forcing herself to rein in her emotions. The humid air and searing morning sunshine of another steamy August day did not bother her. Yet, the sense of loss that swept through her felt like a black stone in the pit of her stomach. Without Ginger's help, she would have to leave Clam Creek.

She had known from the first that Ginger wouldn't make a suitable assistant, but since nobody else had applied for the position, she had been forced to hire the flighty young woman. Waves of heat shimmered from the roof of her blue Chevy as she approached it. She had parked her car in the brutal sunshine, but with the weather forecast for clear skies, and sleepy Clam Creek's almost nonexistent crime rate, she felt safe in leaving the windows open. Nobody had to worry about anyone stealing anything in the tiny town. So when she opened her car door and saw someone in her vehicle, it startled her so badly that she dropped the keys she held in her hand.

A small boy holding a chocolate ice cream cone sat on the passenger seat of her car. Melted brown ice cream covered his chin and he looked at her with wide, round eyes as full of fear as those of the timid deer that occasionally wandered into the field station. The child had straight, black hair falling into his eyes, which were the same hazy blue as the summer sky. Samantha didn't have any idea who he was.

She slowly bent down to pick up her keys, keeping her gaze fixed on the child. "Hi," she said. "Where's your mom and dad?"

The little boy's face crumpled. At almost the same moment, Samantha heard the frantic sound of a deep male voice calling.

"James! James! Where are you?"

Samantha rose, turned, and saw a man running down the street toward her.

The boy wailed. "Daddy! Daddieeeeeee!" His ice cream cone tilted and a large brown glob landed on the car seat. The youngster screamed louder.

"I'm here, James!"

As the man raced toward Samantha's car, she noticed that the ice cream shop owner followed him in hot pursuit.

"Hey, Meester. You no pay me!" The rotund ice cream entrepreneur shouted. The young boy's father skidded to a stop when he reached Samantha's car. He yanked open the passenger door, reached in, and quickly pulled his son into his arms.

"What are you doing with my kid?" he demanded.

"What's he doing in my car?"

The boy sobbed. "My ice cream, Daddy! My ice cream!"

"Hey you! You owe me a dollar feefty!" the shop owner roared, creating more of a ruckus.

"Look, I told you I had the money in my car!" the father growled back.

Samantha shook her head and then studied the scruffy pair of father and son. The dad hadn't shaved in a few days, though the stubble on his chin didn't detract from his good looks. At some point in his life, the man must have lifted weights because he had wonderfully broad shoulders, which his T-shirt only seemed to emphasize. She felt a blush heating her cheeks. "Thees your car?" the angry proprietor asked.

"No," the father answered. "Mine's blue…"

His voice trailed off as he blinked in the bright sunlight at the car's finish.

"Hey, thees one is blue," the shop owner pointed out.

"Yeah, well—mine's a Chev…Samantha saw the puzzled frown cloud the father's face.

He paused as his gaze moved from one end of the car to the other.

"Okay," he muttered. "This car looks almost the same as mine. Is that what happened, James? You thought this was our car?"

The boy nodded his head and took in a ragged breath.

The father glared at Samantha. "You should have rolled up your windows and locked your car."

"You should have been holding your son's hand." Samantha reached under the seat for a roll of paper towels to remove the brown glob of ice cream, which spread out as it melted.

The shop owner boomed, "You shoulda keep the money in your pocket, not in your car!"

"All right!" the father grumbled. "Can't you be patient a minute? It's not like you have a long line of customers in that shop." He pointed to the deserted ice cream parlor up the street.

"You gonna cheat me!" The shop owner shook his fist in a threatening manner.

The harried father swore. "I'll see if I've got any change." He walked back up the street with his son sobbing softly on his shoulder and the shop owner dogging his footsteps.

Samantha tugged a few more towels off the roll and dropped them on the chocolate goo. She glanced up and couldn't help but notice how the father dragged his feet along the street. It appeared as though he didn't have just the weight of his son on his shoulders but the crushing load of the world. An odd suspicion set her nerves on edge. Maybe the father really didn't have the money in his car.

She swiped once more at the mess on her front seat. She couldn't ignore the lost look in the child's eyes. He reminded her of herself at around the same age. A small chill wound its way up her spine despite the heat of the day.

Suddenly, the father and the shop proprietor commenced yelling at each other all over again, loud enough for the entire town to hear.

"This is one dollar and ten cents!" The shop owner had his teeth bared. "I told you it was one-feefty!"

"So I'm a little short." The man clutched his son against him. "I really thought I had the exact amount."

Samantha dropped the messy paper towels in a nearby garbage can. Without a moment's hesitation, she dug in her handbag for some change and hurried up the street to the scene.

"I think you must have dropped this when you bent over to take your son out of my car." She held out the coins in her hand.

"No...I..." The father shot her a wary look. "Uh. Yeah, that must be mine." He reached out and she dropped the change into his palm.

Samantha saw the relief break out on his face as he stared at the coins.

"Thanks...I..." His eyes narrowed and he peered at her for a moment with such suspicion that she took a step back. He turned to the shop owner and dropped the money into the man's beefy paw.

"Well, that's all settled then. Here's your forty cents, sir. No hard feelings."

The shop owner carefully counted out the coins and closed the money tightly in his fist before heading back to his store, mumbling loud enough for everyone to hear. "Hmmph! I know the minute I see him—he's a bum!"

"My ice cream fell," the boy whimpered.

"Yeah, sport." The father patted the child tenderly. "Sorry."

His shoulders slumped in defeat as he began to turn toward his own blue Chevy. Samantha followed him.

"There's plenty of doughnuts and cider at Holy Redeemer," she suggested.

"A church?" The father turned a mocking smile toward her, marring his face. "I don't think so."

"I like doughnuts." The little boy looked ready to burst into tears again. "I'm hungry! Doughnuts, Daddy. Doughnuts."

He muttered a curse and ran his hand through his hair.

Samantha drew her mouth into a thin line and tried to ignore the foul language. The child was hungry and should be fed.

"Everyone at Holy Redeemer is very friendly, and really, there's a ton of leftovers. They'll just go stale if you don't eat them. They're homemade."

"I don't want to listen to a lot of scripture verses while I'm eating."

Samantha took a deep breath and glanced into the interior of the man's car. Pillows, blankets, boxes and clothing had been stuffed haphazardly inside. It seemed all too obvious to her. The man and his son were living in that automobile.

She made a mental note of the brand-name labels on the clothes and shoes the two wore. They hadn't always been destitute. While they could be moving, or vacationing on a shoestring, they could be running, too. The very thought of her own miserable youth made her ball her hands into fists.

She shrugged as casually as she could, trying to push the bad memories to the back of her mind.

"Too bad about the doughnuts, then. The members of Holy Redeemer do have a tendency to sprinkle Bible verses and proverbs into everything they say."

"I want a doughnut!" James voiced his opinion loudly.

The father stared down at the sidewalk for a moment. Samantha saw his jaw clench.

"No one is going to tie you up and force you to become a Christian." She could not prevent the touch of exasperation that edged into her voice.

The father narrowed his eyes and glared at her, but then his son sobbed.

"Daddy, my belly hurts."

Samantha's heart squeezed painfully at the boy's cry. She clutched at her waist and remembered the times she, too, had felt that gnawing hunger. Her temper rose. How could that man allow his son to go without food? But when she looked at him again, she saw that his features had softened. He rubbed his son's back to soothe the child.

"I'm not afraid of becoming a believer any time soon," he scoffed. "So lead us to those doughnuts."

* * *

My name is not Alan Nugent! It is David Halpern. Had he stuttered when he introduced himself? Yes. His face grew hot despite the cooler air in the church basement. How could he erase thirty years of being Alan Nugent? But he had to—for Foster's—*James'* sake. He had created new identities to protect his son and himself, but the boy seemed to have an easier time making the adjustment than he did.

David Halpern. DAVID! David and James Halpern. Alan Nugent must vanish.

He watched James down four doughnuts and at least a half-quart of cider. Two elderly women in the kitchen seemed delighted with his son's prowess in packing away the gooey treats. After the second one, David tried to end James' binge, but the women would not hear of it.

"He's a growing boy!" they scolded.

David ate two doughnuts. He didn't doubt that he could have finished off an even dozen himself, but he didn't want to appear desperate, even though it took every ounce of his restraint to walk away from the platter.

The coffee helped. He closed his eyes and smelled the heavenly aroma wafting out of the hot cup in his hands. Yesterday, he'd been robbed, but a man in trouble with the law could hardly go to the police to demand justice. When he called his lawyer, he'd learned the counselor had gone on vacation.

Leaving a message on the answering machine had wasted most of his precious change. So what now? He couldn't blow his cover, not when he was so close to saving his son from Linda.

"Are you just passing through?"

David opened his eyes warily and studied the blond beauty who had introduced herself as Samantha Lyons. Her light hair looked genuine, a shade more like honey. He didn't detect any dark roots, so it couldn't be bleached as Linda's was. It had to be real, he decided.

But that fact alone did not make her trustworthy. He couldn't trust her. He couldn't trust anybody.

He didn't like the way she twisted a rubber band around her fingers, over and over, staring at him in a most expectant manner. He'd seen that look before from some of those overly zealous Christians eager to bring him back to the fold.

"I wasn't planning to hang around here," he answered.

"It's a lovely town, very quiet."

He found himself staring at her lips. Unadorned by any garish color, they were small but nicely shaped. In fact, with her sandals, gauzy skirt, and sleeveless blouse she radiated a sort of wholesomeness, reminding him of a television commercial for an all-natural soap or herbal shampoo.

"Nothing happens here. Clam Creek doesn't even have its own police force." Her voice dropped to a whisper.

An alarming suspicion swept through David. He rubbed his neck to try and wipe away the prickles of apprehension.

"You need cash and I need an assistant," she said softly.

The sudden proposition hit him with all the force of a head-on collision. He choked on the coffee.

"W-what are you talking about?" he sputtered.

"I'm doing research on mosquitoes in the marsh," she explained. "I need someone to catch them."

He drew his brows together. Was she some kind of lunatic? "You shouldn't have a problem with that. There are zillions of mosquitoes out there."

"Yes, but there are other insects, too."

In a graceful movement, she pitched the rubber band she had been toying with into a nearby garbage can and then folded her arms across her chest. David watched the color of her eyes harden to a steely gray.

"I need someone to specifically catch mosquitoes. Once they are caught, I have to spray them with an experimental pesticide and document the results."

Okay, maybe she wasn't a nut case. Testing pesticides sounded reasonable. David looked at James. His son needed a roof over his head, clean clothes, and food. Since they'd been on the road, David hadn't dared to use his credit card because the purchases could be traced.

"What's the pay?" he asked.

She turned her gaze to the floor and he tensed. Her evasive body language meant she was hiding something. So what? He was a wanted man. The irony of the situation might have struck him as comical, if he hadn't run out of options. "Well, there's plenty of food, a clean room with bunk beds—"

"Bunk beds!" James picked up on the word. "Kyle has bunk beds. I got to climb to the top. I could touch the ceiling!" He smiled.

"Kyle?" David asked.

A sudden look of fear widened James' light blue eyes. "My friend."

David's jaw clenched. What kind of father had he been? He didn't even know the names of his son's friends. A wave of remorse washed over him for all the time he had wasted. Still, he reminded himself that he hadn't really known. He hadn't truly understood the kind of mother Linda had become. Thinking of her sickened him and he nearly missed hearing Samantha softly mumble her wage offer. David was shocked at the meager amount.

"Lady—I can make more than that bagging fries and burgers."

He saw her stiffen.

"But I won't ask for your social security number. This will be strictly under the table. Cash."

Her remark knocked the wind right out of him. She had a sharp mind, and obviously she was just as desperate as he was.

Which couldn't be good. He threw the Styrofoam cup into a trash can.

"Let's go, James," he ordered his son.

"Daddy! No!" James snatched another doughnut and scurried under a table.

As David went after his son, Samantha darted in front of him and blocked the way.

"Look, my assistant quit and I just need someone for two weeks. That's all, I promise! I know it's boring work, but it's really important."

For a moment, David felt mesmerized. The woman's gray eyes held him entranced. He wanted to reach out to touch the delicate blond tendrils that framed her face and quivered as she pleaded with him.

Then he suddenly realized that the room had become silent. The elderly ladies shot disapproving stares at him. He cursed himself for being such a fool. He had known he would have to pay a price for seeking sustenance in a church.

"James!" he rumbled. "Get out from under that table,

now! And you," he growled at the woman impeding his escape. "Get out of my way!"

She didn't flinch. She glared at him with those gunmetal gray eyes and the sweat beaded up on his brow. It felt like he was staring into the barrel of a rifle.

"How can you drag that child around when he needs a roof over his head and food in his stomach?"

Her voice sounded so cold that a shaft of ice went right through David's heart. He wanted to shout at her, to tell her that he loved his son so much he had walked out of his job as vice-president of a major insurance firm, leaving one day without telling a soul in a frantic effort to save his son. However, the lump in his throat prevented him from saying anything. If he hadn't been robbed, if he hadn't been reduced to the status of a homeless man, everything would have been fine.

"Do you know I could report you?"

At that threat, David swallowed hard and found his voice.

"Look lady—"

"Samantha," she reminded.

"It doesn't matter what your name is!" he shot back. "I don't know anything about you. I don't know whether this 'study' of yours is legitimate. Maybe this is just some crazy scheme you dreamed up, maybe you intend to test the pesticide on me and my son like some mad scientist…"

He ended his tirade when he saw her shake her head. A sad smile touched her lips.

"I've been called dedicated *and* crazy, but never mad." A mist clouded her eyes, melting them into a gentle soft fog. "For what it's worth, I can guarantee that you will not be affected by the pesticide. You won't have any contact with it at all."

David stared at her with his heart hammering. He felt like an idiot.

Her unhappy smile turned tight and brittle. "If I don't finish this study, I will have wasted two years of my life plus I lose my happy little home."

Her eyes turned misty. Either she had the makings of an Academy Award winning actress or she was telling the truth.

David thought about the weeks he and James had already spent running: sleeping in a different motel room every night, buying a different car once, reading the papers and watching the television news, fearing that they would be the subject of the headlines. Living in a state of constant tension, hoping that the sound of a baying dog in the distance wouldn't be a bloodhound hot on their trail.

Now, without any money, they could wind up sleeping in the car every night, as they had done last night. With empty pockets, he might have to resort to stealing food. He was in enough trouble. Did he want to add burglary to his record? He realized he had no choice but to accept her offer.

"Okay, I'll catch some of your mosquitoes," he conceded.

Her smile widened, reminding him of the silver crescent moon that hung in the sky only last night when he thought all his hope was gone.

Chapter Two

Samantha's palms dripped with sweat as she drove to the field station with David's car following along behind her. Had she made one of the worst decisions of her life? Nobody hired a total stranger. Until now, she would never have even considered it. While it was bad enough that she knew nothing of the man and his son, what would happen when her new male employee met Cassie? A tense knot formed in her stomach.

She knew Cassie would take an immediate dislike to him. It was all Samantha's own fault. She had no one to blame but herself for Cassie's outrageous behavior. Though Cassie adored women and children, men brought out her baser instincts. Still, Samantha wouldn't have to worry about anyone in town starting any slanderous rumors with Cassie on guard. But if David was frightened away, all Samantha's hopes would disintegrate.

She carefully thought out her options and her shoulders slumped. She really didn't have any alternatives. Her grant ran out at the end of the month and without a documented conclusion, she had no chance of getting another grant. She would have to look for another job and leave her beloved home in the marsh.

No. She sat up straight and squared her shoulders. She would not quit. No matter what, she would struggle to finish her research and remain in her home—with or without David's help—even if it meant not sleeping for days on end.

She had prayed long and hard in church. David Halpern's arrival in Clam Creek seemed to be the answer to her petition, since the likelihood of anyone else breezing into the backwater town was remote.

Besides, she couldn't possibly let young James Halpern suffer. She sighed and the old pain stabbed at her heart.

Seeing that little boy started her mind whirling with
flashbacks of her own young life, which certainly hadn't
dimmed with the years. There had been very little joy in her
childhood.

She comforted herself with the idea that maybe she could
talk some sense into David's head, though suspicions crowded
her mind. Could the child be the prize in a custody battle,
just as she had been? Or was she merely assuming that
because she had been a victim herself? She intended to search
the Internet to see if she could find any information about the
pair, but she sincerely hoped that her fears were way off track.

Then again, David could have committed some other
crime, something even more horrific.

No. She swept her hair off her shoulders and cast her
doubts to the back of her mind. David was the answer to her
prayers—a way out of her difficulty.

Samantha recalled a verse and God's promise. *God is
faithful and will not let you be tried beyond your strength; but
with the trial he will also provide a way out, so that you may be
able to bear it.*

As she drove over the rickety wooden bridge that
spanned the creek, the weight of her car on the old beams
made a series of familiar clunking sounds. She checked her
rearview mirror to be sure that David didn't become
unnerved by the archaic crossing, which had no railings or
guards. He eased his car slowly over the bridge, but he did
not stop or turn around. Samantha realized that she had been
holding her breath as she watched him.

If he was brave enough to cross that bridge, could he face
Cassie without blinking an eye? She gritted her teeth and
prayed that she could change Cassie's mind concerning men.

The field station came into full view as the level of the
dirt road rose another foot above sea level by a copse of
stunted cedars. The sight of the three gray buildings in the
afternoon light gave Samantha a catch in her throat. In only
two short years, that little cluster of simple shelters had
become her life. Two window boxes burst with the bright

magenta of impatiens. On the side of the cottage, tomato towers supported the lush foliage and tempting fruit she had coaxed to grow from a small plot of precious earth. White sheets fluttered in the breeze on a line strung between the cottage and a stunted lone pine.

She pulled up beside the cottage with her eyes growing misty. She had dared to put down roots here. Leaving it would be too painful to bear. She closed her eyes briefly and offered up another silent plea that David Halpern would help her finish her research. When she got out of her car, she saw James already scrambling across the yard.

"Daddy! I hear a dog barking! And look! There's a boat! Can we go for a ride?"

Samantha couldn't help smiling at the young child's innocent delight, but her smile faded as David emerged from his car and glanced around the small enclosure.

"This is a research facility?"

Though he wore a vague look of confusion, Samantha couldn't prevent the surge of anger rumbling through her.

"Your tax dollars, or lack thereof, at work." She could feel the flush burning on her cheeks. "It's funny how nobody wants to get bitten by a mosquito carrying a deadly virus, but the good, hard-working citizens of this state don't want to invest much money in preventive measures."

"I don't live in this state," he grumbled in his defense.

Immediately, Samantha saw a look of consternation steal across his features. It seemed obvious that he realized he had made an error. He had let slip one small detail, one undisguised fact about his life.

She crossed her arms and studied him carefully. "So, where are you from?"

"Kansas."

She doubted the answer he blurted out, but she didn't intend to press him now. That might scare him away, and she didn't want to do that, although Cassie might.

"It looks like this is about as far from civilization as you can get."

His features relaxed into an easy grin, successfully disarming Samantha. Until then, she hadn't known what a smile would do to his face. It made him devastatingly attractive.

"Mrs. Lyon?" James tugged at her skirt. "Do you have a dog?"

Samantha felt her heart sink as she gazed down at the boy's eager face. The moment of truth had arrived, so she faced it with a valiant smile and evaded the question.

"Why don't you call me Miss Samantha? I'd like that."

"Miss Samantha, don't you have a dog?" he tugged at her skirt with both hands.

Samantha bent down to the child's level and wiped her damp hands on her skirt carefully before answering.

"Yes, I do. I got her at the animal shelter. Nobody wanted her, even though she is the sweetest, most beautiful dog in the world. If you give her a hot dog, she'll be your true friend forever."

James' face fell. "I don't have a hot dog."

"I have an extra."

James' eyes opened wide. "You do?"

Samantha nodded. "But my dog will lick you with her tongue. Do you think you will mind that?"

James shook his head vigorously from side-to-side. Samantha stood up and took James' hand to lead him to the cottage.

"You didn't tell me you had a dog." David fell into step behind them.

Samantha stopped and faced him with her mouth feeling as dry as the reeds in the summer sun. She decided that the way to begin would be to extol her dog's virtues.

"She's quite mild-mannered with children," Samantha emphasized. "She adores them. They can even step on her and she won't complain. She absolutely loves having kids annoy her. They can pull her tail and her ears and she just laughs at them. She rolls on her back so they can pat her tummy."

David's right eyebrow shot upward.

"So the dog runs free?"

"Unless we have company," Samantha added hastily and felt a chill twist around her heart as she thought about losing the only extra pair of hands she would probably get. Her own tiny glimmer of hope evaporated.

"Daddy, Kyle's dog used to lick me all the time, even if I didn't give him a hot dog."

Samantha prayed that the pure happiness glowing on the child's face would convince his father to stay.

"Look, I'll introduce James to the dog first. She's old and I don't want to confuse her or wear her out or...well, you'll see, they'll get along fine." She forced a light note into her voice, though the tightness in her chest made that difficult. "You'd best stay outside until I call you."

Leading James by the hand, she went up to the cottage door and opened it. Cassie danced around them with happy barks, wagging her entire tail end.

James laughed. "She's licking my hand!"

"Let's get a hot dog," Samantha said as she hurried into the kitchen and opened the refrigerator. Cassie and James followed at her heels.

"Sit," Samantha ordered. Cassie obediently sat on her haunches and stared at her mistress expectantly.

James patted the dog's forehead. "I'm going to give her a hot dog now. Right?"

"Yes." Samantha pulled out her pet's favorite treat and handed it to James. "Hold it out to her and she'll gobble it down in nothing flat."

James squealed with glee as Cassie downed the hot dog. Cassie then licked him, waiting for another treat while raising her eyebrows inquiringly and wagging her tail the entire time.

"No more," Samantha told the dog. "You don't want to spoil your supper."

Cassie sighed as if she understood and lay down on the floor. James knelt beside her and patted her gently.

"I like Cassie," he said. "She's a good dog."

Samantha found herself wringing her hands repeatedly. How was she going to handle introducing David to Cassie? Maybe she could skip it altogether.

"Have you ever seen guinea pigs?" she asked James.

The boy shook his head.

"They're much smaller than Cassie, but they're nice animals. I have four in the lab."

"Do they bite?" James asked with a suddenly serious expression. Oddly enough, the young boy's face reminded her of all the old anxieties and paranoia from her past. The unexpected ache of it surged up from deep within her and nearly swamped her while her heart thudded ominously in her chest. She reached for the crucifix at her throat and held it. *Lord, let me help this child.*

Fighting to remain calm, she replied. "They only bite if you put your finger in front of their mouths. They think it's a carrot and they love to eat carrots."

James nodded. "Dogs don't like carrots."

"Correct, they like meat," she admitted.

* * *

David walked up to the screen door. He could see his son kneeling on the floor, patting the dog's head. The animal appeared to be a rather nondescript common mutt with a white and tan coat, thin and scrawny without the classic form of any pedigree.

He shivered despite the sweltering temperature as the old painful memories weighed down on his shoulders. He and Linda had a dog, a magnificent Irish setter, when they were first married. He had named it Blarney and had taught it to sit and beg and roll over. But Linda had let it out one day, because she couldn't be bothered walking it. Blarney got hit by a car and died.

He should have known then that a woman as irresponsible as Linda would never make a good mother.

David could see the back of Samantha's head from where he stood. Her honey-blond hair, lush and thick, like molten gold waves cascaded down her back. Samantha wasn't Linda. For a moment, he pictured himself caressing the burnished ripples of Samantha's hair before he thrust that dangerous image to the back of his mind.

He reminded himself that Samantha was a practicing Christian. With all their sanctimonious airs, they couldn't be trusted. Hadn't the minister told him that he shouldn't divorce Linda?

David knew he didn't have many choices at this point. Food and a bed for James and himself for two weeks was a good deal. Well, he could just as easily have a bed and food in prison, but then James would be back with Linda.

Bile rose in his throat as he thought of the way she had abused and neglected James.

No. She would not get their child again. Ever.

He reached for the doorknob. Immediately, the dog jumped up and ran toward him, snarling and baring its teeth.

Startled by such a vicious show, David held the door shut as the dog threw itself against the screen.

Samantha rushed over and grabbed the dog's collar.

"I'm sorry." Her troubled gray eyes met his only briefly. "Cassie doesn't like men. She's a marshmallow for anyone else."

David laughed. "You're telling me that dog will chew me to bits because I happen to be male."

"I would never allow her to do such a thing!"

David found it amusing to watch Samantha struggle with the scrawny mutt, trying to keep it in check while it continued to growl and snap. He could swear the dog was salivating.

"And how will you prevent her from making mincemeat of me?"

"I'll put her in my bedroom."

With that, she dragged the dog away. Another shiver went through David at the irritating sound of nails screeching along the tiled floor. Samantha shut the animal into a room and closed the door. Returning to the porch with her face beautifully flushed, she continued to apologize for her dog's antisocial behavior.

"There's a room in the lab building where you and James will sleep, but you have to eat here. When you do, I'll just keep Cassie locked up."

David shrugged. "Hey, I can understand that you would need protection out here, all by yourself."

"So will you stay, even if Cassie doesn't like you?" Her voice sounded strained and anxious.

"I'll give it a shot."

He noticed her shoulders shake slightly as her gaze went to the floor. David frowned. Was his help that important?

"Daddy, come see the television!" James shouted.

David opened the screen door and stepped inside.

Samantha wheeled around. "Oh yes, and I don't have any television in the lab, so you'll have to use the one in my living room." Though her voice was as soft as the breeze that blew against the linens on the clothesline, David heard a slight tremor in it. From the living room, they went to the kitchen and James skipped along behind the woman as if she were some Pied Piper playing a special tune that only children could hear.

David sighed deeply. He heard the tune himself. Samantha Lyons had some mysterious quality about her that made him want to know more about her—to spend time with her—to touch her—to listen to her hypnotic voice. She was attractive, but not gorgeous. She should have gotten braces on her teeth when she was a kid, yet that didn't matter. David had dealt with enough women to know that outer beauty didn't necessarily make for a nice disposition. Linda had been a cover model for all of the most prestigious magazines, but she had been impossible to live with.

*   *   *

Samantha's tour of the house turned out to be rather brief. David hadn't realized how small the cottage really was. A kitchen, a pantry/utility room, a living room, one bedroom, one bathroom, and a screened-in porch. No basement, no attic, no den.

A cooling breath of air fanned David's face as they stepped back out onto the porch, the best feature of the tiny house. Four wicker chairs and a low table formed a cozy seating arrangement.

Samantha sank down onto one of the chairs and David did the same. James crawled into his lap.

"So how am I supposed to catch the mosquitoes?" he asked.

"You stand outside and naturally, some mosquitoes land on you."

She gave him a tremulous smile and he blinked to prevent himself from being mesmerized.

"I have a straw-type device and you sort of suck up the mosquito—"

"What if I swallow it?" David interrupted.

"It won't hurt you."

He watched her long, thin fingers smooth out her gauzy skirt. Everything about her seemed so soft and feminine that he almost felt he could relax. He wrapped his arms more closely about James. No. He couldn't let down his guard. Not with her. Not with anyone.

He glanced outside at the endless miles of salt hay and at the blue water beyond that. It would be safe enough, he guessed.

"Anyhow, then you put the live mosquito—because, of course, it must be live to test the pesticide—into a small cardboard trap—with a screen on it, so it can't get out. I'll do all the rest. It isn't difficult."

"So I'm a sitting duck. I stand outside, get eaten alive by bugs, maybe catch a few—"

"You have to catch a lot," she broke in. "This part of the

study is very important. I have been breeding mosquitoes in the lab and testing the pesticide on them, but I need a control group, a totally unrelated batch of mosquitoes."

"Can't you just take your vacuum cleaner outside and draw in a million of them?"

Her archaic method sounded ridiculous to David.

"You would hurt them!" She frowned.

"Heaven forbid," he stated in a mocking tone.

Her eyes sparked flint at him. He leaned back in the chair, feeling the heat from her searing gaze. James sighed as his eyes began to close.

"It's extremely important research," she reminded him.

David didn't doubt that the earnestness in her face could convince Congress to appropriate trillions of dollars in funding for her cause. Then he reminded himself that right now, he and James needed a safe haven, and this could be an ideal situation.

"Okay, okay." He tried to sound apologetic. "There are nasty viruses and we must do something about it. So when do I start my human pincushion routine?"

"Tomorrow. Today is Sunday…" Her voice trailed off and she glanced into the distance.

Simply the thought of anything religious made him defensive and he stiffened. He had seen nothing but hypocrisy in his dealings with supposed "Christians".

"It doesn't matter to me what day this is," he said. "I don't believe there is a God."

She whipped her head around and stared at him with such surprise in her expression that he had an urge to touch the top of his head to make sure he hadn't sprouted horns.

"Not at all?"

With a voice that sounded hard and bitter, even to his own ears, he gave her his version of the world. "Everything that happens here on this earth is random. Good people meet up with terrible tragedies and very evil people do remarkably well during their lifetimes. Why would a god, who supposedly loved his creations, treat them so cruelly? Why would he make them suffer? The good guys don't win. Honesty is not the best policy. The clever liar will always have a better life."

He didn't add that women who are monsters get custody of their children. He couldn't say it because he knew he was guilty of not spending enough time with his own son. He should have known, but he had been too busy.

"I can understand how you might feel that way."

Her voice had such a tender quality to it that for a fleeting second he actually believed her and thought she might be capable of understanding his predicament. Then his better judgment returned and he glared at her, fully expecting her to clobber him with sermon number one, a compassionate plea aimed at getting him to come back to the fold.

However, she surprised him by not saying another word. The silence hung between them like the heavy atmosphere on the muggy afternoon. She turned her head to stare off into the distant, hazy horizon. He hesitated. She seemed so vulnerable for a moment. He noticed her hands tremble slightly and she bit her lip.

He shook himself mentally. She was probably feeling tainted by sitting in close proximity with a heathen. She might be regretting the fact that she had hired him.

He glanced down at James. His son had fallen fast asleep in his arms.

"I guess I better show you to your room," Samantha whispered.

Though he tried not to move suddenly, the moment he got out of the chair, James woke up again.

"Put me down, Daddy!" James insisted.

David sighed. From this point on, he knew James would be completely wired and impossible to deal with unless he got a nap.

Samantha led them across the yard to the lab building, a low concrete structure. She ushered them into a small hallway and then unlocked the door on the left. When she swung it open, David sucked in his breath as an overwhelming sensation hit him. The small, austere room reminded him of a cell—maybe it was the color of the walls, a sickly, institutional green, or maybe it was the cheap metal furniture. Or maybe it was a premonition. He struggled to recover his regular breathing rate and force down his fear.

Samantha crossed over to the small window and opened it. "I'm sorry it's so stuffy in here. I have a fan in the lab you can use."

Meanwhile, of course, James bounced into the room and opened the wardrobe along with every drawer. He lifted a black book out of one.

"What's this?"

"A Bible." Samantha answered.

James opened it. "There aren't any pictures."

"No. But there are lots of stories."

James frowned at the dull-looking book and dropped it back into the drawer. "Bunkbeds!" he squealed as he clambered up the ladder. "Can I sleep on the top?"

"Sure," David replied hoarsely.

"Look, I can touch the ceiling." James reached up with just his index finger.

"You're taller than your father, now." Samantha smiled.

"I am!" James looked ready to burst with delight.

David felt a painful squeeze around his heart at the unbridled joy in his son's face.

When Samantha showed them the tiny bathroom, James grabbed the faucet and turned it on full force. Water splashed out over the sides of the small bowl.

"James! Stop it!" David roared. He slapped at James' hand and switched the faucet off. James' tiny shoulders shook and his face crumpled. David clamped his jaw together. He knew that James' tears would be next. Would Samantha decide that she had made a mistake in bringing him and his son here? However, Samantha simply turned to a small closet and got out a bucket and a sponge.

"This is Mr. Spongy, James, he can wipe up any mess."

"Hello, James." Samantha, using a silly voice, folded the sponge in her hand and made it open and close like a mouth.

One tear rolled down James' cheek, but he immediately started to smile. "Hi Mr. Spongy."

"I am so thirsty, James, can you help me drink up this water?" Samantha handed the sponge to James who eagerly tried to make it talk, too. Then David watched in amazement as she patiently showed James how to wipe up the mess.

Once that was finished, Samantha left them to settle into their new surroundings. James went back to the drawer with the Bible. He took it up to the top bunk with him and started turning the pages.

"The big lion ran after the little boy to eat him up." James made up a story for himself.

David went to the window and looked out over the desolate marshland. He could see nothing but miles and miles of short grass interspersed with narrow waterways stretching to the blue sea beyond. Would he be safer in a forest, or at the top of a mountain? He shrugged. For two weeks, this would probably be okay.

When he turned back to check on his son, he found the child fast asleep with the Bible beside him. David eased the book away and put it back into the drawer. Just the sight of the book irritated him. Based on it, he was destined to a fiery eternity. Well, better that than watch his young son suffer. He stood beside the bunk bed and listened to the child's even, light breathing. Suddenly, he felt wearier than he had in weeks. He lay down on the bottom bunk and soon drifted off into a deep sleep.

* * *

David woke up with a rumbling stomach. On the breeze drifting in from the window, he smelled the odor of frying onions.

"Hey, Daddy!" James shook his shoulder. "Miss

Samantha said supper is almost ready."

"What?" David glanced at his watch and groaned. He had slept solidly for at least two hours. He sat up quickly and bumped his head on the bunkbed frame. Biting back a curse, he rubbed at the sore spot and slid carefully out of the bed.

"I helped Miss Samantha pick tomatoes," James said. "Only the red ones."

David continued to rub his head as he stumbled around groggily trying to find his shoes. After he located them under the bed, he sat down again to put them on.

"When did you wake up?" he asked his son.

"When I heard the fish man. He has a *big* boat." James smiled. "He could take me for a ride!"

David's heart rate sped up. "You are not to talk to strangers! And you will not get on a boat with a stranger, either."

"He's the fish man," James scrunched up his face. "He's not a stranger."

"I don't know him," David tried to explain in a calm manner though the sweat on his brow turned to ice. "He is a stranger to me."

"Miss Samantha says he's an old friend," James stated in a very matter-of-fact voice for one so young.

David combed his fingers through his hair while fear prickled along his shoulders. Who was the fish man? What if he had seen a news report about James? What if he called the police?

"The fish man gave me a minnow." James held up a tin can. "See, it's a baby fish."

David squinted into the muddy water. He could barely see the silver flash of the fish as it swam around the small container.

"Hey guys!" Samantha knocked on the door. "Supper's on the table!"

"Neptune, you stay here." James set the can down on the desk.

"Neptune?" David questioned.

"The fish man said that's his name," James explained. He grabbed his father's hand. "I set the table."

David's head reeled while he followed his son across the yard to the cottage. The kid had picked tomatoes, set the table, met someone, and acquired a pet minnow all while he had been dead to the world. He had thought this place would be totally isolated and safe. His nerves bunched into tight knots.

James led him around to the back door and they stepped into the kitchen. Though David frowned at the mismatched plates and utensils sitting on the table, whatever sat in the big serving bowl smelled heavenly and David's stomach rumbled loudly.

"I've got some lemonade," Samantha said as she drew a pitcher out of the refrigerator. "How does that sound?"

"Yummy!" James shouted as he scrambled into one of the chairs.

Samantha had changed into jeans and a green T-shirt. The green brought out the highlights in her honey-blond hair, and the jeans showed off the length of her legs. David's pulse started to race.

"I think I could use some coffee." He cleared his throat.

"Instant okay?" Samantha asked.

"Sure. Fine." David glanced around the kitchen. That was preferable to staring at Samantha. She had a potent effect on him but he sure didn't need any complications right now.

The kitchen, though small and cramped, nevertheless boasted an array of appliances, including a microwave oven and a washing machine. Then he noticed that one important item wasn't there.

"Where's the dishwasher?" he asked.

Samantha's laughter sounded light and beautiful. David fought against the ethereal quality in her voice. He realized he could enjoy listening to her.

And that was very bad.

"Since I cooked this meal, my dishwashers are you and James." She poured out the lemonade into two tall glasses and then reached into a cabinet for a mug. "But if you want to cook tomorrow, then I'll be the dishwasher."

"My culinary skills consist of boiling soup or zapping hot dogs in the microwave." David muttered.

"Hot dogs sound good." Samantha grinned. "Cassie would love that meal."

"So who's this fish man?" He knew his voice sounded gruff. His mouth felt like it had been lined with flannel.

Samantha filled up the mug with water and shoved it into the microwave. "Fish caught a huge shark, so he gave us a chunk of it. That's what I put into the soup."

"His name is 'Fish'?"

"An old nickname," Samantha explained. "I think his name is really Herbert or Henry or something like that. His father owned a fishery and that's how he got the name."

"Look, I don't want my kid talking to some crazy old fisherman—"

"Fish is not crazy." Samantha glared at him, her eyes full of flint sparks. "He's a dear, sweet old gentleman and my nearest neighbor."

The timer on the microwave beeped. Samantha removed the mug, stirred in a spoonful of instant coffee, and brought it to the table.

When she moved to sit down, David remembered his manners and gently pulled out the chair for her.

"Why…th-thank you."

Her face took on a rosy hue that only enhanced the wholesome freshness of her beauty. He heard her take in an audible breath before she went on.

"I'd like to say grace before we dig in."

David should have known that was coming. He sat down and saw James put his hands together.

"You don't have to pray, James," David whispered softly. "Just bow your head and listen."

"But I like to pray." James shot his father a puzzled look. "Kyle showed me how. He said you just have to ask God to fix things for you."

David clenched his teeth together. His son had a lot to learn about the world. God didn't fix things or change things or set things right. If He did, David and James wouldn't be running as if they were the ones who had committed a crime.

Samantha bowed her head and blessed the food, thanking the benevolent generosity of Fish and God. When she finished, she and James both said, "Amen."

"This is cioppino—fish stew, although this time I used shark, so I don't know how that will affect the flavor, but the tomatoes are getting ripe so quickly, and I had to use them up." She ladled out a portion into her bowl. "I didn't make it too spicy. I don't know if you and James like spicy things." She passed the bowl to David.

So far, he knew only that James liked fast food. That's all they had been eating.

"I like spicy food, but not too hot," he said. "Medium." The fish stew looked like manna from heaven as he dished out a generous portion for himself. It felt good to sit at a table and eat, rather than grab a bag from a take-out window.

"I like chicken nuggets," James piped up.

David spooned the stew into James' bowl.

"I don't want that," James pouted.

"It has your tomatoes in it," Samantha pointed out.

"Which ones?" James peered at the stew suspiciously.

"All of them."

David thought her eyes had a mischievous light in them as she answered James' question. A tiny glimmer of warmth spread around his heart. How ordinary this all seemed—like Samantha, warm, simple, and honest.

That last thought jarred him. No. She wasn't honest. She had hired him. He shoved that idea away and tried to keep his mind on more immediate concerns.

"Try Miss Samantha's stew, sport," David urged. "It probably has a lot more vitamins than chicken nuggets."

"Would you like to tour the lab after supper?" Samantha asked pleasantly.

"It's as good a time as any." He dug into the stew and

savored a mouthful of sheer joy. What a difference there was between fast food and the real thing!

"Three of the women from Holy Redeemer will be coming over this evening around eight," she explained. "We have a Bible study every Sunday."

"Then I guess that will be the time for me to go out and catch some mosquitoes." He didn't mean to agitate her, but when he saw the tight lines around her mouth, he knew his remark had irked her.

"We'll be sitting on the screened-in porch since it's going to be a lovely evening. However, it won't disturb us if you sit in the living room and watch television."

"James will like that."

James nodded his head up and down enthusiastically.

David did not press his point. He did not intend to be anywhere near a bunch of churchwomen while they carried on about sin and judgement. Still, his irritation with all things holy didn't have any effect on his appetite. He had three helpings of Samantha's fish stew. James ate some of it, though he seemed fonder of the bread and butter. It was the best meal that either of them had eaten in weeks.

Afterwards, Samantha showed them how she wanted her dishes washed and wound up doing more than half of them in the demonstration. He and James mostly dried the dishes. It didn't seem like work. Samantha entertained them by humming a vaguely familiar tune. It sounded so light and happy that David felt compelled to ask her what song it was.

"Simple Gifts," she answered. "A hymn."

David turned the ends of his mouth down and shook his head. He should have known.

The tour of the lab proved to be a hit with James. He got to meet the guinea pigs: Max, Mocha, Pansy, and Kiszka.

"Kiszka?" David questioned.

"It's a Polish sausage," Samantha replied. "A big, fat Polish sausage. Doesn't Kiszka look like a big, fat sausage?"

"If sausages had legs," David commented.

Samantha gave him another of her golden laughs and

David felt a tug on his heart. She had to stop doing that. He fought against the spark of hope.

"What do you use the guinea pigs for?" he asked.

"The female mosquitoes must have a blood meal before they lay their eggs, so the guinea pigs provide that," she explained. "They don't seem to mind too much—as long as I give them plenty of carrots."

"Can I give them a carrot?" James asked.

"Tomorrow," Samantha promised. "It's nearly their bedtime and I have to show your father how to catch mosquitoes."

"Can I catch some, too?" he asked.

"But they'll eat you all up." She tickled James and he laughed.

"You can watch television for a while with Cassie. It's time for her favorite TV show—it's all about a dog."

"You let her watch TV?" James had an incredulous look on his face.

Samantha nodded. Her mood could only be described as infectious. David found himself daring a genuine grin. Where had she learned to handle kids so well? James had spent a lot of time whining as they had driven from place to place. Though he had to admit that all of their traveling had been boring, miles and miles of road interspersed with drab motel rooms and greasy take-out food. They had gone swimming a few times in the motel pools, but most of the time they had been constantly on the move. David feared someone would recognize them. He wondered how many people studied the "wanted" posters in the Post Office.

He had never done anything like this before in his life, but he didn't think he could have handled it any other way under the circumstances. James' safety came first.

Being with Samantha Lyons felt like a vacation. No doubt, James would make a fuss when it was time to leave this little haven. With a start he realized that he, too, would loathe parting from this odd research station in the middle of the wide-open marshes. If he could start all over again, he would like to get to know Samantha Lyons.

Sure. Like he needed to get involved with another woman. Who was he kidding? Besides, Samantha wouldn't have any use for a fallen man like himself. Or would she?

He narrowed his eyes and studied her as she led James out of the lab by the hand. It appeared as though nothing made her happier than entertaining his son. There had to be more to this generosity of hers, more than the fact that she needed help with her research.

Did it matter? He hated the running. He hated the mindless fear that gnawed at his mind in the darkest part of the night.

If Samantha Lyons was desperate for help, then he would help her. He knew he could not trust her, but for tonight and maybe tomorrow, he would not run. And neither would James.

Chapter Three

Samantha's heart beat rapidly against her ribs as she demonstrated the simple, though tedious, chore of catching mosquitoes. She could feel David's gaze fixed upon her, coolly appraising her as she stood surrounded by salt hay in the glow of the cottage's floodlight.

"That's all there is to it." She forced her voice to remain steady. "The mosquito lands on you, you suck on this tube and then blow the live mosquito into the trap. There's enough light to help you see what you're doing."

"It should also help the mosquitoes find me."

At his sarcastic remark, she bristled with indignation. After all, she was doing him a favor! Then her conscience stung her with the sharp twinge of truth. Without his help she didn't stand a chance of keeping her home. Abashed, she took in a ragged breath.

"This is a critical research project." She handed him the small trap and a clean tube. When their fingers touched, the warmth of him shimmered up her arm, a reaction she could well do without.

Being alone with a male employee in such a remote location wasn't the wisest plan, but then a few notes of happy laughter from the cottage drifted to her on the evening air. She reminded herself that she was doing this for James. The child needed some stability in his life and hopefully, his father would come to his senses with some encouragement.

"I'll watch while you try it." She swatted at the mosquitoes that had landed on her arms.

"Want me to get rid of the ones on you?" A devilish gleam shone in his dark eyes.

"No!" She took a step backward and tripped on a piece of driftwood. He caught her elbow before she fell.

"Hey, I was just teasing."

As he steadied her, Samantha felt a hot flush on her cheeks and yanked her arm away from him. Her composure crumbled as her pulse raced at his nearness.

"Please, hurry up. I have to see if you're doing this correctly. Then I have to get things ready for the ladies," she stated sharply, hoping that her face, turned away from the harsh glare of the floodlight, lay in shadow too deep for David to detect the high color that must surely be there.

He shrugged and got to work, deftly drawing a mosquito into the tube. In a matter of minutes, he became as efficient as anyone else she had taught to manage the task.

"This could get boring real fast," he commented.

"It's a vital link in a necessary study that could prevent the spread of infectious disease." She deliberately injected a serious note into her voice even while she stood there enjoying the little thrill that wound its way to her heart as she observed him.

"Are you always this dead serious about your work?"

His question caught her off guard and she stuttered.

"W-why, of course."

"Trying to win the Noble Peace Prize?" His mouth quirked up a notch in amusement.

"Um. Well, working with insects isn't usually the kind of earth shattering—"

"I was pulling your leg!" he interrupted and let out a deep, rich laugh.

"Oh." She smiled, enjoying his good humor even if it was at her expense. "It's just that I'm not a rocket scientist, after all."

"If you were, I'm sure there would now be astronauts on Pluto."

She frowned in confusion. He really didn't know her. How could he make such a preposterous assumption?

"How many of these mosquitoes do you want tonight?"

A flash of despair swept through her as she recalled his attitude about God. His negative opinion caused her to question the wisdom of hiring him.

"It-it is still Sunday," she reminded him lamely. "You don't have to do this until tomorrow."

"Hand me a few more of those cardboard traps." His expression turned grim. "I'd like to see what my personal best is."

She merely nodded and hurried back to the lab to gather several more traps. She chastised herself for acting like a schoolgirl with a crush. Nevertheless, she reassured herself that the feeling would quickly dissipate, and even if it didn't, the two weeks would fly by. She would most likely never see him again.

That thought brought on a stab of sorrow. Laden with traps, she walked slowly back to where he stood, magnificent in the glow of the floodlight, with his long shadow spreading out over the salt hay. Samantha closed her eyes for a moment and prayed for strength.

* * *

"How is the dear little boy?" Marion Gregory stepped in the door reeking of lilac cologne, dressed in a pastel polyester outfit that made her appear far older than her fifty years.

"He's fine." Samantha smiled. "He's asleep in front of the TV with Cassie right beside him."

"Do you think I would disturb him if I took a peek at his dear little face?" An ebullient sparkle glowed in Marion's eyes.

Agnes, Marion's mother lumbered in the door with her four-footed cane.

"Stop making a nuisance of yourself," Agnes scolded. "The poor thing's probably exhausted."

Marion's right eye twitched. "I suppose you're right, Mother."

"Of course I am." Agnes eased herself into her favorite chair. "Where's that extra pillow?"

Dear Lord, grant me patience, Samantha prayed as she hurried off to the linen closet for the requested pillow. It distressed Samantha to hear Agnes berate her adult daughter, but there didn't seem to be much hope for the situation. After all, Agnes had just turned eighty and perhaps it was all her aches and pains that caused her to be so ornery.

Returning with the pillow, Samantha tucked it behind Agnes' back.

"Fish stopped by with some spare shark for us to eat and gave James a minnow in a tin can. He told him that the minnow's name was Neptune."

Marion's shy smile looked wistful. "That dear, dear man—"

Agnes loudly cleared her throat. "Don't go feeling sorry for that shiftless old rascal. Besides, he's not of our faith."

Samantha caught the sharp look that Agnes delivered to her daughter. Marion's face turned pale.

"Fish is my nearest neighbor and a very good soul." Samantha countered. "And he is Christian."

"He's one of those other kinds of Christians." Agnes banged her cane on the floor with emphasis. Then she glared at her daughter again. "Did you do your preparatory reading?"

The nervous tic in Marion's eye jerked rapidly, but she spoke softly. "As you know, I worked late last night. Then this morning I had to make your breakfast, take you to church, make your lunch, and since you insisted on visiting the Pitts' sisters, I didn't have a single moment to myself."

"Don't give me your excuses." Agnes pursed her lips. "Your sister, Gracie, was always a much better student. Look how far she's gone with her education."

At that point, Winnie Dale raced in. The deacon's wife balanced a tray of cookies in one hand and a folder stuffed with a haphazard array of papers in the other.

"Honestly, I dropped the whole folder in the yard, but that nice young man out there helped me pick them up, though I doubt that they are in any kind of order now."

As the neon-colored chrysanthemums on Winnie's skirt went swirling by Samantha, her heart seemed to hitch up into her throat. The disturbing apprehension that the ladies would rain down condemnation on her because of David had gnawed at her all day, but Winnie had other things on her mind. "I thought I'd never get out of the house tonight. The kids bickered all day long." She ungraciously plopped her folder and the tray of cookies down on the coffee table and collapsed upon the wicker sofa.

"You should give them a sound spanking." Agnes' jowls shook with self-righteousness. "Spare the rod and spoil the child."

Winnie simply groaned and covered her eyes with her hand. "Do you have an ice pack, Samantha? I feel a migraine coming on."

"I'll get one right away." Samantha hurried into the kitchen.

"I'll help get the tea ready, then." Marion followed on Samantha's heels. As soon as they reached the kitchen, Samantha heard a deep sigh from Marion. "Mother really can't take this muggy weather. It makes her cranky. Dr. Peller and I both suspect that Mother is 'slipping'—just a bit mind you, but now and then she does forget things and behave in a rather irrational manner. Not enough oxygen getting to her brain, you know."

Samantha nodded and opened the freezer to root around inside for the ice tray. Marion went on chattering, freed from her mother's caustic reprimands.

"And I'm sure Winnie needs a vacation. It's hard enough raising three children, but she is on every committee from the Ladies' Altar Society to the Social Concerns Ministry."

"It must be rough being the wife of the deacon. He is overworked, too." Samantha located the tray and pulled it out. She popped out a few ice cubes and slipped them into a plastic bag.

"If we only had more young people at Holy Redeemer..."

Marion's pensive wish seemed to echo in the little cottage kitchen.

Samantha thought of her missing intern. Ginger Blaine

swore that Clam Creek was stuck in a time warp.

"There aren't many jobs here, or amusements."

Marion opened the refrigerator and got out a carton of milk. "If someone would open the fish factory again..."

"Didn't Fish's father own that?" Samantha wrapped a soft towel around the bag of ice cubes.

"Yes, but after he died, nobody wanted to keep the place going. It was the lifeblood of this town."

"Why didn't Fish take it over? He still likes fishing."

Marion paused before she poured the milk into the pitcher on the counter. Her eye twitched again. "There were other things that happened—and well, perhaps that's all best left unsaid."

Samantha pouted as she filled the kettle and turned on the burner. She knew it wouldn't do her any good to press Marion for more information.

Everyone in town had welcomed Samantha as one of their own. They had generously given photographs to her, and the family who now lived in the house where her mother had grown up allowed her to walk through it. But when the citizens of Clam Creek had a secret, they kept it. The history of Fish's past was obviously one of those secrets. She couldn't help noticing the evasive action used whenever she mentioned Fish's name, which piqued her curiosity even more. She hoped that one day everyone would feel comfortable enough to reveal that privileged information to her.

A sad, little ache touched her heart. But what if she had to leave Clam Creek?

Her throat tightened as she pictured the place where her mother had been laid to rest in the cemetery behind Holy Redeemer. Samantha had replaced the simple stone that had originally marked the site with a more elegant one. Visiting her mother's grave every week had become part of her routine and she had plans to plant crocus bulbs there in the fall, if she was still here.

All her hopes would be destroyed if she didn't finish her research.

Marion startled her from her reverie by knocking over the sugar bowl as she placed it on the tray beside the pitcher of milk.

"Dear me, I'm such a ninny sometimes." Marion's hand trembled.

"No you're not!" Samantha hated to hear Marion demean herself. She righted the sugar bowl and dusted the small spill into the sink with a flourish. "There, see it's not a problem."

"There is something I wanted to talk to you about..." Marion's eye went into a frenzy. "I don't think it's safe to allow that man to stay here at the field station with you."

"B-b-but..." Samantha sputtered as she fought to keep the heat out of her cheeks. She had suspected that somebody would object, but they didn't understand the problems that faced her! "He's the only help I'll probably get!"

"He is a total stranger. You don't know him from the man in the moon."

"He's well-mannered and intelligent." Samantha poured boiling water into the teapot, and though her hand trembled slightly, she didn't spill any of the hot water. "Also very respectful. Anyhow, Cassie will keep him in line."

"Yes, but he'll be working with you in the lab."

"It's only for two weeks. He's an employee and I am twenty-five years old and very capable of watching out for myself."

"Some men have silver tongues, my dear." Marion carefully folded the napkins. Her eye had stopped its spasmodic jerking and her voice had a measure of steel in it.

Samantha realized that Marion's questions mirrored her own concerns. "I'll be very, very careful."

"Is he a Christian?"

Samantha froze and swallowed hard. "He—he says he doesn't believe in God."

"Hmmm." Marion placed four spoons on the tray in a neat row. "I suspected as much when I saw the way he behaved in the church basement."

"But you should have seen the way James folded his hands beautifully and joined me in the 'Amen' when I said grace at supper," Samantha hastened to add.

Marion's face brightened at the mention of the boy. "Let me sneak in real quick and look at him."

Samantha nodded. Marion had never married and had no children of her own, though she'd been blessed with a passel of nieces and nephews. Still, working at Dr. Peller's office as a receptionist and caring for her mother left her little time to spend with youngsters.

Samantha set her homemade ice pack on the tray along with everything else before Marion tiptoed back into the kitchen.

"He's the picture of peace," Marion cooed. "He's dreaming of angels, I'm sure."

"He's probably dreaming of dogs, guinea pigs, and little minnows," Samantha explained to her older friend. "I hope we have a few cookies left over tonight for him."

"Dear me, no." Marion looked horrified. "Winnie baked the cookies tonight and you know she can't cook to save her life. I mean, they always look so beautiful, but you take one bite and you know she must not have been paying attention to what she put into the dough. Even the birds won't eat the leftovers. I tried to be polite and ate a few more than I should have once and my stomach wasn't right for a week."

A chuckle floated up from Samantha's throat. Winnie hadn't been gifted with even a smidgen of talent in the culinary arts. She knew her Bible verses backwards and forwards, and she knew how to organize a meeting, but whenever she tried her hand at cooking, the results left a lot to be desired. It didn't surprise anyone that Winnie's husband had the look of an ascetic.

Samantha and Marion walked back out to the porch. Agnes had continued to spout off her views on parenting during their absence. Winnie lunged for the ice pack.

"Thanks for the advice, Agnes." Winnie smiled weakly as she applied the wrapped ice to her head, neck, and eyes. "Oh, this feels so much better."

Before Agnes could begin a different monologue about headaches, Winnie directed everyone in a rather strident voice.

"Turn to the reading for today and then Samantha, if you could start us off with the prayer tonight, I'll begin the discussion."

The women flipped through their Bibles to find the assigned page. Then Samantha poured the tea. She took a deep breath before she intoned the prayer.

"Dear Lord——" The phone rang.

Samantha went to answer it. The call was from the deacon, who asked to speak with his wife. Winnie wore a puzzled expression when she took the phone from Samantha.

"He can't handle those three, I know. But he doesn't usually interrupt me."

Within seconds, Winnie rushed back to the porch in hysterics. "Theresa stepped on a nail in the neighbor's yard and it went right through her shoe! Bob called the doctor but he hasn't called back yet."

"Dr. Peller left for a conference in Philadelphia," Marion explained. "He won't be back until Tuesday."

Winnie gasped. "Should we take her to the hospital?"

"She should be soaking it in Epsom salts," Agnes suggested.

"She had her tetanus vaccination, so I'm sure you don't need to worry about that," Samantha said, trying to calm the obviously distraught woman.

"Though there's still a danger of infection," Marion reminded her.

"My son, Andrew, nearly lost his leg after he stepped on a nail and the wound festered. Had red streaks going up his legs." Agnes pursed her lips.

Winnie paled. "Red streaks?"

"Blood poisoning." Agnes nodded gravely. "The doctors were certain gangrene would set in, but those doctors didn't know a thing about poultices. It was my poultices that saved him."

Samantha watched as Winnie started to shake. The deacon's wife let out a sob.

At that moment, David appeared at the screen door with the mosquito traps.

"Excuse me?" he asked. "Where do you want these?"

Samantha was just about to run for a box of tissues.

"In the lab."

"It's locked."

"Right." She shoved her hair behind her ear. Winnie wailed. Marion patted the emotional woman's hands ineffectively.

Samantha dug in her pocket and opened the door just enough to slip him her key ring. "Okay, it's the one with the black L on it. I know I showed you where to put the mosquitoes. Just be sure to lock the lab after you put them away."

"Sure thing." He glanced over at the mayhem with a sardonic look in his eyes. "Interesting Bible study."

Samantha glared at him as her temper flared, but then Agnes grew more vociferous in her explanation of exactly what went into a poultice, and Marion lost her patience. She yelled at her mother to stop, and her mother shouted back at her.

Samantha feared that the elderly woman would have a stroke right there on her porch.

Naturally, all the commotion woke up James and he wandered out to the porch rubbing his eyes.

"Is somebody crying?" he asked.

"Mrs. Dale's daughter stepped on a nail," Samantha told him, and then she suggested that it was time for him to snuggle into his bunk.

"Can I have a drink of water first?" he asked.

Samantha recognized the familiar delay tactic, but she went to the kitchen to get him the water. After he took a sip of water, he had to go to the bathroom, of course. When he emerged from the bathroom, he appeared to be fully awake and quite intrigued with all the hubbub.

Meanwhile, it had been decided that Winnie should definitely go back home to care for her daughter, but since she had become so terribly upset, nobody thought she should drive, even though she had driven both Agnes and Marion to Samantha's cottage.

Marion wrung her hands. "I do wish I had learned to drive when I was younger but there didn't seem to be any reason for me to do it then."

"You could never drive! You're too nervous!" Agnes pounded the floor with her cane.

Marion's eye twitched spastically.

"I—I'll be f-f-fine." Winnie sobbed again.

Samantha could feel a tight knot of tension bunching up on her shoulders. Driving through the marsh took a fair measure of skill and concentration. Driving through it in the pitch blackness with swollen eyes, bleary vision, and a migraine would not be wise. She covered her eyes with her hand.

At that point, she heard a knock on the screen door.

"The mosquitoes are all tucked in for the night," David announced. He dangled the key ring in his fingers.

Like a beast in a nightmare, Cassie came running and leaped at the door.

"Mrs. Dale's daughter stepped on a nail," James called out above the noise of the raging animal.

"I'm very sorry to hear that."

David's conciliatory tone sounded genuine to Samantha, though it was difficult to tell under the circumstances. She glanced at her watch. He had been gone fifteen minutes. That seemed rather long for a stroll out to the lab and back—unless he hung around outside for a while waiting for the excitement to die down.

Samantha grabbed Cassie's collar and dragged the dog along to her bedroom while struggling to dismiss her uneasiness about her new employee. David didn't look like the type of man interested in destroying two years of research.

Or did he? Could he be the kind of man who had abducted his own son? Or could he be running from some other crime? That thought sent a shiver zinging up her spine. She had every right to be suspicious about him.

By the time she returned to the porch, David had joined the ladies.

"I heard part of this discussion," he explained. "I could follow you in my car while Samantha drives you all home. Then I'll bring her back. You other ladies will have to have an early evening but Winnie will be able to take care of her daughter."

"But Daddy." James crinkled up his nose. "You said there isn't any more gas in the car."

Samantha watched David nervously tousle his son's hair.

"That's right, sport. I almost forgot. It's a good thing you reminded me. Then we can have Samantha lead the way while I drive Winnie's car."

Samantha frowned. What if he was a car thief? What if she was being paranoid?

"What about James?" Marion asked. She dabbed at a few tears on her own cheeks. "The boy shouldn't be here alone."

"But Cassie is here!" James told her. "She's my new friend. And I've got Neptune, too!"

"You can ride with me, Mrs. Dale, and the other ladies," David suggested.

"Cassie is an old dog and it's way past her bedtime." Samantha spoke to the child. "I don't think she can stay up and watch you. Besides, who would be here to keep Neptune company?"

"Yeah." James frowned. "He'd be lonely."

Samantha offered up a silent prayer and then herded everyone along to the cars. She led the caravan slowly through the inky night along the marsh road. No streetlights had ever been placed along the dirt road, but Samantha had memorized the twists and turns quickly when she had first moved into the field station.

She thought about James as she wound her way through

an extensive patch of tall reeds that hemmed in the narrow road. James had blurted out the truth about the lack of gasoline in David's car. The child might accidentally divulge more of his past while he stayed at the field station, if she managed to gain his confidence and get him alone for awhile.

Did she really want to know his whole unhappy situation? A little shiver of fear crept up her spine. Who *was* David and what had he done? By the time they reached Winnie's house, Samantha's thoughts had returned to the necessary steps that still needed to be documented before her research would be complete.

Getting out of her car to say goodbye to the ladies, she felt relieved to find that the deacon's wife had calmed down, though her eyes would be swollen for quite some time by the looks of them. Deacon Bob came to the door of his house carrying his daughter in his arms, and Winnie rushed to them. Marion, loaded down with Winnie's papers, and Agnes, still mumbling her advice, invited themselves into the house.

David carried his now sleeping son into Samantha's car and they headed back to the field station in silence.

Thoughts about her own young life intruded and left a bitter taste in Samantha's mouth. She doubted whether her own father had truly loved her. If he had, he would never have snatched her away from her mother. He had effectively stolen her childhood in the process of punishing his ex-wife. With the help of the people in Holy Redeemer, Samantha had begun to heal, but there were still times when she felt angry and depressed. The thought of leaving Clam Creek tore at her. Her last hope to remain there rested with David Halpern, but could she count on him?

She glanced furtively to her right and caught David's eyes fixed on her. Unnerved to find him staring at her, she quickly turned back to focus on the road ahead as her pulse raced madly. She tried to calm herself with the fact that David would soon vanish from her life. Then her heart twisted. And what would happen to James? Would the child get the proper nourishment? The proper rest? What should she, as a Christian, do? Her kindness, if she could call it that, had been motivated by her own needs.

What would happen if she reported David as an unfit parent to the authorities?

She needed to pray about this matter and confide in someone, but couldn't it wait for just two weeks?

"I need to make a phone call."

His voice, though hushed, still startled her in the quiet interior of the sedan. Her hands trembled as they gripped the wheel.

"Oh, okay, you can pay me back." She winced. No chance of that, he would be gone. "Or-or maybe we can make some sort of arrangement—" Her words trailed off. She seemed to be tripping over them anyway.

"Deduct the money from my paycheck," he suggested with a touch of exasperation in his voice. "It shouldn't cost more than five dollars. I'll make it brief. I want to let someone know where they can reach me."

Unexpectedly, a flood of optimism washed over Samantha.

"Okay," she found herself grinning in the darkness. Obviously, she had gained his trust. Then her heart sank. Getting someone to trust you and then destroying that faith by reporting him as an unfit parent could hardly be considered benevolent. Her concern for James continued to weigh on her mind. What would be best for him?

"I'd like to make the call in private," David stipulated.

"That will be fine," she assured him. "I need to make a few notes to myself in the lab before I go to sleep tonight. So why don't you call as soon as we get back."

"Thanks," he said.

*   *   *

After he had tucked James into bed, David made the call

from the phone in the cottage. He left a message on his lawyer's machine, repeating the phone number where he could be reached three times. Slowly. Not that it would make much difference. If his lawyer had flown off to Hawaii, he wouldn't be hearing from him for a while. He had no choice but to stay put until his lawyer returned. At least, he and James wouldn't starve. He didn't particularly enjoy catching mosquitoes and being eaten alive by them, but the more he thought about the situation, he realized that he couldn't have gotten much luckier. The field station sat out in the middle of nowhere and relatively few people stopped in to visit.

Glancing out the window, he noticed that the lights were still burning in the lab. He certainly hoped he had caught enough mosquitoes for one day.

He went out to his car and dug around in the trunk for his shaving kit and a change of clothes. He would have to throw some things in the washing machine tomorrow. He had reached his last pair of clean briefs.

He noticed a light fog rolling in as he walked back to his room in the lab building. The mist carried with it the putrid odor of methane fermenting in the marsh. David covered his nose but it didn't help.

For the tenth time that day, he wondered why someone as intelligent as Samantha would choose to live here. The shops in town appeared to be small, offering little variety beyond the basics. Clam Creek didn't have a movie theater. Or a bar.

The majority of the citizens looked well beyond sixty.

He couldn't envision himself happy in a place like this.

He frowned, but he realized that he hadn't been happy in Connecticut either. Being a member of the country club grew tedious after a while. Shows, movies, restaurants—he'd been to the best and none of those diversions ever satisfied him. After separating from Linda and filing for a divorce, he had buried himself in his job, rising to the vice-presidency in record time. But what good had it done him?

He shook his head. He had made a desperate move to

save his son and for tonight, at least, James could sleep peacefully.

He glanced up at the dark sky. The fog had obliterated the moon and constellations. Not one tiny, faint beam shone down on him. He had no star to make a wish upon.

He felt as if he stood at the end of the world in this god-forsaken swamp. It was the last place on earth anyone would ever look for him. He shrugged. He could be happy in a place like this if it kept James safe. He smiled.

* * *

David felt wonderful after his shower, almost human again. Sure, he had a few mosquito bites, but with his fresh shave and clean clothes, he really didn't care about a few itches. James lay in peaceful slumber on the top bunk.

Due to his long afternoon nap, David didn't feel very sleepy. He thought about watching television in the cottage, but he had already discovered the channel selection to be extremely limited. Samantha Lyons didn't have cable. He had checked through the shelf that held her small library of videos. However, none of the titles appealed to him; they were all kids' stuff. An odd collection for a grown woman, in his opinion.

Then he thought about Samantha, her natural beauty, and her gentle manner. Everything about her shone with the same light as her tumbling hair. He furrowed his brow. Obviously, she followed the dictates of her faith in her choice of entertainment, but there was more to it than that. She had some childlike quality about her—some innocence that most women her age had lost. He glanced out the door of his room and saw the lights still burning in the lab. He hoped his mosquitoes had survived capture. What if he had treated them a little too callously?

He turned to check on James again and found his child resting in such tranquil repose that his throat started to ache with love. He wanted only the best for his son. Unfortunately right now, the best happened to be hiding from Linda.

He slipped outside and walked around the yard. As he passed the window of Samantha's bedroom in the cottage, he heard a little guttural sound from the dog.

"Can't we be friends, Cassie?" he asked.

The dog snarled at him. It struck him funny for some reason. Perhaps a former boyfriend of Samantha's had messed up the crazy animal's mind. He decided that he would try to get the dog to like him, or at least tolerate him.

He thought of his own wonderful Blarney and the pain came back. Linda had a gift for ruining everything.

Trying to distract himself, David decided to see how his mosquitoes had fared. It would be interesting to watch Samantha at work. Would she morph into a mad scientist? An old hag with warts and a cackly laugh?

He strolled back across the yard. The swamp gas didn't bother him so much now; maybe he was getting used to it. He listened with interest to the evening sounds, even though he couldn't identify them all. Feeling relaxed for the first time in weeks, he sighed deeply.

He tapped on the screen door of the lab and saw Samantha sitting at her workstation in front of the computer. When she heard his knock, she swung around, looking startled. Then in a swift move, she hastily groped for the mouse to turn off the machine. But he had seen what she had been studying so intently. She had been online looking at one of the many sites with photos of missing children.

"D-david," she stuttered. "I thought you would go right to bed."

Her cheeks had a blaze of color on them and he could see her trembling, but he could not feel sorry for her.

At first, he simply stood there in shock, too frozen to do anything. However, anger fired up quickly. He opened the unlocked door and strode toward her. He had been a fool! A wretched, trusting idiot!

"Did you find my picture there? Are you going to call the

cops now? Are you going to watch them throw me in jail and give James back to his mother?"

The pain almost swallowed him up.

Chapter Four

Samantha did not cry out. She couldn't. The sound of alarm lodged in her throat, and for a moment, she couldn't even breathe. Aside from ruining her chance of finishing the research, she now had a desperate man on her hands. And a desperate man was dangerous.

With an effort, she steeled herself for the worst and stared up at him. Torment and anguish were clearly written in his face. Struggling with her own fear, she took in a ragged breath and managed to quell the stirrings of panic for the moment.

"I did not 'find' you and James," she said. Slowly, she stood up, clasping her hands together so that he would not see them shake.

"So far, I checked the sites for Pennsylvania, and New York. I had no intention of notifying the authorities." At least, not yet. The lie nearly choked her. She inched away from him with a barely perceptible movement.

"Then why did you look? Why would you bother if you didn't plan to report me?" His face grew threatening as the veins bulged in his neck.

She felt her skin grow cold and clammy while her stomach churned with nausea.

"It was obvious that you were living in that car of yours. I wanted to know why."

From the moment she met David, she had her suspicions, but she could not be sure until now, when he, himself, confirmed it.

"Besides, you could be wanted for something other than abducting your own child." She kept her voice soft and smooth, though she thought she would suffocate.

He drew his hands into fists and she saw the pulse throbbing along his jaw.

"Do I look like a criminal?" His black eyes burned her with reproach.

She felt sick with the effort of maintaining her deceptively calm demeanor. She leaned against the counter as a wave of dizziness threatened.

"Murderers are rather ordinary-looking citizens."

Her bald statement had its effect. He stepped back, his mouth slack. The fury in his expression faded.

"I-I would never—" he stammered.

Her heart pounded in her chest, but she continued with an almost daring bravado. "Don't all murderers claim that they are not guilty?"

She watched the uncertainty flicker in his expression.

"You know I'm not that kind of man."

The stress of the day bore down on Samantha's shoulders. She didn't think she could hold up much longer.

"I can't be sure."

Silence fell like an icy curtain between them. Seconds ticked off slowly as time waited in suspense, until finally he began to speak in a husky whisper.

"I was robbed yesterday and when I tried to call my lawyer, I found out that he is on vacation. I used up the last of my change making the call. I don't know what I would have done if you hadn't come along."

She nodded. Was that an apology of sorts? Or thanks? Had the crisis passed so quickly? His decision to abduct James would mar his son's future forever, just as she continued to carry the scars of her past on the run. She wanted to hate David for what he was doing to his son, but she couldn't.

Showered, shaved, and dressed in clean, though wrinkled, clothing, he presented a handsome picture, one that she knew she would not be immune to. The look of his black hair silky and still damp, along with the fresh scent of soap on his bronzed skin made her pulse beat faster. She locked her arms in front of her and stared at his shoes. She must resist his appeal. She must not fall under his spell.

"James' mother neglected and abused him."

She watched David shift from one foot to the other.

"She—uh—well, I don't have proof, but he had a broken arm last summer, that's when it started—or I noticed—"

She heard the hollow note of grief in his voice before he suddenly turned and rushed back outside, slamming the screen door as he went.

She sank back down on the chair. ...Or I noticed... Could she truly believe whatever he told her?

Samantha's father had made similar claims against her own mother, but none of his accusations were true. Samantha's father had wanted to make his ex-wife suffer, and he had succeeded in that goal.

She massaged her temples, wishing she could rub the awful scene with David out of her mind. The demands of this single day had completely shattered her nerves. Forcing herself to move, she checked the lab, turned off the lights, and went outside, locking the door securely behind her. Glancing about the yard, she saw David's silhouette in his car, outlined by the floodlight.

That meant that James was all alone. She peered into the room where the boy slept. David must have put a nightlight into one of the electrical outlets because a gentle glow lit the room. James lay curled on the top bunk looking like the cherub she didn't doubt he must surely be.

She crossed the yard to the cottage, careful to avoid looking at David in his car. Knowing she would never be able to sleep just yet, she went to her bedroom and opened the door. Cassie yawned and stretched.

"Want to watch a movie with me?" Cassie got up wearily and padded off to the living room as if she understood.

Samantha pulled out the video of *The Wizard of Oz*. After popping it into the slot, she settled onto the couch. Cassie jumped up beside her and she stroked the animal's long, soft fur as the film flickered on the television screen.

After a few minutes, the sound of a car door closing started Cassie barking ferociously. The dog rushed to the porch while Samantha ran after her. She struggled to pull her pet back, and scolded her to be quiet. She didn't want Cassie to wake James.

It took a few minutes for Cassie to calm down again, but then she watched the movie with Samantha in companionable silence. Finally, at the end, when Judy Garland clicked her ruby slippers together and said, "There's no place like home," Samantha hugged Cassie and whispered to her pet.

"It's only a fairy tale." But she couldn't stop the tear rolling down her cheek.

*   *   *

Cassie woke Samantha early the next morning by whining. Samantha tried to tune out the high-pitched sound at first, but Cassie persisted. Aware that the dog only used that tone of voice when she needed to go outside, Samantha groaned and threw back her faded coverlet.

Groggy from a restless night, she opened her eyes to the gloom of a rainy day. She sighed and hoped that, at least, the rain might lower the temperature outside.

"You aren't going to want to stay out there long," she told her furry pet.

Cassie ignored the warning and danced around, looking frantic.

Samantha tossed off her thin cotton nightgown and pulled on an oversized T-shirt along with a pair of cutoffs. Cassie barked impatiently at her. Hurrying to the door, she let the dog out.

Cassie dashed outside eagerly, but before Samantha had even begun fixing the coffee, her pet returned, whining piteously to be allowed back inside.

As Samantha opened the door, Cassie rushed in and promptly shook herself. Samantha squealed as droplets of water sprayed all over the room.

"I wish you wouldn't do that!" Samantha wrinkled up

her nose as the heavy odor of wet fur assailed her nostrils. "I should give you a bath with lavender soap."

Cassie cowered in the corner with a fearful expression in her dark eyes. Samantha laughed.

"Sometimes, I think you understand every word I say." She petted the dog's head. "Okay, I didn't mean it. No bath today."

Cassie sighed and laid her head down on her paws.

Samantha started the coffee brewing and then cooked up a pot of oatmeal. While she worked, her mind whirled with the statistics of her study. She had a million things to accomplish before she could consider her research completed. The documentation had to be painstakingly detailed. Just thinking about it gave her a headache. Wondering if David would be a reliable helper might turn it into a migraine. She hoped last night's confrontation hadn't altered anything.

"Neptune isn't moving."

James' small voice intruded on her thoughts. He came into the kitchen carrying the tin can that Fish had given to him yesterday. Samantha peered into it. The silvery minnow floated on its side at the top of the water. It might be dead, or near death. James looked up at her with his huge blue eyes full of sadness. Samantha couldn't be sure of how he would react to the truth, and she really didn't want to find out.

"Maybe he's sad because he misses his friends," she offered.

"Yeah." James nodded his head. "I miss Kyle."

"We could put him back in the water and then he could go back home," she suggested.

"Okay," James agreed.

Samantha put a lid on the oatmeal and turned off the heat. She bent down to tie the laces on the sneakers the boy wore. He had evidently slipped into them himself. Then, she put on her own duck boots and led Cassie back into her bedroom in case David showed up while she and James were outside. Finally, with her umbrella, she and James went out into the rain together.

A thick fog hung over the marsh, shrouding James and Samantha as they walked in the gray gloom. The usual calls of the birds sounded muffled and mournful in the dense air.

"We'll put him back in the creek at the little wooden bridge," she told James.

James nodded. He walked along solemnly, carrying the tin can.

Though not a long walk, it seemed a lonely one, as if they were the only two in the world with their heart-heavy burden. The rain beat harder on the umbrella and soon the puddles soaked through James' canvas sneakers.

Once they reached the bridge, Samantha bent down near the edge and asked James to hand her the can.

The boy brought the can up near his chin and whispered, "Bye, Neptune."

The clear note of finality in the young boy's farewell made Samantha's own throat ache. James handed her the can and she poured the minnow into the tidal stream. Fortunately, the tide was going out. Neptune, caught in the rushing water, appeared to be swimming away.

"He's swimming again!" James smiled. "He's going fast! Maybe his mommy is looking for him."

Samantha felt a cold stab in her heart at his words. She returned the empty can to him.

"Do you think Neptune's mommy will be happy now?" she asked in a whisper. "What will his mommy do when he gets home?"

James clutched the can to his chest. "She's going to slap him. He was bad."

Samantha managed to stifle a gasp. Could David's accusation be true? Or had he coached his son to respond in that way? Had he made James' mother the villain?

As they walked back in the rain to the cottage, her spirits sank lower with every step while last night's dispute weighed heavily on her mind.

In less than twenty-four hours, James had wound his way into her heart and she knew that when he left, she would be bereft. She felt an incredible empathy for the young boy, which probably wasn't healthy. But she couldn't help being concerned about the boy's safety.

They stepped back into the cottage and found David pouring himself a cup of coffee and looking like he hadn't slept a wink.

"Where have you been?" he grumbled. "James, I've told you not to run out like that. Wake me up when you get up."

"Good morning to you, too," Samantha said in a deliberately cheerful tone as she knelt to remove James' wet sneakers. "We went to the bridge to put Neptune back in the water. He had stopped swimming. In fact, he looked rather lonely sitting on the top of the water."

"He went back to his friends," said James.

Samantha frowned. The boy failed to mention anything about the minnow's mother.

"In other words, he D-I-E-D." David spelled out the word very quietly.

Samantha nodded and dried James' feet with a towel.

"He swimmed away." James stated.

The child omitted the fish's destination and Samantha felt an icy shiver race up her spine. Young James knew the forbidden topics. Undoubtedly, he was already psychologically scarred. David had done that to his own son and the thought made her physically sick.

She finished her task and rose to get breakfast on the table, avoiding even one glance at David.

James went over to the table and set the tin can down.

"Put that can in the trash," David ordered.

Samantha saw James flinch at David's gruff words. The child's face went white.

Samantha turned to glare at David, but found that a thundercloud had settled on his brow and seemed more threatening than any in the cheerless sky.

"I'll wash the can," she stated between clenched teeth.

"No. I don't want to be toting around an old tin can." He sounded sharp and bitter. "Put it in the garbage."

"It's my can and I'm washing it." She forced her lips into a false smile. "As long as James is here, he can use it."

She bent down to James' level and spoke in a softer tone. "I'll keep it forever, and when you grow up you can visit me and I'll give it back to you."

James threw his arms around her neck and Samantha had to struggle to keep her tears in check.

"You should not make promises like that," David warned.

"I always keep my promises." She kept her voice low, but it held all the conviction in her heart. With an effort, she put on a smile that defied the sunless day.

"I've got oatmeal for breakfast—with raisins and cinnamon and brown sugar," she told James as she very gently extricated herself from his hug. "It's really porridge you know—just like the Three Bears were going to eat until Goldilocks came along. Do you know that story?"

James shook his head.

"I'll tell you the story while we eat breakfast, then." She reached into the cabinet for bowls and said softly to David. "Why don't you fill in on Papa Bear's part? You have a very authentic growl."

He scowled at her and whispered hoarsely, "Don't come between me and my son."

She felt the black chill between them. Though the tension knotted in her shoulders, she plunged on with recklessness.

"Don't tell me what to do with my can."

Her haughty retort seemed to confuse him. His eyebrows shot up in a quizzical way. Apprehension crept through her, tightening every nerve. In truth, she knew so little about this man. How had he treated his wife?

"I don't care about your can." The wry twist of his mouth marred the perfection of his face.

"Okay! So at last we have some sort of agreement here," she quipped with a gaiety she did not feel. "You don't care about my can. That's great. Now I can wash it!" She tossed it into the sink where it rattled noisily.

"How can you be so happy on a day like this anyway?" David grumbled.

"What's the matter with rain?" She doled out a generous glob of oatmeal into each bowl.

"It's wet," he snorted.

"So's orange juice," she commented. "But I know you've had some now and then. And I bet you liked it."

When she went to sit down, David pulled out her chair as he had done last night. The deferential act unsettled her. She would probably never be privileged to learn of his true background, but his simple gesture seemed to speak volumes about his upbringing.

She and James said grace and then as they ate, she entertained with her best rendition of the Three Bears. James, completely caught up in the story watched her in awe with his wide, blue eyes as if she had hypnotized him.

David's eyes had a different look in them and she had to fight a constant battle to keep from getting lost in their smoldering depths. She could feel his gaze burning a path along her skin. She reminded herself that he had a wife, James' mother, and that he had committed a crime by stealing the child away from that poor, unhappy woman.

In two weeks, though, he and James would be gone. She might never know what had become of the sweet child. Desolation cloaked her with the heavy weight of despair and her shoulders slumped.

Her home would feel so empty when they left. While she and Cassie had spent many long evenings in the cottage on the marsh, until now she hadn't realized how bleak and barren their existence had been.

*   *   *

David could barely stomach the odor coming from the guinea pig cages. The stench could bowl a man over! While

James sat on the floor with Max in his lap, David had been assigned the task of cleaning out the animal's cage. Samantha had informed him that he had to pick out the droppings and then add some fresh pine bedding.

"This is menial labor!" he complained.

"The guinea pigs are an invaluable part of this study," Samantha stated. "Besides, they are the dearest creatures. Right, James?"

James stroked Max's long hair. "He likes me."

David burned with resentment. He was vice-president at one of the biggest insurance firms in the country! Well, he *had been* vice-president and the odds were that he would probably never get his job back. A black cloud of depression hovered over him.

He held his breath and thrust his hand into the cage. Nearly gagging a few times, he nevertheless managed to clean out the cage. When he finished, he gingerly picked up Max from James' lap and put the animal back where it belonged. When he tried to corner Mocha, the wily animal slipped away from him.

"Excuse me, but I can't catch this little guy," he called out to Samantha, who stood at a lab table on the other side of the room.

"Okay, I'll be there in a minute to show you how to do it." she promised. "But in the future, you must remember that you are the boss in that situation."

The irony of her remark actually brought on a humorless smile. "Did you hear that you guinea pigs? I'm your immediate supervisor."

Samantha's laugh echoed in the lab.

David felt better somehow. A phrase from his childhood came drifting back to him. *...the fruit of the Spirit is love, joy, peace, patience, kindness, generosity, faithfulness, gentleness, self-control.* He counted them off on his fingers. All nine.

Shaking his head, he wondered why he had remembered that particular verse. Somebody must have drummed it into his young brain. He didn't believe a word of it.

He studied Samantha while she worked. Perhaps, to him, she seemed to epitomize all those qualities. However, he believed that her disposition was a fortunate mix of genes, not the gift of a nebulous spirit. Her parents must be exactly like her, he decided. He would like to ask her about her family, but he knew he could not because then she might start prying into his past. And he did not want to go there.

He did not understand why he could not stop staring at the woman. She looked every bit the scientist with her long white coat and her hair pulled back tightly in a clip. Efficient, business-like, and completely captivating. Whenever they were in the same room together, he felt like one of those obnoxious mosquitoes seeking out a warm human. The more he thought about it, the more he decided that she had a "presence", a charisma that would charm the pants off most men.

It had already occurred to him that she must have a boyfriend. With her optimistic nature, brains, and natural beauty, she had to be attached to someone. More than likely, the very terrific guy was currently scouring the world for the most perfect diamond to place on her delicate finger, which was why the lucky fellow didn't happen to be anywhere in the vicinity.

Old memories began crowding in on David. There could be no happiness for him. The future held no hope, other than the fact that his son was safe—for now. Maybe. He narrowed his eyes at Samantha and studied her some more. Would she inform the authorities about him and James?

Not until she finished this study, he decided.

"Hey, Daddy." James held up a carrot he had gotten out of the small refrigerator in the lab. "You can make Mocha come out if you give him this."

"Good idea, sport." David ruffled the hair on his son's head. "We'll lure him out."

"It just might work," Samantha called out cheerfully from the lab table. "Let me know, because I'd love to get this part over with." She bent her head to look in the microscope.

"Hold it just in front of him, but don't let him grab it," David told James. "I'll put my hands inside and you see if you can get him to walk onto my hands."

David found out that guinea pigs actually had some intelligence—not much—but enough to thwart the good intentions of humans trying to clean their cages.

Still, David and James would probably have succeeded in their ruse if the slamming of the screen door hadn't startled them. James dropped the carrot, and Mocha snatched it, dragging it to the very farthest corner of the cage.

Biting back an oath, David turned to see a petite young woman standing in the doorway, shaking out her dripping umbrella. She tossed back her long, curly red hair and stamped the mud from her platform shoes onto the tiled floor.

"My boyfriend told me I should apologize."

Her affected drawl grated on David's nerves. Linda spoke in that manner.

"So, like, I'm sorry already," the young woman went on.

David heard a loud sigh from Samantha as she slowly straightened up. She turned away from the microscope to walk over to where the young woman stood.

"I'm sorry, too," Samantha said. "This internship would have looked very good on your résumé."

The young woman's eyes narrowed. "Don't you understand? Like, I'm back already. I'll finish the job." Her voice grew more shrill.

David felt a cold lump form in his chest. What job was this young woman talking about? The job that Samantha had given to him? He felt James' arms curl around his leg and he patted his son's back comfortingly. David thought about the angry words he had spoken to Samantha and wished he could take them all back.

"Ginger, this is my new assistant, David, and his son, James," Samantha's voice sounded smooth, polished, and coolly professional. "I hired David after you left. As far as I'm concerned, you resigned."

Ginger stamped her foot. "I did not resign! I just-I just had a hangover. Okay? Can't you understand that I didn't really mean what I said? I had, like, this massive migraine. You should have a drink now and then. You're, like, so anal."

David watched Samantha's lips press into a grim line. He held his breath. In his estimation, Ginger just shot herself in the foot, but he suspected that Samantha had a very forgiving nature. He couldn't be absolutely sure she would tell Ginger to take a hike.

Samantha crossed her arms over her chest and spoke slowly, "I would not be doing you a favor if I allowed you to return and finish this internship. From what I have observed, you do not have the necessary skills—or temperament—required for this type of research. In fact, I would suggest you change your major to one more suited to your talents."

Ginger's face turned red with rage as every curl on her head shook. She wheeled around and stormed back outside, slamming the screen door so hard that the walls reverberated with the force of it.

"Wait till I tell my father," she yelled. "He's a lawyer!"

David covered his eyes. "Terrific." He still had a job, but the sheriff's office would soon be snooping around and serving warrants.

"I'm sure that's just an idle threat," Samantha commented softly. Then she added with a note of entreaty in her tone. "Please, don't let her intimidate you. Stay and help me finish this project."

Dragging his hand from his face, he gazed down into the somber gray of Samantha's eyes, nearly getting lost in the haze. Needs he had buried away menaced him by striving to burst back into life. He struggled for a moment to hold himself in check.

"I promise I won't do anything to jeopardize your safety," she went on. "I'm still very sorry about last night."

"Y-yeah," he stuttered. "It's okay. I owe you."

That much was the truth. She had done him an

enormous favor. He blew out a gust of air. "Well, I suppose it would take more than two weeks for the wheels of justice to get rolling." Truthfully, it seemed the wheels of justice never seemed to roll in his favor. Still, without a dime to his name, he didn't have any choice.

*   *   *

Lunch turned out to be last night's leftovers or macaroni and cheese. James went for the macaroni and cheese. David opted for the cioppino. Samantha had a little of both, after, of course, she had said her blessing first.

James had memorized most of the words to the simple prayer already, and David couldn't think of a single concrete reason why listening to his son intone grace made him angry, but it did. Maybe the fact lay in the unhappy truth that God had never been there for James. Nobody had stepped in to help his boy who had been a victim of not only Linda's wrath and negligence, but the stupidity of his own father along with agencies designed for the protection of children.

If there was a God, how could He allow someone like Linda to mistreat her own child? How could a loving God have allowed David himself to be so blind to the truth? How could a supposedly benevolent God have permitted so many people to be fooled by Linda's deceptions?

David could only come to the conclusion that God was a figment of a lot of people's imaginations, and that all this praying business was just a waste of breath.

"I have to go into town to do some grocery shopping." Samantha's words drew David away from his dismal thoughts.

"Can I come?" James begged.

David caught Samantha's questioning look. Logic demanded he and James stay put, but after a whole day of total isolation, the call of civilization, however quaint, drew him.

"Why not?" he shrugged.

Samantha gave him a smile that made him forget all the rain outside. He decided he had been wrong about her needing braces as a kid. When she grinned wide, she needed each and every one of her teeth.

He found himself smiling back, much to his surprise.

"Cassie is going to be lonely without Neptune," James said.

"Cassie isn't allowed in the store, and she would get terribly bored waiting for us in the car but she loves dog biscuits, so we'll buy her some," Samantha suggested.

"I'll go say goodbye to her." James slid off his chair and ran to Samantha's room.

David had a sudden sinking feeling in the pit of his stomach. If Samantha had a tough time holding the dog back, James certainly couldn't do it. He stood up and, sure enough, within seconds, the dog rushed into the kitchen with all her teeth bared, snarling in the most menacing way, and giving him the definite impression that he was going to be her next meal.

"Cassie, sit!" Samantha ordered.

Cassie did not sit. She snapped and growled until she had David cornered up against the refrigerator. His heart pounded and his mouth felt like he hadn't swallowed a drop of water in a week.

"Bad dog!" Samantha grabbed the dog's collar. The dog lunged forward, knocking Samantha off balance. She landed on her knees with a cry of pain.

At that point, David knew it was every man for himself. He yanked open the freezer door, grabbed a round container of ice cream, tore off the lid, and threw it on the floor.

Cassie yelped and jumped back as if he had thrown a hand grenade, but she only cowered for a moment. She walked up to the ice cream and sniffed, gave David another malevolent bark, and then dug in.

David took a deep breath and wiped the sweat off his brow.

"Hey, that's my Haagen Dazs!" Samantha grabbed the edge of the counter and pulled herself up off the floor with a moan.

"Are you okay?" Keeping his gaze fixed on the dog, David moved carefully over to where she stood rubbing her knees.

"I need that ice cream for—for medicinal purposes."

"You put it on your skin?"

"Of course not!"

She lifted her face to his, and he could see a rim of tears ready to spill over.

"It's just that sometimes—sometimes—well I just need ice cream!" She sniffed.

"Uh-huh." David raised one eyebrow. "I figured it was the ice cream or my leg."

Samantha grabbed a tissue on the counter and dabbed at her eyes. "Don't think Cassie's going to like you because you gave her my ice cream. The mailman carries those cheesy dog treats with him, but Cassie still abhors him."

"So, you trained her to hate men."

He heard her draw in a sharp breath, obviously insulted by his accusation.

"I did not! She's always been that way."

"Cassie loves ice cream, just like me." James smiled as he knelt beside the dog and stroked its shaggy coat.

David bent down slowly next to the dog and held out his hand. Cassie glanced up briefly, but she was too involved trying to stick her nose all the way down into the container while holding onto it with her front paws.

David patted the dog lightly. She tensed and gave him a little growl, but she wanted every last drop of that ice cream, so she continued frantically licking the container.

"We're going to be friends, Cassie." David ran his fingers along the fur. It felt silkier than old Blarney's bright red coat.

He clenched his jaw. He hadn't saved Blarney, but he had saved his son—so far.

"We'll teach her to catch sticks, Daddy. Right?"

"Maybe even a Frisbee." David nodded. "Yep, she looks like a dog that can catch anything."

After they cleaned up the table and the dishes, they all piled into Samantha's car. David noticed the brown stain on the front seat and remembered the ice cream. He really should try to scrub it out. He thought about the Haagen Dazs as they drove out of the field station.

"I'd like to replace the ice cream the dog ate and get a spare carton. Could you deduct it from my paycheck?"

"With that sort of financing you could wind up having no paycheck."

"If ice cream can prevent me from becoming a chew toy, I think it's worth it."

He heard her deep sigh.

"I was going to replace the ice cream anyway."

"For medicinal purposes only, of course." He pursed his lips to prevent a smile.

She shot him a fierce glare. "You're going to spoil Cassie."

"I'd like to think of it as a positive attitude adjustment."

He watched her cheeks blaze with color, and he grinned.

The rain stopped as they drove along the muddy dirt road and the sun spread through the openings in the clouds.

"This isn't supposed to last," Samantha commented. "I checked the weather online this morning. There's the possibility of severe thunderstorms."

David stiffened. She might have checked out a few more websites with missing children while surfing for the weather.

"We'll do some more work when we get back," she told him. "I like to take a break in the afternoon because the grocery store is air-conditioned."

He sure couldn't call her a slave driver. He frowned as he thought of all the employees he had pushed to the end of their rope as he had clawed his way closer to the top of the corporate ladder.

"How did you manage to put up with Ginger?" he asked.

"I prayed—big time," Samantha admitted. "To Ginger,

having a great time meant that she drank so much, she passed out."

"She looked underage," David commented.

"She is, but she's got a fake ID," Samantha sighed.

"So all your praying didn't change her." He couldn't hide the heavy dose of cynicism in his tone.

"My prayers brought you and James."

David shifted uneasily in his seat as he watched her smile into the rearview mirror at James. It wasn't her prayers! It was chance—dumb luck! He had wandered into Clam Creek because it had a strong resemblance to a ghost town. He had thought they might be safe in the backward hamlet.

As Samantha continued driving, David gave her a few surreptitious glances. She had taken to James like a mother hen, and she had been kinder to his son than David had expected. Would it break James' heart to leave her?

He turned his head and stared out the window as the car passed a clump of cattails. He closed his eyes for a moment as the image of his son, bruised and frightened, gripped him with horror. The memory nearly took his breath away before he shoved the fear to the back of his mind.

As they pulled into the parking lot of the grocery store, James bubbled with excitement.

"Do they have candy?" he asked. "I like candy."

"Candy is bad for your teeth," Samantha reminded.

"I brush my teeth," James informed her. " See." He bared all his choppers.

Samantha's tinkling laughter rippled through the air like music borne on the wind. The sound of it lifted David's spirits.

"Maybe if we buy just a small amount..." Samantha hinted.

"The red ones!" James nodded his head frantically. "The red ones are small."

"The red ones then," Samantha promised.

They went into the wonderfully frigid store and cruised up and down the aisles. James skipped through the store pointing out all the food he had seen on television commercials. Samantha allowed him to choose one box of breakfast cereal.

David groaned at his son's choice. From the photo on the box, it looked like the cereal was made of brightly colored rocks.

"You sure you want to eat that? It looks like it will glow in the dark." He glanced at the ingredients on the side of the box. "Yep. It has artificial flavors, artificial colors, artificial vitamins, uranium—"

Samantha interrupted him with another of her infectious laughs. He glanced at her and the store didn't feel so cold anymore.

"What's uranium?" James asked.

"It's radioactive," David explained. "You eat this cereal and you can run a nuclear power plant all by yourself."

"I'll be strong!" James bounced up and down holding onto the side of the cart.

"And I'll never need to buy another light bulb," David quipped.

He saw the tender curve on Samantha's lips. The look of radiance on her face reminded him of...Chernobyl. He turned away, swallowed hard, and put the box of cereal into the cart. With that expression, she could cause a meltdown and he didn't want to be a part of it. Besides, he reminded himself that he really couldn't trust her.

Nevertheless, when she placed three cartons of ice cream in the shopping cart, he felt enormously relieved.

At the checkout counter, David automatically pulled out his wallet before he remembered that it didn't have anything in it. His face burned with shame as Samantha paid for everything.

As they pushed the grocery laden cart back outside, the clouds above them turned ominously black.

"Looks bad." David could smell the ozone in the air. All hell was about to break loose and standing in the middle of the parking lot would make them prime targets. "We should wait here a few minutes."

Within seconds, the first flash lit up the area, followed by an immediate crack of deafening sound that shook the ground.

Almost immediately, another ear-splitting boom rent the air. Then came a high-pitched shriek. He turned to see Samantha pointing a trembling finger at a distant spot in the parking lot.

"The lightning hit him!" Horror had washed all color from her face.

David looked across the wet blacktop and saw a figure lying on the ground. Immediately, an old familiar surge of adrenaline and instinct took over.

"Call for help," he barked. "James, you stay with Samantha!"

Then he rushed out across the lot as the rain poured down on him.

Chapter Five

Samantha felt rooted to the spot as panic gripped her. "911." James yanked at her hand. "911!"

The child's persistence shattered the cold wall of fear that held her immobile. With James dragging her along, she stumbled into action. Her whole body shook as she rushed into the store. Her words tripped over each other as they tumbled from her lips, but judging from the look of shock on the manager's face, she knew her message had gotten through.

Someone thrust an umbrella and a blanket into her arms, and told her that help was on the way. Hurrying back outside, she and James found that the lightning storm had moved on. They splashed through the pounding rain to the spot where David straddled the fallen man and rhythmically pumped his chest.

Samantha held the umbrella over David. Her throat felt raw and her stomach knotted. She stared at the ashen face of the victim. She knew him. He was a member of Holy Redeemer; a gentle soul, who enjoyed teasing her by telling jokes about scientists.

Dimly aware that the rain had slackened, Samantha wondered if David could keep up his efforts much longer. Time didn't seem to move at all. Wouldn't anyone come to help?

She didn't even hear the sirens until they pulled up alongside of her. A squad of emergency medical technicians materialized like a group of earthly angels in orange jumpsuits. David staggered away as the squad members took over the rescue effort in a flurry of activity.

"It sure took them a while," David muttered. James latched onto his father's leg, throwing him off balance. Samantha's shoulder took the rest of David's weight as he lunged toward her for support. As she struggled to hold up his heavy frame, she gave him a pitying glance. He kept gasping for air.

"Are you going to be okay?"

The fresh scent of the rain mingled with the musky scent of his skin. It smelled honest.

David nodded and let out a big sigh.

She guessed that his heartbeat was slowing down, but hers sped up. She patted his back, tentatively at first, and then she allowed herself to give him a tender squeeze. She had taken a chance that deep down inside David Halpern was a good man, and now she had her intuition confirmed. He really had done something extraordinary.

"You were wonderful. Where did you learn CPR?" she asked.

"I spent several summers as a lifeguard."

Samantha saw David's gaze turn toward the victim. She could see grief etching itself into the lines of David's face when the EMTs loaded the man on the stretcher into the ambulance.

"Up until now, I only lost one." He shook his head.

Samantha felt the blood drain from her face.

"Can I have my candy now?" James asked in a small voice.

"Yeah. Sure, sport."

David's words came out as barely a whisper, but Samantha saw the hope beaming in James' eyes.

They all turned to retrieve their shopping cart from the front of the store. After they loaded the groceries into the trunk of the car, Samantha handed James the candy. His eyes brightened with an almost reverent joy.

"I'll eat two."

Samantha ached at the child's cautiousness. He knew he might not get another box of candy and this one should be savored slowly. She thought of herself and her own usually prudent behavior. She would have done the same thing as James. Until now, she had always been so careful, so guarded in her approach to any situation.

The possibility of losing her cottage changed all that. For her, hiring David had been a rash move taken only in desperation. Though now, after seeing his selfless action, she felt better about it. He was a good man, an honorable man— Suddenly a bright flash startled her. As spots swam before her eyes, she realized that several people had gathered nearby and one of them had taken a snapshot. Turning to glance at David and James, she saw shock plainly written on their faces.

"We're out of here!" David gave a harsh bark. He grabbed the keys she had tossed on the seat of the car. "Get in. I'll drive."

"It's just a snapshot!" Samantha ushered James into the back seat, as David revved up the motor.

"It's one snapshot too many." David growled.

As soon as she slid into her seat and shut the door, David sped off on the slick surface of the blacktop.

"Slow down!" Samantha found her voice rising. She couldn't believe he was doing this.

"If they put my picture in the papers, I could be in jail tomorrow." He drove like a madman on the wet pavement.

"But that wasn't a newspaper reporter—"

She gasped as the car skidded around a corner when he swung the wheel sharply.

"All they have to do is give it to a cop."

Samantha felt sick.

"You'll be in jail tomorrow for reckless driving!" She clutched the dashboard as the hysteria tightened in her throat. "Or we'll all be in the morgue!"

Her anxious words finally had David easing the car into a more moderate pace.

Tense silence charged the atmosphere between them. She could understand his fear, but he had created this crisis by abducting James in the first place.

David swore. "I should never have helped that guy—"

"But I know him." Samantha interrupted as her voice choked with emotion. "He's a dear, sweet fellow, who makes me laugh—"

"I need money," David broke in. "Until I can get in touch with my lawyer—"

"No!" Samantha reined in her sorrow and narrowed her eyes. Folding her arms across her chest, she glared at him. "Is this what you've become? A common thief."

"I'm not going to steal it!" David thundered. "I'm asking for a loan!"

"I am not going to let you do this to James. I am not going to facilitate this insanity." She couldn't stop herself from shaking. She glanced at James in the back seat. His face had gone totally white. Motionless, the boy stared out the window, clutching his box of candy. She saw a tiny tear roll down his cheek.

Fighting to control the anguish that threatened to overwhelm her, she prayed. *Dear Lord, help this little one.*

"Nobody is going to come all the way out to the field station to do a media interview on you." She kept her voice as even as she could manage. "And if they did, there's a million places for you to hide. You are far better off in the marsh than on the road."

"You are only saying that because you need a helper to finish your research," David's voice lashed out at her.

If he had punched her in the stomach, it wouldn't have hurt as much. She slumped down in the seat. Cold, weary and out of options, she admitted to herself that she had been wrong. She should not have gotten involved with David and James. She should have notified the authorities directly and immediately.

As they neared the field station, David slammed down on the brakes unexpectedly.

"Whose truck is that?" he growled.

Samantha looked up. Her heart warmed when she saw her old friend wave to them.

"Fish man." The soft answer came from the back seat.

"Fish," Samantha corrected. "He's brought us supper."

"We're leaving."

The stern, hard tone in his voice could have cut

Samantha like a knife.

Fish walked up to the car as soon as it pulled in. He carried a big white bucket.

"Sammie, look what I've got—blue crabs." His raspy voice chuckled. "Sold two buckets of 'em to some tourists but I saved the best for you and your helpers there."

The grizzled old fisherman gave Samantha more fresh seafood than she could ever possibly eat by herself. Fortunately, Cassie had developed a liking for seafood leftovers.

Samantha opened the car door and got out to look at the crabs. The bucket brimmed with an incredible bounty.

Taking a calming breath, she struggled to act as if everything was fine.

"What did you use for bait?"

Perhaps her voice came out too soft and too whispery because Fish gave her a barely perceptible nod, as if he guessed some of her trouble.

"Chicken. They love chicken," he replied.

James climbed out of the back of the car and stared down into the bucket with an air of resignation, an odd emotion in one so young. Samantha's heart ached.

"Do they bite?" he asked in a dull tone.

"Oh, they snap at your fingers something terrible with those claws." Fish pulled out a can opener from his overalls and dangled it in front of the crabs. One crab lurched at it and hung on, even as Fish lifted the creature out of the bucket. "Make a grown man cry if one of those held on to his finger."

James' eyes widened in interest for a moment. Then David came around from the other side of the car and the youngster's shoulders sagged. Samantha wanted to hug James and never let go.

"Um, this is David Halpern, Fish." Her heart felt wooden as she twisted a stray lock of hair around her finger. "James' father."

Fish dropped the can opener with the crab still attached.

He stuck out his hand to David. "Pleased to meet you."

A few seconds passed by before David reached out to grasp Fish's hand. The reluctance on David's part seemed awkward and obvious to Samantha, like a social snub, but apparently it didn't bother Fish.

"You got a nice boy there," Fish noted, grinning at James.

David cleared his throat. "Thanks."

"Neptune stopped swimming in the can," James stated quietly.

"That can happen," Fish rumbled sympathetically. "But I found you some new friends. A whole bunch of 'em. They're as lively as any of God's marvelous creations."

James lifted his face, and Samantha saw the light of hope spark ever so faintly.

Fish lumbered back to his truck.

"We aren't taking any souvenirs with us," David warned in a low voice.

"Miss Samantha will keep them for me," James responded with confidence.

"Yes, I will," Samantha said firmly. "Forever."

They followed Fish to the truck. He slid another big bucket out of the back, and then lowered it below the level of James' chest.

"Hermit crabs," Fish said. "Crazy little things. They don't have a home of their own. They go creeping around looking for empty shells that some other animal left behind. Then they crawl inside and make it their own."

"Squatters," David commented, giving a sardonic twist to his mouth.

"Nah." Fish shook his head. "They're just using shells that are already empty. Doing what the good Lord wants 'em to do. Nothing goes to waste in His creation." He stuck one hand down deep into the bucket and picked up one of the small creatures.

"Here ya go, son. They don't bite. Open up your hand and let this little guy tickle you."

Samantha saw eagerness shining in James' eyes as he reached out for the hermit crab.

"What's his name?" James asked as the animal sat in the middle of his palm with all of its spindly legs drawn up inside the shell.

"Why, that one there you can name yourself, son," Fish decreed.

James' smile spread slowly. "He's gonna be Kyle, like my friend."

"Any man with a true friend is a king," Fish said.

Samantha saw the old man's eyes water a bit, and found a lump welling in her own throat. Fish had the tender heart of a poet, and Samantha wished she knew what had hurt him so badly that the pain still plagued him. Undoubtedly, any probing questions would upset him further and she would never do that.

The little animal in James' hand gingerly stretched its tiny legs out from under the shell and started to scurry across James' palm.

James giggled. "He's tickling me."

"Now don't let him fall down." Samantha cupped her hands beneath the young child's.

"Hey, Kyle," James laughed. "You re so funny."

Fish pulled a red bandanna out from his pocket and blew his nose.

"Well, I better get moving," the old man said in a gravelly rumble. "I was up at three this morning."

"Why don't you join us for supper?" Samantha offered.

"No, thank you. But it's mighty kind of you to ask."

"Oh, Fish," Samantha sighed. "You've given me so much, it would be nice if you would help me eat some of it once in a while."

Fish gave her a shy smile. "Those are from God's bounty. You best be thanking Him and not me."

"Miss Samantha always thanks God," James piped up.

"She's a good woman." Fish nodded. "A special gift for some lucky man."

Slowly, Fish's gaze turned to David. He stared long and hard, without saying a word for several moments. Samantha watched as David shifted uneasily from one foot to the other.

Then Fish, obviously finished with his assessment, scratched the beard on his chin and turned to push up the tailgate on his pickup.

Samantha stole a quick glance at David. His eyes had a stony resignation in them that chilled her. Tension crackled in the air as she watched David's jaw stiffen.

The old fisherman shuffled around to the front of the vehicle and pulled himself up into the driver's seat. "Won't be any rain now for a good long time. Gonna dry up the marsh, keep an eye out for smoke."

Samantha nodded. She'd become used to Fish's warnings, and had learned to heed them. He knew the signs to watch for in this strange little corner of the world. She bit her lip to stop it from trembling. With David leaving, there would be no hope for her to finish her research. Her heart felt as if it had a band around it and each second the band tightened.

"Bye Kyle," James said as he lowered the little critter down to the bottom of the bucket.

Samantha reached for James' hand and they moved closer to the cottage, well away from the truck. Fish turned on the noisy engine, and with a deafening intensity of sound, he shifted the gears. The truck pulled away from them, splashing through the puddles on the dirt road and sending off wide arcs of mud.

For a stretch of several minutes, nobody said anything. Samantha knew it would be hopeless to argue. The only option left to her was prayer. She closed her eyes for a moment and offered up her most heartfelt petition.

"I need to get our stuff," David broke the silence. "And I'll be expecting the pay you owe me."

Samantha opened her eyes and wearily went to the trunk of the car. Grabbing a bag of groceries, she walked across the yard to the sounds of Cassie's ecstatic barks. The dog's greeting didn't make Samantha smile as usual. When she unlocked the door, Cassie seemed to sense that something had gone wrong, and she whined in a most sympathetic manner.

"We forgot the dog biscuits," James said sadly.

"That's okay. I bought more hot dogs," Samantha tried to keep her voice light, but the effort seemed almost impossible. After years of wandering, she'd found her own beginning and come home. Now she would have to leave once more.

Cassie followed Samantha and James into the kitchen.

Samantha ordered the dog to sit but when Cassie obeyed, she shot her mistress a questioning look. James patted the dog tenderly.

"I'm really sorry that we didn't get you the biscuits," Samantha explained to her pet. She clipped a leash on the dog's collar, so she could hold onto the dog in case David walked into the room.

"I'll miss you, Cassie." James knelt down and threw his arms around the dog. She licked him and then cried so pathetically that Samantha felt like joining in.

Fighting back her emotions, she reached into the refrigerator, pulled out a hot dog and handed it to James.

Then the phone rang. Samantha gave James the end of the leash and hurried to answer the telephone. The person on the other end turned out to be David's lawyer.

When she called him, David rushed in, carrying two bags of groceries. She couldn't mistake the relief she saw in his eyes as he put the receiver to his ear. Miserable, she turned away. If David's lawyer gave him good news, she would still lose her house.

Unable to bear listening to the conversation, she asked James to come along with her to the lab to say goodbye to the guinea pigs. Cassie trotted along with them as James held the leash.

As she entered the lab, the heavy weight of Samantha's woes lifted slightly. The familiar work environment calmed her. She knew she could find work in another lab, doing similar research. Unfortunately, it wouldn't be here in Clam Creek. Most likely, it would be far from the sleepy little town.

She could still visit Marion, Agnes, Fish, and all the others she had grown to care for at Holy Redeemer church. However, she knew that time and distance would make her trips to Clam Creek short and far apart. The town where she had spent her early years and where her mother's grave lay had given her roots and quenched her soul's longing. Still, she had to face facts. She had come to the end of this brief, idyllic sojourn.

"The guinea pigs are hungry," James stated.

Sure enough, the crazy critters were gnawing at the bars of their cages and squeaking their loudest to get attention.

"They are always hungry," Samantha sighed. "I keep hay for them in the closet. You can give them each a handful."

She walked over to the closet, opened the door, and pulled off the top of the plastic bin where she kept the hay. But when she turned around, she didn't see James. A small sliver of panic chilled her.

"James?" she called out. "James?"

Swallowing a lump of fear, she raced around the lab table and the animal cages, but he wasn't there. She stood still, with her heart pounding nearly loud enough to be heard.

She forced herself to think logically and realized that if the child had run out of the lab, she would have heard the screen door slam. James still had to be there, and Cassie was probably with him.

"Cassie!" Samantha called.

The dog whined from a far corner of the lab. Samantha followed the sound. Cassie sat on the floor next to a stack of cartons that held mosquito traps. Behind the cartons, crouched down low with his arms around his legs sat James.

"Are you hiding from me?" she asked.

He gave a small shake of his head.

"From your father?"

He nodded.

Samantha's mind filled with her own bitter past. She knew the kind of torment that was tearing at the child's heart, but she could do so little to help him.

She bent down at his side. "Here, I have some hay. The guinea pigs love this stuff as much as they love carrots."

James did not lift up his head, but he snatched at the hay and clutched it tightly.

"Are you sad about leaving?" Samantha asked. James didn't answer, and his total withdrawal ripped at her. She rose and went back to the guinea pig cages. Capturing Kiszka without too much trouble, she carried the small animal to James and held it so that it could nibble at the hay clenched tightly in his little fist.

In a few moments, James lifted his head to watch the ravenous creature tugging valiantly at each strand of hay. Soon he had Kiszka in his lap, quietly offering it more hay with one hand and stroking its soft fur with his other hand.

Samantha felt his pain. Memories of her childhood spilled out as if a keen knife had cut through her. She knew what it was like; the insane paranoia of life on the run left a soul empty and isolated. If James asked to take Kiszka with him, she would let him. She would give him anything if it would ease his suffering.

And then she remembered the one thing that was worth more than any material gift.

"I remember you telling me how Kyle said God could fix things for you."

James nodded as he continued to stroke the guinea pig's soft coat.

"Did you know that God has a son?" Samantha continued.

James lifted his eyes to hers at that point and shook his head.

"His son's name is Jesus and he wants to be your very best friend, an even better friend than Kyle, because he wants to go everywhere you go and stay with you wherever you are."

James gave a sad, little sigh. "Daddy said there's no

room."

"But there's always room for Jesus." Samantha smiled. "Because he can live right in your heart."

James frowned at her for a moment and her heart plummeted. Had he become so worldly at his tender age? She wanted to give him hope, but could she? Had James become so savvy that he would think it merely another fairy tale like the one she had told him that morning?

"Kyle has a Jesus song," James said.

Warmth flooded through Samantha. God bless Kyle, wherever he was.

"Do you know the words?" she asked.

James shrugged his meager shoulders.

Samantha guessed at what Kyle's Jesus song might be. She sang "Jesus Loves Me," soft and sweet, praying that the simple tune would touch James' heart and guide him on his way.

James lowered his head as he listened. When Samantha finished, he asked her to sing it again.

The third time she sang it, James joined in on the chorus. He had an angelic voice and carried the melody well. Samantha could barely hold her tears back at the beauty of the moment, but then they both heard the screen door open. James jumped as his father walked into the lab. Cassie growled menacingly.

"Stop trying to 'save' my son," David accused. His face wore an angry flush.

"He needs an anchor for his soul." Samantha took Cassie's leash and the dog barked in agreement with her.

"Religion isn't going to help him at all. I want him to grow up strong and independent. I don't want him to think that God is going to perform any miracles for him, because He won't!"

Samantha stood up to face David. "Are you blaming God for all your troubles?"

Cassie snarled.

"No. He doesn't exist!"

Samantha had never met anyone so adamantly opposed to God's very existence. There seemed to be an abundance of souls who readily acknowledged that God was up there, somewhere, in His heaven, though they really didn't think He did much here on earth.

Samantha stood up to face David. "He's real. You simply feel that He's failed you."

"Stop it!" Fury laced his command. "Not another word about God or Jesus or I'm out of here."

Samantha blinked in confusion. "You were leaving immediately anyway."

David's hand shook as he ran it through his hair. "My lawyer wants me to stay put."

A surge of relief coursed through her, leaving her knees with all the stiffness of seaweed. She reached out to brace herself on the counter while her emotions careened up and down. After taking a deep breath, she managed to sputter out one word. "W-why?"

His gaze turned toward James. Worry furrowed his brow before he answered in barely a whisper.

"There's been some progress. The private investigator has a video that could be damaging to James' mother. It proves she isn't the saint most people seem to think she is. We probably won't be able to use it in court, but it could provide some leverage."

Samantha clasped her hands tightly around Cassie's leash, remembering the horrible things that her father had claimed her mother had done, but her father had lied.

Could she believe David? She knew that a parent who resorted to abduction created a full-scale war that left nothing but casualties littering the battlefield.

Nobody won.

She glanced at James. He appeared to be deep in thought while toying absently with Kiszka's fur. What sad musings occupied his young mind? "Is your lawyer going to send you money?" she asked.

David gave a short, harsh laugh. "No. And he isn't going

to cut his vacation short either." With that news, Samantha took another deep breath. One minute, despair held her in its grip and then, without warning, she had hope again. She didn't know how much more of this she could take.

However, James again had stability in his life, even if only for a short time. That thought cheered her immeasurably. She straightened her spine.

Cassie, who had settled down beside her, sighed, yawned, stretched, and delivered a token snarl.

"If you're staying, you'll have to get to work. Let's cook up those crabs before they get wise and crawl away."

Before bustling off to work, she paused and fixed David with her most piercing look.

"But you can expect me to talk about God and Jesus as often as I feel the need," she warned. "Faith has been a comfort to me."

She saw David glower back at her, but she didn't care. She could no more deny God and His Son than she could stop breathing.

Chapter Six

David stood at the door of his room and glared at the bright lights still shining in the lab. Eleven o'clock had come and gone five minutes ago, but Samantha remained at work. All week, she had pushed herself relentlessly on the research project. She got up with the sun and crawled into bed during the wee hours of the night. Despite the dark hollows which had settled under her eyes, she continued to be committed to her grueling schedule.

She had taken a few hours off to go to the funeral of the man who had been struck by lightning, but other than that, she plunged on with such focused determination that she reminded David of himself in the months following his separation from Linda.

Samantha's clothes hung more loosely on her already thin frame. Though Fish dropped by each day with some kind of fresh seafood, Samantha ate little of it, always rushing back to the lab as soon as possible.

David grumbled to himself as he scratched several of his many mosquito bites. He couldn't help but admire Samantha's dedication, but he knew she was wearing herself out with her punishing regimen. He shouldn't care. He didn't care. It just annoyed him.

The week hadn't been all bad, of course. He had enjoyed exploring his new surroundings with James. Because he still feared that he might be recognized, whenever Samantha went off to town in the afternoon, she went alone, which left David and James free. They had discovered a small beach on the edge of the marsh where James had met all the denizens of the shoreline. With a small textbook that Samantha had loaned them, he and his son looked up the names of the resident creatures. James seemed to have an aptitude for remembering facts, even though he hadn't learned to read yet and his retention of the tiniest details often amazed David. At Samantha's urging, James had begun a shell collection, which naturally Samantha promised she would keep for him.

Nevertheless, it was Saturday night, and David had tired of the monotony. He craved a beer, he wanted to sink his teeth into a steak, and he wanted some lively entertainment, which could not be found on the few channels available on Samantha's non-cable television or in her assortment of very tame videos. He wanted to bust loose.

He pounded the doorframe with his fist as he thought about how he and Samantha had barely spoken to each other all week. Well, it wasn't his fault. At mealtimes, she talked to James about Jesus. David sat there seething in silence while she deliberately indoctrinated his son.

James enjoyed her Bible stories as much as he would any other fairy tales, and eagerly anticipated meals just to hear another story. So far, David had held his tongue, but he didn't know how much longer that would last.

His son adored Samantha. David pounded the doorframe again. She was driving him nuts.

At work in the lab, Samantha constantly gave David orders. Sure, she did it in her soft and lilting voice, and she always remembered to say, "Please," too. But he was used to giving orders, not getting them, and it grated on his nerves.

David briefly considered whether prison could be compared to living at Field Station Number Thirty-Seven. But his conscience bothered him at the thought because he knew that Samantha couldn't ever be considered a cruel taskmaster. No, she had simply been cool to him. Unfailingly polite, but decidedly reserved. Why should he expect more? She knew what he was. She had done him a huge favor. Still, David felt almost desperate enough to risk using his credit card to escape the tedium despite the fact that his lawyer had called again that morning and warned him once more to stay put. The private detective had filmed more of Linda's escapades on video. He claimed the footage was so detrimental to Linda's case that she would be a fool to persist in her allegations against David. David almost groaned aloud. He knew Linda better than the private detective. Linda was a fool, but worse than that, her vindictiveness had no limits.

Restless, David walked back to the bunk to check on James. He had so many hopes for the boy. He had even begun to think of what college James should choose. Since David had not been accepted by Yale, he hoped James could get in. Then his foot kicked over the can that James had left at the bottom of the ladder. The metallic clang brought with it the vivid image of prison bars and for a brief moment panic spun through him. Adrenaline pumped into his veins and he wanted to run again, to clutch his boy close to him and escape into the darkness.

He drew his hands into hard fists and forced the fear away by visualizing Blarney, his goofy dog. His pet had been full of crazy antics and hopelessly stupid when it came to training. Recalling all the difficulty of trying to get his dog to heel left him ready to laugh and cry at the same time. As much as he had loved that dog, he knew the dog loved him even more. The terror eased as his mental trick calmed him.

Then he thought of Cassie. She loved Samantha, but unlike Blarney, she seemed serious and intelligent—much like her mistress. How could it be that dogs had such different personalities?

Supposedly, no two snowflakes were alike and no two grains of sand, either.

David scratched his arm again. What about mosquitoes? Were they all different?

Did earth and all its inhabitants just happen by chance?

David clenched his jaw. Why not? If there was a God, shouldn't He be doing something to help all the disenfranchised souls in this world?

David watched as James slept peacefully, probably dreaming about hermit crabs, mole crabs, snails, and jellyfish. He had gotten a nice tan during the week and looked like he put on a few pounds. He had eaten as much ice cream as Cassie. He smiled a lot more, too. Samantha only smiled at

James. Or Fish. Or the mailman. Or Cassie.

Okay, she smiled at everybody *except* him. So what? He didn't care.

...love, joy, peace, patience, kindness, generosity, faithfulness, gentleness, self-control.

He shook his head remembering the fruits of the Spirit again. It seemed that all week Samantha had been practicing self-control with him. He had the feeling that she wanted to jam Jesus down his throat, too, but it wasn't working and she knew it. He glanced at his watch again. It was almost Sunday. Annoyance and frustration warred inside him. Finally, he decided to do something about it. Leaving his room, he crossed the short hallway and stood at the door to the lab. He itched for an argument, or anything that would break the dull monotony of the past week.

The screen door slammed behind him as he walked into the lab.

"It's Sunday, your day of rest," he called out. "Take a break."

Then he spotted her next to the microscope, slumped in the chair with her head cradled on her folded arms which rested on the counter top. For a moment, he hesitated. She hadn't stirred at all despite his boisterous entry.

Swallowing hard, he quietly moved closer. He could see the rise and fall of her shoulders with each breath she took. Relief swept through him. Evidently, she had fallen very soundly asleep.

"Samantha, wake up," he insisted as he gently shook her shoulders.

She mumbled something that sounded like, "Leave me alone." Then she tried to settle herself comfortably again.

"This is ridiculous!" He shook her again. "Quit for tonight and get some real rest!"

She lifted her head, looking dazed and confused.

"Oh no," she whined. "What time is it?"

"Time to go to bed, obviously!" Irritated, he spat out the words. He had been ready to walk in and demand that she buy beer, steak, and a better selection of videos, but it was tough to argue with someone who was asleep.

He watched her push the hair out of her dreamy gray eyes with a languid motion, as if the silken strands had been weighted with lead. Seeing her so vulnerable disturbed him.

"I've got to finish this," she muttered with a sigh. "It'll just take a few more minutes." Her fingers fumbled with the papers that had lain beneath her head.

"No!" He kept his order curt. He doubted if she would really understand anything more since he didn't believe that she was fully awake yet. "You are going to close this place up for the night, or I am going to carry you out of here and put you in bed."

Her eyes grew round and wide as she stared up at him.

"I can bench press one hundred eighty pounds." He stated the fact quietly, which somehow gave it more emphasis. "Picking you up would be a piece of cake."

She gasped as if he had finally gotten through to her foggy mind, and obviously realized that he would certainly carry out his threat if need be.

Clumsily, she got up from the chair and stumbled around, turning off the microscope, filing away her papers, and closing the cabinets.

"You are murdering yourself over these stupid mosquitoes," he complained as she puttered around the lab. "Who is really going to care?"

She covered a weary yawn. "Haven't you heard of West Nile Virus?"

"As a matter of fact, I was wondering what happens if I catch it out here while I'm being eaten alive by those voracious bugs." He paced the floor, restless and bitter. "Do I get workman's compensation?"

She blinked her eyes and frowned as if the question puzzled her momentarily. Then she rubbed her eyes with her fists. "Hey. I hired you off the books."

He stopped pacing and put his hands on his hips. She made such a pathetic figure; her eyes were red, her hair had tumbled out of the clip that usually held it securely in place, and her face looked pasty. He had a terrible urge to take care of her.

"I'm turning out the lights and locking the door, right now, before you collapse." He kept his voice firm, that no-nonsense tone that had always had subordinates jumping to do his bidding.

She attempted to hide yet another yawn. "I have to say good night to the piggies and give them a little more hay."

"I'll take care of them." He opened the screen door. "You get off to bed."

She shuffled to the door obediently. "Thanks. I might have been here all night."

Her lips spread into one of her wide smiles, but this one was just for him. His alone. Her eyes were still embraced by the cloudy softness of dreams. For a moment, she held him mesmerized. A lazy warmth shimmered through him and robbed him of breath.

He touched her shoulder as she stood grinning up at him, and strands of her honey-colored hair fell across his knuckles. He wondered how many nights Samantha had fallen asleep next to the microscope. How many lonely evenings had she spent in this god-forsaken wasteland when she had all the sweet goodness of the sunshine glowing from within her?

His hand went from her shoulder to cup her chin. Her tender lips drew him, and before he realized it, he tasted her and found the warmth of the sun along with the nectar of summer wildflowers in her kiss. Somehow, he had known it would be special, like her. He had never met a woman quite as unique as Samantha Lyons.

He came to his senses when a stray mosquito landed on him, intent on drawing blood. As he slapped the annoying bug, he drew back and saw shock engraved on Samantha's face. A flaming blush blooming on her cheeks made her only lovelier, and he bent towards her again.

"N-no!" she sputtered. "No! I—I…"

Then she rushed out the door and hurried across the yard.

David watched her enter the cottage. He frowned as his mouth turned as dry as all those grains of sand on the beach. Realization slammed into him like a direct hit on the solar plexus. He swept his hand over his face. In a moment of weakness, he had let his guard down. Would Samantha dismiss him as coldly as she had the unfortunate Ginger?

He had to stay here! Right now everything hung in the balance, and he had to keep James safe. Nothing mattered more than that.

...*self-control.*

David ran his hand through his hair and paced the floor. How could he have done this? His shoulders drooped as he reasoned that any man would have attempted the same thing. She had looked so luscious, like a peach ripe for the harvest. He licked his lips and still tasted her flavor there.

A dull ache, like that from an old wound, gnawed at him. How could he have forgotten that he wasn't just any man? Right now, he was a criminal. Samantha had only to pick up the phone and call the nearest police station.

Bleakly, he knew the truth was that he had been a little bored after one week and went asking for trouble. Furthermore, he had gotten it, risking his own son's future. What kind of father was he? Would he never learn?

He glanced back outside, through the screen door. The lights were on in the kitchen of the cottage. Samantha had not yet retired.

He threw his shoulders back. He would apologize, forget about his pride, and grovel. He had already thrown everything away for his son's safety. He didn't have anything else to lose.

* * *

Samantha stared at her reflection in the dark window

above the kitchen sink. She ran her fingers under the cold water and touched them to her blazing lips, but that didn't wash away the feeling. Fully awake now, she heard the blood roaring in her ears as her heart raced double time.

What had happened? Had she just ruined everything?

She felt the heat on her cheeks and splashed more cool water on her skin. She had been so groggy when David woke her up. If he hadn't been so insistent, she really could have been there all night. When he promised to give the guinea pigs more hay and close up the lab for the night, her heart had warmed at the consideration he had shown for her.

How had that kiss happened? Though she had been half-asleep, she shouldn't have allowed it! But she wasn't quite sure that she had even known it was coming until his lips touched hers and the dreamy, blissful warmth coursed through her.

Samantha closed her eyes and tried to slow her heartbeat with deep, even breaths.

Her stomach churned. What would David do next?

Samantha opened her eyes and turned off the water. She wasn't sleepy anymore. In fact, she didn't think she would be able to lie down for the rest of the night. Keeping her mind on the exacting statistics for her research would be equally impossible at this point as well.

She reached under the sink for a bucket, a bottle of potent-smelling pine cleaner, and her scrub brush. She poured a dollop of the cleaner into the bucket, then added hot water. She glared at the floor, bent down on her knees, dipped the brush into the water, and applied it to the floor.

Within a few minutes, she had lots of soapy bubbles swirling in wide arcs on the tile floor. Her mind kept circling with the brush in her hand. She could not deny that she enjoyed that brief kiss. The echoes of it continued to reverberate in her heart.

Nevertheless, it was wrong!

She scrubbed furiously, ignoring the protest from her tired muscles.

"Like I said before, isn't Sunday your day of rest?"

She heard him speak softly from behind her, but she didn't turn around.

"Cleanliness is next to godliness," she spat out and scrubbed even harder.

"Hey, I'm sorry."

She paused for a moment. Could she accept his apology? If she did, would he think he could kiss her again? She swallowed hard.

"Sure you are." She ground out the words between her teeth, using every ounce of sarcasm she could muster.

"I really mean it."

She heard his big shoes plop down on her sudsy lather and whirled to glare at him. A tumult of conflicting emotions swept through her when she saw the sincerity in his eyes and a feverish surge of excitement threatened to undo her completely. Grasping for a way to conceal her inner turmoil, she lashed out at him.

"Stop stepping on my bubbles!"

"Oh, sorry." He moved to a dry section of the floor, but, of course, his feet spread a film of muddy slime wherever he went.

"Now see what you've done." She pointed to the offending area with her brush.

"Uh. I'll fix that up." He rushed out of the kitchen, trailing large, patterned footprints behind him.

Samantha sat beside the bucket and felt the tears filling her eyes. He had made a mess of everything! Her heart, her floor, and her quiet peaceful life had been turned upside down by this one man! Still, she had no one to blame but herself. She had brought David and his son into her home.

But what else could she do? She had to finish her research or she would lose her lovely little cottage. Besides, there was James. She had done this for him, too.

At that point, David raced back into the kitchen carrying one of her nice, fluffy bath towels—a brand new one she had purchased not long ago that had a pattern of seashells on it.

She knew he intended to wipe up the mud with her beautiful towel!

"No!" She called out and waved her hands in the air.

David put one huge shoe down on the soapy tiles and slipped. Both of his feet went up in the air, and the rest of him seemed destined to land on her bucket. In one quick move, she snatched the bucket out of the way. However, in doing that, she slopped all that pine-scented, mud-tinged water on herself.

David crashed with a resounding whump on the floor and lay there quite still for a moment. Samantha quaked inside, wondering how badly he had hurt himself.

"I'm so sorry!" Her voice quivered as shock set in. "I should have warned you that the floor was slippery." Tentatively, she touched his arm with her hand.

She leaned forward, anxiously searching for a good sign, hoping he hadn't broken every bone in his body. Slowly, he turned his head to look at her, but unexpectedly she saw his eyes widen and his mouth drop open. When he quickly closed his eyes, turned away and groaned, Samantha wrung her hands together as raw panic nearly overwhelmed her.

"Okay. I understand. You can't move. There's probably internal injuries and fractures." Her voice trembled with hysteria, but she couldn't help it. "I-I'll call the ambulance."

"No!" The rough edge in his voice startled her.

She placed her shaky hand on his arm. "I know you're worried about being discovered—"

"I'm not hurt," he interrupted. "Much."

She noticed that he kept his eyes tightly shut, as if something pained him.

"You're in shock," she decided, trying to remember the signs and symptoms.

"Yes, I am definitely that," he muttered. He tossed the towel at her that he still had clutched in his hand. "Cover yourself up, will you, before I go into cardiac arrest."

She caught the towel, glanced down at her clothing, and gasped. Her gauzy cotton shirt, now sopping wet, clung to every one of her natural curves. Hastily, she wrapped the towel around her body.

"Go away," he begged.

"B-but are you okay otherwise?" she asked.

"Yes," he hissed with what sounded like exasperation.

"Are you sure?"

"Get into something dry!"

Samantha gulped. "Right."

Stepping carefully, so she wouldn't become another casualty on the wet floor, she went to her room. Cassie got up from a snooze and sauntered over to her.

"Oh, Cassie," she whispered to her pet, "look at me. So far, I haven't done anything right tonight."

Cassie raised her eyebrows sympathetically and cocked her head to one side, looking as if she was ready to listen to the whole tale.

"Everything's hopelessly messed up," Samantha sniffed as she reached for her bathrobe. "We worked fine together and then all of a sudden. Boom. He kisses me."

Cassie opened her mouth. Samantha knew the dog was grinning from ear to ear.

"So you think that's funny?" Samantha sighed. "You should have been in the kitchen."

Cassie whined.

"Yeah, it had to hurt." Samantha tossed off her wet clothes and wrapped herself up securely in the robe. "So I'll go check on him now, before I wash up I smell like pine-scented cleaner, don't I?" She bent down and hugged the dog.

Cassie sneezed.

Samantha laughed. "I love you, Cassie. I don't know what I'd do without you."

Cassie licked her.

Leaving her room, Samantha very nearly bumped into David. He was pulling towels out of the linen closet. A huge wave of relief swept over her.

"How do you feel?" she asked. She wondered if he had been listening to her as she talked to Cassie. Nevertheless, she hadn't said anything truly earth shattering to the dog.

David turned to look at her. "I suppose I'll live."

Samantha frowned. He didn't seem too happy about the prospect of surviving.

"You really should see a doctor. I'm sure you got a few nasty bruises or maybe you hit your head."

"I'm a lot tougher than I look. The only part I've wounded is my pride." He twisted up his mouth in a mocking smile and recited, "Pride goes before a fall."

Samantha blinked in surprise. "That comes from the Bible."

"I know. I'm not totally ignorant," he said.

Samantha bit her lip. How little she knew about this man! He shut the linen closet door.

"I'll mop up the mess for you," he said.

Samantha rolled her eyes. "I own a mop. Towels are for drying hands, faces, and other human body parts."

She watched his gaze slide to where her bosom lay covered by a half-inch of thick terry cloth.

He cleared his throat. "These will work just as well."

Samantha sighed. It was too late to argue with him.

"I'm going to take a quick shower," she said.

"Good. Women should smell like flowers, not pine trees."

His boyish grin returned and the power of it totally disarmed her. Her heart whirled and danced, leaving her feeling far too warm.

She had an overwhelming urge to reach out and touch the impish smile, but she willed herself instead to hurry into the bathroom. Once safely inside, she hoped to slow her wild pulse with a cool shower. However, when she turned on the water it flowed out in a tepid stream as it usually did all summer long.

As she rinsed away the pine-scented cleaner, she couldn't stop thinking of that one gentle kiss. It had changed everything and made it all so much more complicated.

She knew she would have to be very careful in the week

ahead. She already loved James and would be broken-hearted when he left, but she must not fall for David. She would have to be very cool; friendly, but distant, in dealing with him. She must always keep him at arm's length so that he never got close to her again.

That would be the best thing to do, she told herself, but she came out of the shower just as warm as she went in.

Chapter Seven

"Daddy, wake up!"

David winced as James yanked his shoulder back and forth. Evidently, his fall in the kitchen last night had caused some damage. He felt as if he had jumped out of a plane without a parachute.

He rolled over, groaning as he discovered a few more tender spots.

"It's Sunday. Get back in bed," he grumbled.

"But Daddy!" James' voice became more insistent. "My arm growed."

"*Grew.*" David corrected absently. "Get in—"

Grew? The word flashed a warning in David's groggy mind.

He blinked several times but it seemed impossible to open his eyes beyond narrow slits. When had he closed his eyes and drifted off?

He had sopped up all the water on the kitchen floor and then hung the soggy towels outside on the line. Afterwards, he lay in his bunk trying to forget that kiss. Not that Samantha's lips hadn't been—well—great, but she obviously had not felt quite the same about the experience. And who could blame her? He was, after all, a wanted man.

Slowly, he sat up, but the effort seemed like a Herculean task. Somehow, he managed to prop his elbows on his knees and hold his head in his hands.

"See, Daddy!" James put his arm next to David's nose. "My arm's fat."

David heard the tremulous quiver in James' voice. Making a valiant attempt to clear his foggy brain, he peered at his son. James' distended limb indicated that something had gone drastically wrong. David's heart thundered as he held off a wave of panic. He reached out to draw James closer and study the condition of his arm. When he pressed down on the bulging skin, it felt hot to the touch.

His stomach clenched in a spastic knot. With James' arm swollen way out of proportion even his knuckles seemed to have been swallowed up

"My fingers are stuck," James said.

"What happened?" David's heart slammed against his ribs. He ground his teeth together. He wanted James to be safe, and now this! He didn't know if he could deal with another cruel twist of fate.

"A bug bit me." James took in a ragged breath as he pointed to a small, red patch. "Right there."

David's mind raced. What if he needed anti-venom? How many minutes did he have? "Was it a spider?"

"No. A green head." James let out a sob. "He bit me hard."

David tamped down his anger to hug James and give him a reassuring pat despite the fear that crept along his own spine. James had been bitten by lots of green-headed flies before, but until now, the insects hadn't affected him.

"Miss Samantha said Jesus makes people get better." James sniffed.

David pressed his lips into a thin line and felt his blood pressure rise. He had heard Samantha rattle on about Jesus' miracles. Fury simmered beneath the surface whenever he listened to her attempting to brainwash James, but it would only be for one week more, he reminded himself.

Unexpectedly, a heavy stab of remorse sank into him. Evangelizing was Samantha's only negative trait, he enjoyed everything else about her. Everything. Especially her lips. He shoved that dangerous thought away and stumbled out of the bunk bed.

"We have to find a doctor for you." Then David remembered that it was Sunday and swore. "I bet there isn't a doctor's office open anywhere."

"Miss Samantha will say a prayer for me."

David ignored James' solution. "The emergency room!"

He snapped his fingers as the idea burst into his thoughts. Grabbing his wallet off the desk, he started searching through it. "There's got to be a hospital around here. I'll use the insurance card—okay, maybe they won't accept it. But my credit card, my ATM card!" He held it up triumphantly. "What if they trace it? But this is an emergency!"

He turned around, and saw that James had gone out the door. He raced across the yard and found James in Samantha's kitchen. The boy sat in a chair beside the table while Samantha examined his arm.

"It's fat," James told her.

"Yes, it is, like a balloon." She smiled at James who lifted his eyes in adoration.

David could not possibly mistake the love he saw in his child's face and his heart sank because he knew James would believe anything Samantha said.

"Jesus can fix it." James nodded.

The glimmer of hope shining so plainly on his son's sweet face wrenched David's gut out of place. He cursed under his breath. He couldn't have James relying on mystical mumbo-jumbo to get him through life. Asking Jesus to fix anything was ridiculous.

"We'll say a prayer," Samantha said softly. "But you'll have to go to the doctor for some medicine. I had the same problem once. There are bad germs in your arm, and you need special medicine to make them go away."

David realized that he had been holding his breath. His shoulders sagged with relief when he heard Samantha's practical advice, but then he saw James' mouth quiver and knew exactly what would happen next.

"No!" James cried. "No, I won't go to the doctor! I won't!"

James jumped off the chair with the surprising agility of the young, and ran out the door before Samantha could stop him.

David bounded past her and raced out the door after James. He caught his son in a matter of twenty yards or so and scooped him up in his arms.

"Don't go running off like that!" he scolded

"No!" James screamed. "I won't go to the doctor!" He pounded David with his good arm and tried to kick him with his feet.

Desolation swept over David, crushing his soul. His throat tightened with grief. He had no idea how to handle James at times like this. His inadequacy as a father left him feeling so miserable that his head started to throb. He had bungled everything, leaving his life a disaster, all in a desperate attempt to protect his son. But he hadn't solved anything. He had only made everything worse.

Closing his eyes and clenching his teeth, he withstood James' frail beating and admitted to himself that he didn't know how to raise a kid. He felt he deserved every blow.

"James, stop hitting your father." Samantha's voice sounded stern. "You get time out for that."

Surprisingly, James sagged in David's arms. Opening his eyes, David tried to avoid looking at Samantha, which wasn't easy since she stood less than two feet away from him.

He cleared his throat. "Right, time out," he reiterated gruffly and headed back to the cottage.

Samantha walked beside him. "Dr. Peller will be at Holy Redeemer for the service. I'll call now and see if he can look at James' arm beforehand."

"James is not going to church." David spoke in bitter defiance. Almost at once, he regretted his virulent tone. The morning sunlight gleamed in Samantha's hair and gave it the dazzling appearance of spun gold. He could not take his eyes off her, and the memory of last night's kiss nearly robbed him of coherent thought.

She had given them food and shelter when they needed it most. She deserved his respect.

"James is only four years old and he hasn't grasped the concept of what is real and what is make-believe." David tried to remain calm and objective, but Samantha's lithe form distracted him as she stepped lightly along beside him.

"God is real."

It was the way she said it, with a soft smile touching her lips that almost made David want to believe it.

Samantha opened the back door and David walked in with his burden.

"James, you will sit on the hard chair in the living room for five minutes, with no television, and think about what you did," she instructed.

David put James down. Though the boy set his lips into a pout, he went willingly into the living room. David followed him to make sure that he did as he had been told.

While James silently suffered through his sentence, David went back into the kitchen.

"I'm making blueberry pancakes this morning," Samantha informed him. "You can help by picking some more blueberries. There's a few low bushes behind the lab." She held up a small dark berry. "They look like this. I only need about a cup." She handed him a plastic container.

"How do you know they aren't some poisonous plant?" he countered. "Blueberries have to be picked by experts."

She popped the berry in her mouth, chewed it briefly and swallowed it. "Fish taught me about the blueberries. He's the expert."

He glared at her but she ignored him. She scooped up a measure of flour, scraped a knife over the top of the measure, and dumped the flour into a bowl.

"I can't understand how you can be a scientist and still believe in God!" David hardened his voice, but his serious tone obviously did not affect her. She gave him a tender glance and scooped up another cup of flour while a generous ripple of her warm laughter floated through the kitchen like the summer morning sunshine.

"How can a scientist *not* believe in God?"

He felt the warmth of her smile all the way down to his toes. If he could spend the rest of the day basking in the glowing rays of her joy, he knew he would turn to mush. He clenched his jaw and fought against the power of her happiness.

"God is nothing more than a legend made up by a bunch of frightened people. Your God is no different than the gods fabricated by the Romans or the Greeks."

She sighed and shook her head. It seemed to David as if a cloud of melancholy had come to hide the sun. "My God has promised everlasting life, in addition to making those blueberries out behind the lab."

David knew that was his cue to get outside and fill the container she had given to him, but he couldn't let the argument drop.

"Stop messing with my son's head. He believes everything you say. He was all set to have Jesus heal him!"

An uncomfortable silence filled the kitchen after his outburst. Samantha didn't say anything, although she chewed on her lower lip. The room seemed to grow warmer as David thought about how her mouth had tasted last night. How would it taste now? Like blueberries?

She opened a small container and stuck a spoon into it.

"If you could try to trust Him—"

"Don't talk to me about trusting God," he interrupted. "Nobody can expect God to reach down and fix the world's problems. Don't you think I prayed for Him to save my son? It was a waste of breath!"

The memory shook him. He ground his teeth together so hard that it hurt.

He saw her put down the spoon and the container and dust the flour from her hands. Then she looked up at him with a sad, wistful expression. He knew she had the power to completely undo him, so he tried to steel himself against her soft, gray eyes, but his effort was wasted.

"Three days ago, while you were out catching mosquitoes, James told me a few interesting facts about his friend, Kyle. From what he said, I'm quite sure that Kyle is really an imaginary playmate."

David had an awful tumbling feeling in his gut, as though a sinkhole had opened up in the marsh and swallowed him. He could not deny that he had thought the very same thing about James' playmate himself, but he had refused to acknowledge it.

He watched her search his face and he knew that she could read into his soul with her probing, silvery eyes.

"James has mentioned Kyle less and less over the past week," she went on. "He doesn't need Kyle as much because he has you helping him search for new friends out on the marsh. He has Cassie, Fish, and me, too. He has security and safety. I prayed for help on my project and no matter what you believe, I know that the Lord brought you here. God is watching over your son, and Jesus is healing him. Right now. That child has been given the gift of faith. Don't you deny him that!"

She choked on the last word and swung away from him, but not before he saw the hot tear roll down her cheek.

A raw, wretched chill shot through him. It didn't feel like August anymore, it felt like January and David could swear that a sharp, brittle icicle had pierced his heart. He did not want to believe her. He would not!

He stood immobile, as guilt ran rampant inside him. Causing Samantha to cry tormented him. He saw her hand tremble as she continued mixing ingredients into the bowl. He heard her ragged breathing and wanted only to circle her in a tender embrace, to bury his face in the flaxen gold of her hair. But he would be a fool to do that, for he knew that a hug would never be enough.

Trying to conquer his conflicting emotions proved impossible. He stamped out of the kitchen and slammed the door behind him, determined to pick every blueberry he could find.

*   *   *

Shaded and cool, the cemetery behind Holy Redeemer rested under ancient, gnarled oaks. David sat on a concrete bench and leaned back against the brick wall that kept the graveyard secluded from the rest of Clam Creek. He stared at the road atlas in his hands, but he couldn't keep his mind on the map. His thoughts wandered off in a different direction.

He knew why James didn't like to visit the doctor and his son had clung to him during their brief visit with Dr. Peller. Nevertheless, the doctor had not been at all alarmed by the swollen limb. He had handed David a batch of antibiotics for the child.

"You never know what that green head bit before it bit you," the doctor shrugged. "Something nasty by the looks of that arm."

Afterwards, when they arrived at the church, James reached for Samantha's hand and headed into the church with her as if he were going to a party. He didn't whine, or beg his father to join them.

"I'll pray for you." His face had fairly glowed with joy. "Jesus loves you, too."

David waited outside feeling overcome with guilt. Attendance at church would be a novel experience for James. Undoubtedly, his mother had never taken him and David winced as he admitted that he had never bothered to bring James to worship either.

Of course, Samantha had made church sound like paradise all week, so it shouldn't surprise him that James had looked forward to the event so eagerly.

Sitting on the cool bench in the quiet graveyard, David sighed. He knew he had never willingly attended church as a child, but his parents had never given him the option of staying home. Despite his protests, his parents dragged him along every Sunday. He had a chance to experience religion before he decided that it had no value for him, but until now, James hadn't been granted the opportunity to see what all this God stuff was about.

What if James had been born with some special talent to understand the spirituality that had eluded David all this time?

What if there really was a God?

David lifted his head and stared up at a sky that didn't have a single cloud in it. It was the same brilliant hue as James' eyes. It hurt just to look at it.

He glanced at his watch. Shouldn't they be done by now? David frowned as an ant walked across the atlas. He brushed the insect away and then pushed the road atlas aside. Resting his elbows on his knees, he glared at the grass by his feet. He didn't care where he went next, anyway. He had gotten sick and tired of running.

Lifting his head again, he noticed a familiar figure bending near a headstone about a hundred yards away. David narrowed his eyes. It could only be Fish. On his knees, the old fisherman appeared to be clipping grass next to the stone, manicuring it with methodical precision. Two pots of yellow flowers sat beside him.

Utterly bored with waiting, David stood up and quietly walked over to where Fish labored with such studied intensity. A cold chill shivered along his shoulders as he drew close enough to read the inscription on the headstone. The name "Susan Mallory Lyons" seemed to jump out at him.

"Good morning," Fish squinted in the morning sunshine. "I know Sammie doesn't have time for this sort of thing with all her research."

David nodded in agreement.

"What do you think of those flowers?" Fish asked.

"They look like—wildflowers."

Fish leaned back on his heels and seemed to smile at the flowers as if they were good friends. "Yes. That they are. Brown-eyed Susans they're called. They remind me of her." He gave a long sigh and turned his gaze toward the solemn gray monument. "She was shorter than Sammie, with hair a shade lighter, more like straw, but her eyes...they were like chocolate syrup."

The old man paused for a moment in silent reverence before returning to his work.

"Did Samantha grow up here?" David asked.

Fish looked up at him with a puzzled frown. Then he picked up a small trowel and dug a hole on one side of the headstone.

"Sammie was born here." Fish's trowel paused briefly as his voice turned gruff. "When she turned three, John Lyons left town. He came to visit every now and then, but one day he simply took off with Sammie and disappeared for four years, until the police picked him up for burglary. But by that time, Susan had passed away." The fisherman sniffed and began to dig with more vigor.

Shock slammed into David and held him in a paralyzing grip. His mind whirled. Now Samantha's devotion to James made more sense.

"Sammie was put in foster care, in Pennsylvania." Fish took out his red bandanna and blew his nose. "But she found her way back here, she did. Been such a blessing."

David knew a beer would go down real easy at that point. His mouth had turned as dry as the dusty street of Clam Creek. It seemed obvious that Samantha saw in James the lost, motherless child she had been herself.

"These flowers come back every year," Fish said as he pulled the root ball out of one pot and then lowered the plant into the hole he had dug. "They'll be blooming here even after I'm gone."

"And what happened to Samantha's father?" David asked.

"John Lyons died in prison," Fish answered tersely.

A crushing weight seemed to press on David's heart. Would he suffer a similar fate? No! He hadn't committed burglary, he told himself. Not yet. But he knew he might have resorted to it if Samantha hadn't hired him. Besides, he still could go to prison for abducting James.

If anything happened to him, what would become of James? He would go back to Linda! David clenched his fists. That must not happen!

Chapter Eight

Marion Gregory came home with them after church. She smiled into the car's rear view mirror as Samantha drove them all back to the field station along the narrow marsh road.

Samantha glanced at David who sat beside her. He stared straight ahead with a dark scowl firmly fixed on his face. She sighed and went back to watching the road, but in her peripheral vision, she was very aware of the way David slouched in the seat with his arms crossed across his chest. A cold knot had settled in her stomach as the tension between them grew. Samantha considered Marion's help a blessing, but it seemed obvious that David did not.

"I'll sleep on the couch, so I won't be a bother at all." The scent of lilacs permeated the interior of the car as Marion chattered happily in the back seat with James beside her. "Dr. Peller told me that James' arm should be soaked in magnesium salts four times a day. It draws out the poisons, as Mother would say. But it would be such a bother for you, and you must finish your research."

Marion's sister had come to take care of Agnes for a few days, leaving Marion free to do as she liked. Samantha realized that for Marion a jaunt out to the field station constituted a vacation, of sorts. Her offer to care for James would certainly be a great load off Samantha's shoulders. Not only that, but after David's kiss last night, she felt that they needed a chaperone, especially since her traitorous dog had totally succumbed to the lure of designer ice cream. However, at the moment, David reminded her of a hydrogen bomb waiting to be detonated. All he needed was one little spark.

"You know Dr. Peller told me I should have been a nurse when he saw how I took care of Papa in his last few months. I always followed instructions to the letter. Never missed a single pill. I had them all lined up and I wrote it all down on a chart to keep track. Well, my goodness, you had to do that since it could get confusing with some of them being given out three times a day and some four times a day. Except for the white pill, that was once a day." Marion paused briefly. "And what about your pills, my little man?"

"My pills are pink and they taste like bubble gum."

James' voice vied with the trill of a red-winged blackbird hovering nearby in the *Phragmites* of the marsh. Samantha's mood lifted for a moment as the bird's song brought back the memory of the hymns they had sung together in church.

"You mustn't think those pills are candy," Marion warned. "Why when my brother was just about your age, he ate a whole bottle of those baby aspirins, you know, the orange ones. Goodness, they had to pump his stomach out. Then my little grandniece, Wesley—I can't imagine why her mother gave her such a name—gobbled up a bunch of grape-flavored painkillers, and she had to get a blood test. They could tell right then and there from her blood that she hadn't eaten too much and we were all so grateful."

David cleared his throat and Samantha started, fearing what he would say.

"James had dialysis once when his mother left her medication out on the table. I'm sure James knows better now. Don't you sport?"

"Uh-huh."

James almost whispered the reply but it jarred Samantha's concentration. Her heart thudded dully and her damp palms slipped on the steering wheel. The thought of the young boy suffering and critically ill because of his mother's carelessness made her stomach churn, though she knew in her heart that even such an incident did not justify the child's abduction.

Still, for the most part, David seemed a decent and caring man—one who truly did love his son. She knew she should not compare him to her father, but she couldn't help it.

She could feel the emotions warring inside her. She

clamped her teeth together so tightly that her jaw hurt.

The silence in the car stretched on uncomfortably until Marion asked James if he would like to sing with her.

"A song makes the miles go by faster."

"I know 'Jesus Loves Me,'" James said.

"That's my favorite!" Marion clapped with as much delight as any child.

The tune of the simple melody had Samantha's eyes turning misty. She couldn't join in the singing because she knew she would certainly cry if she did.

She thought of the agonizing four years of her childhood that she spent living like a nomad without even a hint that her Savior walked beside her all the way. If she had only known then about Jesus, it would have been such a comfort to her. It would have given her hope even in the worst of times.

She prayed that James would keep Christ with him so that no matter what trials came his way, he would be assured that his Creator loved him, even if it appeared that nobody else did. Samantha had been shifted from one foster home to another as she grew, and she had found little affection in any of them.

The memory brought a sharp stab to her heart. She had wanted only to be loved. It seemed such a simple thing, but it had eluded her until she found her way back to Clam Creek where everyone seemed more than willing to give her their heart.

She took another sidelong glance at David. He sat sullenly beside her with his gaze fixed on his shoes. What was he thinking about? How he hated that joyful hymn, or last night's kiss? Was he upset now because Marion would be hovering about? Still, Samantha had to keep him at a distance.

Her misery plunged further down into sorrow. She imagined the pain her mother must have endured, the awful sleepless nights, the hours spent wondering if her child had a bath and a decent meal, the endless waiting while she prayed that her child would soon be in her loving arms again.

All of her mother's unhappiness had been caused by John Lyons, her own father.

Samantha remembered the day she found her mother's grave among the others in the small cemetery behind Holy Redeemer. Only the knowledge that they would meet again in heaven kept her from falling completely apart with grief.

Only with the help of Jesus had she been able to forgive her father and get on with her life. She clenched her teeth together. David and James had brought back too many of the bitter memories.

Once more the qualms she had about sheltering James and his father came to the fore. Had she made the wrong decision? Though David maintained that James' mother had mistreated the child, that didn't make his illegal action a viable alternative. And what if he had exaggerated the danger? What if he had lied?

Samantha's father had been an inveterate liar—a boastful braggart who took advantage of people's trust. She had learned early that her father's words were empty and that only by ignoring his promises could she retain some sense of reality.

David did not behave like her father. So far, he had not tried to bluff his way out of any situation. If he agreed to do something, he did it. However, could she really trust a man on the run?

Even if James' mother had been negligent, wouldn't she still be suffering unendurable agony at the loss of her child? Wouldn't that add to her guilt? She could be dying of a broken heart right now because she didn't have a clue as to where his father had taken him.

"Do you have a roasting pan?"

Marion's question jolted Samantha from her thoughts. She had been so caught up in her musing, she had completely tuned Marion out.

"Y-yes, yes, I do."

"Good. A roaster should be about the right size for

soaking James' arm. And I have something very special in my bag for one good little boy..."

Samantha's mind wandered off again, maybe because she hadn't gotten much sleep at all last night. She had prayed and prayed, hoping for some divine inspiration. What she had gotten was James' swollen arm and now she had Marion's presence to bolster her own lagging personal restraint.

She wished she could forget David's kiss, but nothing could get it out of her mind. It had happened so fast and for a moment, she had gotten lost in the tenderness of it—until reality slammed into her. David was a wanted man. If the authorities caught up with him, he would go to jail.

John Lyons had deserved jail. He had a mean streak a mile wide and believed he had a right to batter his wife. Her mother had divorced her father for her own self-preservation, but that hadn't helped Samantha. He had slapped his daughter countless times as well.

She allowed herself to peek once more in David's direction. Would he beat a woman? He always treated her with a considerable amount of deference, opening doors for her and pulling out her chair at the table. His eyes met hers and for the merest second she thought she caught a glimpse of the agonies that tortured him. The brief impression passed quickly before his eyes narrowed and hardened into sharp, cold stones that accused her with their chill. Samantha turned to focus once more on the road ahead and swallowed against the anxious lump in her throat. *Please guide me, Lord.*

At last, they reached the bridge and Samantha devoted her complete attention to navigating the car over the narrow causeway. She sighed with relief when the wheels touched the roadbed on the other side. She couldn't help thinking how the old bridge was a lot like life; all the trials and obstacles made it difficult to find the straight and narrow path. She could only hope she didn't lose her way, slipping over the edge after a final, critical mistake.

*   *   *

David felt a heavy weight pressing on his shoulders. Fish's revelation concerning Samantha's forced odyssey as a child had brought on a sense of foreboding. He had believed all along that the most important thing in Samantha's life was her research project, but what if she had another game plan? Would she attempt to ameliorate her own caustic feelings with some sort of displaced revenge?

His head throbbed painfully. Psychology had been his worst subject in college. If he had paid more attention to it, maybe he wouldn't be in such dire straits—maybe he wouldn't have married Linda, or fathered James...

Then he heard a giggle from the back seat and felt a sharp stab at his heart. Perhaps fathering James was one of the best things he had done. Despite everything, his son happened to be a nice kid.

Worry and the lack of sleep started to take a toll on him, he couldn't think straight. He rubbed at his mouth, as if he could erase the memory of that one inspiring kiss, but it didn't help.

He didn't believe that Marion Gregory's assistance would be much comfort to any of them. Beneath her shy exterior, that woman had all the trademarks of a steamroller. He could well imagine her killing them all with kindness.

He shut his eyes tightly, and his mind replayed the awful night that James' had swallowed his mother's pills. He could still see his son hooked up to the dialysis machine, looking as pale as death. He clenched his fists as he remembered the anger he felt towards Linda. If there was ever a time he had come close to understanding how one human being could kill another, that night had taught him how deep hatred could go.

The memory poisoned him even now. It had been Linda's fault, of course, but she told everyone it was an accident, and they believed her.

For him, it had been the last straw.

He opened his eyes and tried to calm himself by listening

to James' voice mingling with Marion's delicate soprano in the back seat. It all seemed so ordinary and normal, as if he had somehow become part of a real family once more.

Surprisingly, happy events from his own childhood filtered through his pain. He could recall returning home after church with Grandma in the car singing childish hymns, and suddenly, he felt lonely—so separate and apart from the rest of the world that it pierced him deep inside.

He had lost his whole family in a single day. His father, mother, sister, and grandmother had succumbed to carbon monoxide poisoning from a crack in the old furnace while he had been away at college. That was when he began to doubt the existence of a loving God.

He rolled the car window down all the way as the heavy floral scent of Marion's cheap cologne nearly suffocated him. Breathing in the more earthy aromas of the marsh; the cloying odor of the methane and the brackish water, along with the crisper tang of the hardy cedars and bayberries calmed him. He had come from a different world and stopped by chance in this one which, at first, seemed so alien he could swear it was on another planet. But, the longer he stayed, the more it reminded him of what his own young life had been like. He admitted to himself that he did not miss the glass and steel skyscraper with the plush rugs and mahogany desks. He did not miss the country club with the manicured lawn. Most of all, he did not miss the half million-dollar home with the automatic sprinkler system, the inground pool, and the hot tub.

He doubted that he would ever miss Linda. He had begun to realize that she wanted a child only because everyone else had one, just as she had wanted a tennis bracelet because the other women in the club had them. She had thought of James as a possession, and then the novelty had worn off...

David suppressed a groan, he couldn't stand the solitary ache that gnawed at him.

"We're home!" James gave a whoop of joy.

David saw the cottage, bright and cheerful in the afternoon sunlight. He heard the sounds of Cassie's happy barks greeting them as they pulled up. It was like coming home, but none of it could ever be his. That awful truth wrenched his soul.

*   *   *

Despite the heat of the afternoon, Samantha went outside to pull up a few weeds and pick more of her ripe tomatoes, but when she stepped inside again, she found that Marion had completely taken over her kitchen. From a large pot on the stove the aroma of browning onions and beef wafted through the tiny room.

David sat at the table with James as the child soaked his arm in the roasting pan. A flotilla of small plastic boats appeared to be having a skirmish in the rough, magnesium salt seas. The boats had come from Marion's bag.

"Where did that beef come from?" Samantha asked.

"It was sitting in my freezer waiting for an occasion." Marion sniffed the steam rising from the pot. "I make stew exactly like Mother used to do. It'll take a few hours, but the meat will be so tender—"

"I intended to heat up the leftovers from yesterday," Samantha interrupted.

Marion shot her a horrified look. "Leftovers are for the dog."

Cassie, who had curled up in the corner, lifted her head, gave a sad little moan, and then lay down again.

David turned to the disconsolate dog. "Butter pecan for dessert, Cassie. Don't feel too bad."

Samantha watched the grin widen on her pet's face.

"You need some red meat to put iron in your blood." Marion stirred the contents of the pot with a wooden spoon. "It'll put the color back into your cheeks."

Samantha had a sneaking suspicion that the battle raging

in the roasting pan wasn't going to be the only dispute in the kitchen.

"Let me help you then. What do you need? Should I peel some potatoes or some carrots?" Samantha pulled the potato peeler from the drawer.

"You know what they say about too many cooks!" Marion smiled and emphasized her words by banging the wooden spoon on the side of the pot.

"It's my kitchen."

"But you're looking like a ghost, what with being in that lab all the time. When was the last time you went for a swim? You have an appetite like a bird."

"But Miss Samantha doesn't eat worms and bugs." A quizzical expression appeared on James' face, causing a temporary cease-fire in the naval battle.

"Miss Gregory means that Miss Samantha doesn't eat much," David said softly to his son.

"Hardly enough to keep body and soul together." Marion turned the heat down and put a lid on the pot. "Since James needs to soak that arm again for another twenty minutes or so, why don't you and David get outside and take a walk. A bit of exercise would do you a world of good."

Samantha stared at Marion. The nervous tic in the older woman's eye had vanished and she had become a tyrant—just like her mother!

"I got some exercise while I was pulling weeds and picking tomatoes." The very thought of being alone with David had Samantha's heart beating quicker.

"Humph. By the looks of you, you spent the whole week caged up—"

"Miss Samantha wasn't in a cage." James' arm slapped down in the water, creating a giant tidal wave that capsized three of the battleships.

"Hey!" David rumbled. "Stop splashing."

"But Miss Samantha is not a guinea pig!"

"Of course she isn't and she can go on a walk by herself," David growled as he grabbed a kitchen towel to sop up some of the water that had sloshed out of the roasting pan.

A sinking sense of despair attacked Samantha. She felt as if she were one of the beleaguered battleships headed to the bottom of the sea.

Then James put both hands in the water to plunge the remainder of the navy into the briny deep. "A big monster swallowed up all the boats."

Despite her apprehensions about being alone with David and her frustration at being kicked out of her own kitchen, Samantha found herself laughing at the child's imagination. To her, James was God's little sunbeam, shining on them all.

"When I go for a walk, shall I bring back a big fish for the monster to eat?" she asked.

"Bring back a little fish for the monster to play with," James begged.

"Little fish are hard to catch."

"I know. But snails are slow." James looked up with a hopeful expression.

"Does the monster want a snail for a friend?" Samantha asked.

"I won't keep him. I'll put him back with his friends right away," James promised.

"Okay, I'll see what I can find."

"A beautiful young lady should not be walking about unescorted." Marion fixed David with her icy blue eyes.

"There is absolutely nobody else living on this marsh." Samantha protested. "I'm perfectly safe."

"Three years ago, a young woman's body was found not three miles from here. Simply dumped in the weeds, like garbage. We never learned who she was or who committed the crime."

David swore and then the room became deathly silent except for the slap of tiny waves against the sides of the roasting pan. Samantha tilted her jaw at an obstinate angle. The very last person in the world that she wanted as an escort was David. However, she realized that Marion could be just as stubborn with her old-fashioned ideas of propriety and safety. Under the scrutiny of Marion's cold stare, David caved in.

"All right. A short walk, since James sunk my navy."

"A monster sank the boats and ate them!" James clutched at the tiny vessels and made chomping sounds.

Samantha headed toward the door, intent on escaping before anyone noticed.

"Now don't forget your hat," Marion reminded. "You don't want to be getting a burn—you being so fair and all."

Samantha suppressed a groan. She grabbed an old baseball cap from the rack on the wall and jammed it on her head. She didn't wait for David; she hurried out with her pulse racing.

David caught up to her in a moment and easily matched her quick stride.

"Is this a race?"

"It's for exercise. So I don't eat like a bird."

"Keep this up and you'll pass out from heat exhaustion."

"I will not." Still, she did slow down. She had already started to perspire. In just a week's time, the unyielding summer sun had scorched the salt hay on the marsh into a drab brown. Even the gentle breeze that usually blew in off the water had ceased in the blistering temperatures. Worse than that, Samantha sensed that the friction between her and David had not lessened at all. In fact, she thought she heard his short fuse sizzling.

For several minutes they walked on in silence. Samantha led the way on the narrow path that ended at the small beach along the edge of the marsh. It seemed an eternity had passed since she last visited the secluded spot edged by a mass of tall *Phragmites*.

She hadn't even thought of going swimming during the summer due to her frantic work schedule. But now, with the heat making the air shimmer in waves, the hazy blue of the water beckoned to her and she didn't really care about anything else other than getting wet. When she reached the pristine white beach, she kicked off her sandals, yanked the cap off her head, and cast it down on the sand. Then she stepped into the water.

The soothing coolness felt heavenly. She walked in further until the waves lapped at her knees.

"I should have changed into my bathing suit," she sighed blissfully.

David plopped down on the sand, shaded by the high reeds, and said nothing.

The water felt so wonderful that she continued on until the ripples teased the edge of her shorts. The temptation to enjoy a swim proved stronger than her will to stay dry. She sank down. "This is *so* sublime." She closed her eyes and floated on her back. "Marion is right. I really should do this more often."

She turned over and dove smoothly down to glide along the bottom as gracefully as a mermaid. She loved the sensation of weightlessness as she propelled herself with her hands and feet. For a few moments, she left the world and all its problems on the sandy bank. Too soon she ran out of air and had to surface.

When she did, she saw David standing with his feet in the water.

She smoothed the hair from her brow and swept the drops off her face. "Why don't you join me?"

"For one thing, I'll get my clothes wet. Aside from that, I'm the only lifeguard here."

"I know how to swim. I'll be fine."

"What if a shark attacks you?"

She noticed the frown lines creasing his forehead. Was he really worried about her? "Shark attacks in New Jersey are rare. Come on in and cool down." She swam closer.

"No thanks," he grumbled.

Mischievously, she showered him with a barrage of seawater. She laughed gaily at his outraged roar before she dove under again.

When she resurfaced, she didn't see him on the beach. Had he gone back to the cottage?

"David?" she called out. Only a red-winged blackbird cried out a reply.

"Rats." She swam toward the shore. She supposed she would have to apologize to him for dousing his clothing.

Suddenly, he burst out of the water not four feet in front of her. She let out a yelp of surprise.

"I thought you were afraid of sharks!"

"You said there aren't any."

"I did not! There are sharks, they just don't usually attack here."

Being alone with him in the isolated spot made her skin tingle. She averted her eyes, hoping that if she didn't look at him, maybe she could maintain her equilibrium. Then she saw the whitish blob in the water. As big as a dinner plate, it gently pulsated on the tide toward David.

"Ummm—there's a jellyfish, a really big one—"

"Don't play games with me." His brow creased in deep furrows.

Samantha floated gently away from him. "Look to your right. Jellyfish at three o'clock."

He continued to bore through her with a cold, black stare.

"Fish told me that your father abducted you."

A chill pierced her to the very marrow of her bones. Why had Fish done that? But it didn't matter right now. The jellyfish undulated gracefully closer to David.

"Move to your left, slowly. Jellyfish sting."

With one broad stroke, David drew nearer to Samantha. Caught in the swirling current caused by his movement, the jellyfish followed him.

"Are you going to report me?"

The thunderous pounding of her heart drowned out the barely repressed fury in his words. The milky pink jellyfish poised dangerously near David's right shoulder, waiting only for the next wave to lay its glistening tentacles across his flesh.

"It's right behind you!" She shouted at him. "Move!"

She reached out, intending to pull him away, but before

she could grab his hand, another wave pushed the delicate creature up against the skin of his arm.

The roar of his wounded howl shattered the marsh's peaceful solitude. He bounded toward the little beach while spouting an endless stream of profanities.

Samantha watched as the jellyfish, seemingly unperturbed, throbbed rhythmically on the small swells churned up by David's frenzied escape from the sea.

Lord, please help me through this. She prayed as she hurried after David. When she reached him, she pulled his hand away from the injured area.

"Calm down and stop rubbing. You're firing more nematocysts into your skin."

"This is your fault!"

Samantha picked up her cap. "I warned you, but you didn't pay any attention to me. Let me scrape off the tentacles and pour some seawater on it. That should alleviate some of the pain until we get back to the cottage. Then we can saturate it with vinegar."

"Don't you touch this!" he shouted. "I don't want any home remedies."

"Vinegar works." She crossed her arms and glared at him.

"Jack and Jill used vinegar and brown paper but I think we must have made some medical advances since then."

"Acetaminophen, ibuprofen, and ice are helpful. Plus you have shaving cream, so you can shave your arm—"

"I am not going to shave the hair off my arm!" he interrupted. "I'm going to get the gun out of my car and kill that thing!" He set off at a furious pace on the path back to the cottage.

Samantha felt herself go pale. A gun! She could barely swallow. He could have robbed her! She had been so desperate for help in finishing her research that she had behaved in a totally naive and foolish way, risking far more than her job and her home. Had she gambled with her life?

No. She had never felt threatened by David, at least, not physically. The only danger she feared was the loneliness that would overwhelm her when David and James left. She loved James with her whole heart. Had she been foolish enough to fall for David, too?

She closed her eyes. She would not love David. Then the remembrance of that one kiss threatened to melt her into a puddle of useless emotion. She opened her eyes, scooped up some seawater with the cap and doused her head. It didn't do much to cool her down. She slipped her sandals back on and raced after David, praying for strength all the way.

Chapter Nine

By Thursday morning, both patients' total recoveries seemed assured. Since Marion was signed up to volunteer at Clam Creek's famous Peach Festival which opened that evening, Samantha drove her back to town as soon as the sun came up.

The long, lonely return ride back to the field station gave Samantha plenty of time to pray, but she found it impossible to keep her mind on a conversation with the Lord. Her thoughts drifted over all the events of the past week and a half. She would never forget the moment she had found James in her car. Then there was David's kiss, so brief, but no less earth shattering to her. Amazingly, despite the upheavals in her life, Samantha knew that the end of her research project lay within easy reach. She didn't doubt that she would now be able to keep her home and remain in Clam Creek. Nevertheless, whenever she considered the fact that she had facilitated James' abduction, needles of guilt pricked at her. She had used the situation to her own advantage.

The sun climbed higher in the sky as she drove along the meandering road through the marsh where the stifling heat of another cloudless day turned the steamy swamp into an oven. The mud along the route had already been baked into hardened cakes that cracked as the tires crushed them into a fine powder. Samantha choked while a patch of gritty dust swirled in her rearview mirror.

She coughed and cleared her throat. She wished that she could remove the heavy weight that had settled deep in her heart as easily. She knew that if she hadn't needed someone to help her finish her research, she probably would have reported David to the authorities.

As the cottage came into view, she prayed that she would not be prosecuted for giving David and James shelter.

Shortly after her return, as she poured out a glass of orange juice while preparing breakfast, Samantha asked James to wiggle his fingers.

"I can see your knuckles again."

"Where?" James peered at his hand.

Samantha pointed out the bony protrusions before she filled up David's glass with the juice.

"Do you have knuckles, Daddy?" James asked.

"Yeah."

Samantha saw the veins standing out on David's hands as he gripped his steaming cup of coffee and stared morosely down into the brew. She had begun to wonder if he could see his reflection in the hot liquid. Every morning, he glared into the cup as if he was preparing to do battle with an enemy.

"Let me see." James went to examine his father's hands.

David didn't look up from his cup despite the way his son poked and prodded him.

Samantha poured another glass of juice for herself. Though James' recovery had everything to do with the use of antibiotics, Samantha knew that without Marion Gregory amusing and entertaining the boy every day, the research project would not have made as much progress as it had. Marion had taken it upon herself to keep the youngster happy with cards, books, boats, and cookies while she soaked his arm in the old roasting pan.

"Mother would say it draws out the poisons, but it's really the heat." Marion had said as she and James had acted out the battle of the Spanish Armada.

Samantha couldn't have been more grateful. With both David and herself freed from keeping an eye on James for the past three days, the work had sped along at a fast clip.

She had given David an increasing amount of responsibility, too. At first, she had tried to teach him to clean the glassware properly, but after he broke three of her expensive beakers, she decided it would be prudent to give him another task. When she let him do some data entries on the spreadsheets, his true talent became evident.

The same fingers that now looked like they could crush the coffee mug could tap the keyboard with rapid and accurate grace. His familiarity and skill with the software program she used had started the questions whirling in her mind. What sort of job had he left behind when he had abducted his son?

When she had first promised David that the research would only take two weeks to finish, she had been making a wild guess. Once she had given him the chance to record her endless stream of numbers, her conjecture had become reality. But her soul remained troubled even though it looked like she would truly wrap up everything by tomorrow.

She popped some waffles into the toaster oven and decided she needed some distraction. "Now that your arm is all better, we need to celebrate!"

The child shook his head in agreement.

"Tonight is the first night of Clam Creek's annual Peach Festival and we are going to be there!" Samantha declared with a burst of enthusiasm. She could feel the excitement soaring through her at the thought of all the bright lights, the noisy midway, and the heavenly aromas from all the food concessions.

"What's so special about peaches?" David grumbled as he continued to make a menacing face at the opponent in his cup.

"It's not just peaches! There are rides, lots of food, live entertainment, in addition to lots and lots of things made from peaches—peach pie, peach ice cream, peach jam, peach nectar, peach tea, peach leather, peach chutney, and peach upside down cake."

"Sounds fruity," David dead panned.

Samantha shot a puzzled frown at him. He had been rather quiet the past several days and that worried her. What was he thinking about?

She ran her tongue along her lips and tried to forget that one beautiful kiss, but the memory of it haunted her. She wondered if David thought about it, too. Shoving that idea aside, she rattled off more information about the festival.

"Last year, there was a clown twisting up long balloons into dogs or bunnies and she gave them out to all the children." Samantha pulled the toasted waffles out and plopped them onto the plates.

"Clowns are scary." Tiny furrows marred James' innocent brow.

Samantha bent down next to him. "I'll tell you a secret. The clown at the Peach Festival is really Miss Gregory. You can tell because her favorite color is blue and she will be dressed all in blue. She even has a blue wig for hair."

"Blue hair?" James crinkled up his nose and giggled.

"Yep." Samantha nodded. "But don't tell anybody else."

"Okay," James agreed. "Miss Gregory is my friend."

Samantha's heart warmed. For the last few days there had been no mention of Kyle at all.

"Would you like to pour on your own syrup?" Samantha held out the bottle.

James nodded his head eagerly and she handed the sweet syrup to him.

"I thought you still had a lot of work to do on your research," David grumbled as she stood up.

"The end is in sight!" Samantha threw out her arms and spun around once. "If we work all afternoon, I know it can be finished by tomorrow." She glanced out the kitchen door at the wide expanse of marsh, sea, and sky. She loved every inch of it so much that her eyes grew misty. She would get to keep her house. She would get another grant! She would stay in Clam Creek another year. She would plant crocuses at her mother's gravesite.

Then she remembered that, in all likelihood, David and James would be leaving her very soon. A dull ache settled in her chest and she sat down.

"Tell me that they will have beer at the festival." David glanced up from his coffee with a hopeful expression. "Or maybe peach brandy." A warm smile brightened his face and Samantha's heart lurched.

She lowered her gaze to hide her emotions. Even though she had known from the first that David and James would only be temporary visitors, she could not have prevented herself from caring so deeply for both of them.

Cassie sauntered over and nudged her mistress, as if she understood her sadness. Samantha patted her dog's soft fur.

"Clam Creek has always been a dry town," Samantha explained with a voice that sounded too scratchy.

David let out a moan. "I should have known."

"Fish said the reeds are dry," James small voice piped up. "He said don't play with matches."

Despite the anguish in her heart, Samantha found a small smile tugging at the corners of her mouth. The child had no idea that she had meant the town had no alcohol. How she would miss his dear, sweet face!

Painfully, she cleared her throat. "Right. We have to watch out for fires."

She glanced up and caught the grin appearing on David's face. He winked at her.

With that one simple gesture she realized that she not only cared for him, she did indeed love him. That knowledge sent desolation sweeping through her. How could she bear it when he and James left?

"Will you pay me tomorrow then, when we finish?" David asked.

Samantha could only nod.

"May we stay until Saturday?"

Again she nodded and closed her eyes for a moment. With its full tones and a rich timbre, his voice bore the edge of authority. Where had he come from? And would she ever see him again?

No. She thought once more of her own father and the pain he had caused. For a moment, she could barely breathe. Like her father, David would run until he could run no more—until he slipped up somewhere and got caught. If James' mother was unfit, the youngster might be placed in foster care as she had been. James could wind up just like her, in places where he would never be truly loved.

She had to steel herself against the anguish of knowing what could happen to the young boy. Opening her eyes, she put her hand upon her heart. Had it nearly stopped beating? Would David notice?

She wretchedly admitted to herself that she would be happy to allow him to stay as long as he wanted. Forever.

She stared at her waffle and tried not to gag at the thought of eating it.

"Are we going to say our prayer?" asked James.

Reining in her misery with sheer determination, Samantha reached out to clasp his small hand. "This time, you do it," she whispered.

Solemnly, James intoned the blessing, drawing out each word carefully.

"Please Jesus, I want to stay here with Miss Samantha for ninety hundred more days," James added before he reached the final "amen."

"James, you know we cannot stay here," David reminded.

Samantha cast a sidelong glance at James.

"Daddy, I asked Jesus," James said, giving an exasperated sigh. "You should always ask Jesus."

The next thing Samantha heard was David's fist pounding on the table. The dishes and glasses on the table clattered, bounced, then tilted threateningly.

David charged out the door and slammed it behind him.

Samantha's eyes filled with tears as she saw James' lower lip tremble. Then he slid off his chair and clambered onto her lap. Throwing his arms around her neck, he let loose a heartbreaking sob. Samantha could barely hold back her own tears as she tried to soothe him.

It did no good to cry, she well knew. Some things could never be changed, only accepted. She dabbed at James' wet cheeks and reminded him that they had to trust Jesus and not worry. That somehow it would all work out the way that God knew was best.

"Maybe we can't stay together for now, but with Jesus' help you will come back and visit." Samantha prayed with all her heart that it could be so.

"Daddy's mad." James took in an uneven little breath. The sound tore through Samantha's heart.

"Why doesn't Daddy like Jesus?"

"He doesn't believe in Jesus. He doesn't think He is real. He thinks that the story about Jesus is like a fairy tale, but in fairy tales the animals talk." James sighed. "Everyone knows that pigs and wolves don't talk."

Samantha nodded. Deeply troubled, with her emotions raw and confused, she stroked James' hair and wished she could save him from the very sad future awaiting him. Yes, she would finish her research, but at what price? The question remained as to whether she had done the right thing as a Christian. Should she have called the authorities at the outset? Was she wrong to have offered a temporary respite to James and his father?

Was it foolish for her to have fallen in love with David?

A sudden thought came to Samantha which stirred her heart with hope. Could there be a greater purpose to all this trouble?

"Maybe your father doesn't really understand about Jesus," she said. "But I have some books that might help him to learn about God and His Son."

"I like books." Excitement sparked in James' eyes. His troubles faded in the anticipation of a new activity. "Miss Gregory read books to me."

Samantha went to the bookshelf in her bedroom. Cassie and James followed her. Searching through the shelves, she decided on one of her favorite children's Bibles and a large picture book about Noah's Ark. She had gotten the books years ago in a thrift shop.

"You can keep these," Samantha said as she held out the books for James to take.

James hesitated and frowned. "Daddy said there's no

room."

"But these aren't very big," Samantha reassured him. "I'm sure we can find a space. You could even hold them on your lap."

James eagerly gathered the books in his arms.

"Will you read me a story right now?" he asked.

Samantha thought of the work she still had to finish in the lab. It could wait ten minutes. James needed her now. She had to trust God that this opportunity would be part of His plan.

Samantha led James into the living room and sat down on the couch. James put the books into her lap. She opened the children's Bible to the story of Jesus and the children. Just studying the picture of Jesus with a group of smiling children brought peace to her heart. The light of the Savior reflected in the children's faces. It comforted her to remember how much God loved and protected the innocent.

Hadn't God kept her from harm when she was a child? Surely He would guard James.

She slid her arm around the boy's shoulder and read the story to him.

"...their angels in heaven always behold the face of My Father..." Her voice faded because she could not go on.

"Read me another story," James insisted as he turned the page.

Samantha cleared her throat, but her voice still came out as a whisper. "Later. You can look at all the pictures now."

She gave him a quick kiss on his forehead and left him on the couch while she went to clean up the breakfast that nobody had eaten.

James came back to the kitchen within a few moments and asked for paper to draw a picture. Samantha handed him some crayons and several sheets of paper. He quietly colored while she put things away.

Then David came back. He barely made any sound as he gently opened the door, entered the kitchen, and poured himself another cup of coffee. He sat down at the table and behaved as if nothing unusual had happened, as if he hadn't acted like a raging bull at the mere mention of the name of God's son.

"Hey sport." He sipped his coffee and frowned when James didn't turn to look at him. "What are you drawing?"

"Miss Samantha." James kept his gaze fixed on his artwork.

Samantha blinked in surprise and peered over at the paper. It was so beautiful that she bit her lip to keep it from trembling. With classic child-like symmetry, James had endowed her with a large round head punctured by small dots for eyes and a happy, though thin smile. Her hair, a vivid shade of purple, stuck out haphazardly from her head.

Twig-like arms and legs popped out directly from the circular head, but then she watched as James added two shapes on either side that looked roughly triangular.

"What are those?" David asked, pointing to the unusual shapes.

"Wings," James answered. "Miss Samantha is my guardian angel."

Samantha held her breath waiting for another outburst from David, but none came. She heard instead his deep sigh.

"I'm not an angel, James," she ventured softly.

"You are too," James insisted as he put a big yellow sun in one corner of the paper.

"I can't fly," she pointed out.

"Doesn't matter," David said gruffly. "James is right. You've been an angel to us."

Stunned at David's words, Samantha turned to stare at him. Shocked at the depth of sorrow she saw in his eyes, she took in a quick, sharp breath. Did he care for her? Was he unhappy to be leaving as well?

David reached out to his son and James climbed up into his father's lap.

"Can we stay with Miss Samantha?" the boy asked once more.

David shook his head.

Chapter Ten

David's stomach clenched into a tight knot as he glanced at the out-of-state license plates on the cars, vans, and trucks parked in the open field next to the fairgrounds. The vehicles had come from Pennsylvania, Delaware, Maryland, New York, and even Connecticut. Anger and fear warred together inside him. He and James shouldn't have come.

Why had Samantha suggested this? Was this how she intended to pay him back? With his capture she could avoid the necessity of doling out the cash for his two weeks of work. Had he read her wrong from the very beginning?

Holding tightly to one of James' hands, David halted. Samantha, who held James' other hand, turned to face him with a baffled expression on her face.

"Hey, we've got to grab a table before they're all taken up," she urged.

David glared at her. From their disastrous breakfast onward, she had spoken very little all day. He thought about her past. She had been an abducted child. Could this be her way of exacting revenge? Did she intend to deceive him?

"You didn't tell me there would be so many people," David accused.

"This is Clam Creek's only claim to fame."

Then David noticed a frown settle into her brow and she continued on in a much softer voice.

"You needn't worry about being 'spotted.' Not in this crowd."

She clicked her tongue with an impatience that bothered David. She hadn't been intolerant at all until now. Why?

The smell of sausages, peppers, and onions sizzling on a grill wafted along on the evening breeze, followed by the yeasty odor of frying funnel cakes. The aroma only made David's stomach queasy.

The paranoia grew inside him and he couldn't stop it. His anxiety billowed up into a massive cloud of pure fear. He knew Samantha was probably right—nobody would give them a second glance. But he couldn't be sure because he couldn't trust Samantha. Or could he?

"Think of this as my bonus to you. I really couldn't have finished my research without you. I want to do something special for both of you. You'll really have a good time." Her lips became a thin, grim line. "If you could just relax."

David narrowed his eyes. "I could be risking everything."

Samantha's exasperated sigh annoyed him.

"Okay," she said. "You sit in the car while James and I have a good time. There's no reason for all of us to be miserable."

David rubbed his hand across his brow. Although she had provided a safe oasis for him and James up until this point, he didn't feel he could rely on her caring for James. If anything happened...if James was returned to Linda, he would certainly be abused and neglected until he wound up in the hospital—or dead. Samantha didn't understand the gravity of the situation.

James tugged his hand out of David's grasp and gleefully pointed toward a dizzying swirl of lights.

"Daddy, there's a merry-go-round!"

David quickly captured his son's hand once more. He knew he risked a full-scale tantrum if he turned and left the fairground with James in tow, and that would certainly get them noticed.

"It'll be all right." Samantha whispered close to his shoulder in a voice that reminded him of the waving marsh grass. "Trust me."

David swallowed hard. How could he be so suspicious of those serene gray eyes? His gaze lingered on her mouth and he remembered the honeyed sweetness he had tasted there.

Nevertheless, prickles of alarm crept along David's spine. If he only had some guarantee—

Then a disturbing truth weighed down upon his

shoulders. Life didn't come with any kind of warranty.
Nobody had promises handed to them when they came into
the world. The only certainties were death and taxes. He
knew there were always some people who could be counted
on in an emergency, a few who never went back on their
word.

Samantha had seemed like one of those people. He
couldn't have misjudged her, could he? He clenched his jaw
tightly. If his hormones had done the analysis, it might be
highly probable. After all, he had married Linda, hadn't he?

"Daddy, I'm going to buy Cassie a dog biscuit!" James
called out. "She likes dog biscuits."

David ground his teeth together. "We'll get a little closer
and I'll take a look around first."

James jumped up and down as if he wore springs on the
bottom of his sneakers.

"You'll see, it's really quite nice." Samantha's face glowed
with such delight that David knew he could easily fall under
her spell, just as James had.

Face the truth, man! She fascinated him. He found his
gaze constantly wandering over her graceful curves. He
wanted to touch her again, taste her lips once more, and feel
the warmth of her body next to his.

Enough!

He took a deep breath and tried to clear his head as they
made their way across the rutted field toward the main gate of
the festival. He looked back at the day's events and found
himself remembering how Samantha had showed James the
way to pluck out the weeds in her tomato patch that
morning. After pulling out the offending plants, James had
picked all the ripe tomatoes. For his efforts, Samantha had
handed him a five-dollar bill, despite David's protests.

"He earned it," she had stated with that steely look in her
eyes that told him he would have to accept her generosity or
risk Armageddon.

The fact that she had not given him his own pay at that
time probably precipitated many of the doubts now besieging

him. He reprimanded himself for his own stupidity. He did trust Samantha. He loosened his stranglehold on James' hand. He should not let fear ruin this special day.

"Miss Gregory!" James squealed. Then without any warning, he yanked his hands free from both David and Samantha before dashing away into the crowd.

For a moment David stood there numbly as terror shot through him and turned his blood cold. He didn't see Miss Gregory.

"James!" he called, finding his voice. "James! Come back here!" But James didn't return. In the blink of an eye, his small son had disappeared into the crowd. David didn't think he could draw another breath.

"Come on!" Samantha grabbed his hand and pulled him into the crowd. "We'll find him."

The teeming mass of people hampered their efforts to find James. David called out James' name over and over but the sound of the music blaring from the speakers on the carnival rides drowned out his voice. At last, they came to the crowded midway of the festival. David searched the sea of faces, but he didn't see his son. An icy sweat broke out on his skin.

He barely noticed the whisper-soft touch of Samantha's hand.

"I'll have everyone from Holy Redeemer paged," Samantha said. "They all know what he looks like."

David followed her, though his heart felt like it had been put in a vise. What if someone kidnapped James? What if he never saw his son again?

At an information booth, Samantha spoke into a microphone that miraculously blared out over the din of the crowd and the music. Within moments, at least thirty people hurried to the booth. Samantha explained what had happened and then told the volunteer searchers what James had been wearing.

David stood and studied each small face that passed by the booth, but none of them had the wide, blue eyes and black, straight hair of his own boy. Every nerve in his body felt stretched taut as he stood there, hoping that by some miracle his son would materialize out of the crowd. Time ticked slowly onward and with each minute the torment inside him brewed, until he found himself pacing restlessly. When James did not appear after half an hour, David couldn't stand the tension for another second.

"I'll find him myself!" he growled and started to stalk out of the booth.

Samantha's hand gripped his arm. "No. You stay put. They'll find him."

She spoke with such conviction that while he felt like a drowning man going down for the third time, her life preserver presented a glimmer of hope, and he had no choice but to accept that tenuous line.

Nevertheless, part of him continued to war with the idea that this was her fault. The dark doubts he harbored about her swirled in his mind. He shrugged off her hand before he sat down on a rickety wooden chair which groaned in protest at his weight. He rested his elbows on his knees and put his head in his hands.

He didn't want to think, but he couldn't stop his mind from playing back all the incidents that had led up to this moment. He went through a litany of misery. If only he had known how Linda would treat her son...if only he had sued for custody in the beginning...if only someone in some agency had believed him...if only he hadn't been robbed...if only he hadn't stopped in Clam Creek...if only he hadn't met Samantha...

He lifted his head to glare at her again, but the sight of her softened his anger. She stood a few feet from him, her honey-blond hair cascading down her back, her arms folded across her chest and her head bowed.

David felt a fresh stab of pain in his heart. He knew she loved James as much as he did. It didn't matter why.

She turned toward him. "I'm really, really sorry." The hurt sounded in every syllable. It made David's own throat feel tight.

"I didn't think there would be any danger," she explained. "I just wanted James to have the most fun he's every had. I wanted him to always remember Clam Creek."

Her voice broke. The ache consumed David's soul. He could not bear to see her cry. He got up and surrounded her in his arms.

"Please join me in a prayer?"

He knew it would make no difference. He knew it was a waste of breath, but he couldn't argue with her now. He merely nodded. They did not break apart. He clung to her, feeling totally wretched in the midst of the raucous festival as Samantha begged God for James' return. She seemed so naive, so vulnerable and helpless in placing her absolute trust in an all-seeing Supreme Being who would know where the boy happened to be.

Listening to her made it all hurt more. David couldn't say anything for his throat had closed up all together. This whole "God" business still seemed to him so much like a child's faith in fairy tales. He couldn't even add an "amen" to her gently voiced pleas for James' safety. David shut his eyes and buried his face in her hair which somehow remained scented with sunshine, despite the darkness closing in on him.

He couldn't think how he would get past the next moment or the one after that without James. He didn't want to imagine life without his son. He had tried so desperately to protect his child, but all his reckless measures had come to this—this horrible, unceasing agony that threatened to shatter his hold on sanity.

He clutched Samantha against him as if her delicate frame was the only support that kept him standing. All the doubts he had about her vanished. He sensed that she felt as devastated as he did and while he could not share her gullible belief in an imaginary God, it seemed that they forged a new bond—one that went beyond simple understanding. He knew then that leaving Samantha would shred what was left of his broken heart. So he held on tightly, breathing in time with her breathing; willing his heart to beat in the same cadence as hers.

Then a high-pitched voice, the squeal of an exuberant child, sounded off to David's right.

"Daddy, Miss Samantha, look! I have a tattoo!"

Believing he was dreaming, David dared to glance up. Relief washed through him when he saw a very real James, bouncing up and down while holding onto one of Fish's huge, gnarled hands.

"He told me he had lost Miss Gregory," Fish explained. "He was crying up a storm worse than a hurricane!"

"But Fish gave me a tattoo. See!" James held up his arm where a yellow smiley face turned a thin grin on the world.

"Calmed him down a bit, it did." Fish smiled. "I told him only a real, tough sailor gets a tattoo. ' Course this one's the stick-on kind."

"Fish has lots of tattoos." James' eyes were wide with awe. "One is a snake!"

David felt Samantha stir in his arms and realized he still enveloped her in a smothering hug. A pang went through him as he regretted the necessity of letting her go, but a sudden surge of anger at what James had done came rumbling up from within him. He released Samantha and walked over to his son.

"I have told you a million times that you are never to run off like that!" David's tongue lashed out with all the pent up torment of the past half-hour and though he saw the wonder in James' eyes vanish, David found he couldn't stop his tirade. James didn't seem to understand how serious this had been. He didn't know how much misery he had caused.

"I called your name and you should have come right back to me," David ranted.

James didn't say anything. He lowered his head and stared down at the ground. He didn't cry or tremble, he simply stood there holding onto Fish's hand.

David's wrath burned. The overwhelming ache inside him spiraled into seething fury.

"You are never, never to do that again!" David continued to harangue the boy. "I told you it is dangerous to go running off like that. I warned you time and time again—"

"Calm down." Samantha put her hand on his arm.

"He has to realize the consequences of his actions!" David roared at her.

She didn't flinch. However, her mouth twisted at a wry angle.

"You're making an unnecessary spectacle. That's not a good way to blend in with the crowd."

Her words cut through his ire. He glanced around the information booth. A group of bystanders had stopped milling about the festival to view the drama he had created. David's first inclination was to grab James and bolt, but Samantha had already knelt down and put her arms around his son as Fish stepped away.

"We were so afraid you had gotten lost," Samantha said softly. "We were worried and unhappy because we love you so much. That's why your Daddy is yelling. He was so scared that we wouldn't ever see you again."

That's when James started to cry. He let out a big sob and David felt his own heart splinter into a thousand piercing shards.

"You shouldn't worry about whether he understands what he's done," Fish commented in a gruff voice. "That boy of yours was missing you mighty bad."

Fish's massive hand came down on David's back and the weight of it conveyed the aging fisherman's feelings better than mere words.

David nodded in understanding and walked over to his son.

"See, Daddy wants to give you a big hug, too," Samantha said.

She stood up, freeing James from her arms, and David scooped his son up.

"I'm sorry," James sniveled on David's shoulder.

"It's okay," David croaked as he cuddled his son tenderly

against him. He never wanted to lose James ever again, but he knew he had gone about this whole business in way that was perhaps almost as harmful as Linda's abuse and neglect. He, too, had hurt his son. He had robbed James of the security that a child should have. The paranoia had to stop, both for himself and for James. But how?

"I asked Jesus for help," James stated softly as his sobbing subsided. "And then I found Fish."

David closed his eyes as a raw sense of sorrow swept over him. Perhaps James' unshakeable belief in the idea of a Heavenly Father had been formed because his own flesh-and-blood father hadn't been around much in his infancy. It could be David's own fault that his son had latched onto religion with such a tenacious grasp. If that was true, to forbid his son's faith would be a cruel blow. For David, religion remained simply another collection of legends designed to entertain while indoctrinating people with a set of moral restrictions, though he could not deny that for some people, faith worked. It did seem to give them a more positive outlook on life. It had helped James. He seemed to have replaced his imaginary playmate with Jesus.

David took in a deep breath and lifted his head, noticing that he and James now stood alone in the booth. He gently set James down on his feet and glanced around.

Outside the booth a group had gathered in what appeared to be a chaotic melee of agitated people. Samantha stood at the edge of the small mob. When David finally understood what they were saying, his blood chilled.

"There's a fire on the marsh!" several of the people shouted.

"Way the wind's blowing, it's headed toward the field station."

"The volunteers are asking for mutual aid. No way they can handle it."

Without waiting to hear more, Samantha suddenly turned and ran toward the gate.

"Hey, come on! We gotta help her!" another man called

and the small mob took off after her.

A new anxiety gripped David. He knew that Samantha would do anything and everything to save her research. She might even attempt something foolish and risk her life.

He snatched up James once more, intent on catching up to Samantha, but Fish stopped him with one of his burly hands.

"I got my truck right outside the back gate," said Fish. "If I floor it, and head round on the trail the dirt bikers use, we might catch her before she gets there."

David caught the spark of fear in Fish's eyes and knew that they shared the same terrorizing thought because they both were well aware what that research meant to Samantha.

"Lead the way," David agreed.

Chapter Eleven

Samantha coughed as the acrid smoke swirled into the open window of her car. Her hands clutched the wheel as she drove recklessly over the rutted road. She took each serpentine turn at an outrageous speed because she had everything at stake! She *couldn't* lose it all! Not now!

Perspiration dripped from her brow as she pictured her painstaking work going up in flames. She clenched her teeth together, recalling the endless hours of meticulous research, the testing, recording, and her own exhaustion as she labored long into the night to finish on time. She had toiled so diligently and risked so much, even hiring David against all her better principles.

The thought of David and James brought a stab of pain to her heart. Though James had been found unharmed, David would, no doubt, blame her for the entire incident.

Her throat tightened as tears welled up in her eyes. She had only wanted to bring James some happiness, to give him the things that most children enjoy, but her plan had turned into a near tragedy. David probably hated her now while she loved them both so much. She knew she couldn't hold out any hope for a future involving all of them. She had been worse than foolish to lose her heart.

The road wound around a stand of hollies and Samantha headed directly west. Her stomach churned at the sight of the orange glow lighting up the night sky over the usually dark marsh. A chill of pure panic shot up her spine. She offered up her prayers in desperation. If there was any chance, any chance at all for her to save her research—if she could just make it in time! *Please, Lord!*

She tried to hold back the hysteria that threatened to unravel her completely. Clinging to the steering wheel with all her might, she barely rounded the next bend, almost crashing into the tall reeds that bordered the narrow track.

Far behind her, she could see the headlights of several cars bouncing along the road. They moved with deliberate caution, obviously unsure of the way. She had no doubt that her friends from Holy Redeemer would do all they could for her, but the only fire fighting equipment she had at the field station consisted of two hoses, an assortment of shovels, and a hoe.

She thought of Cassie and the guinea pigs and pressed the accelerator to the floor. The car shot forward, nearly leaping into a bank of bayberry bushes, but Samantha cut the wheel sharply to the right in time and avoided a catastrophe.

At last, she reached the bridge and gasped in horror. On the other side of the creek, the entire marsh flickered with firelight in the night. Tongues of flame licked at the reeds and salt hay. It had a surreal, though lethal, loveliness to it. From a distance it looked like glowing splatters of bright, neon paint on a black velvet cloth.

Then she noticed how the tar-covered wooden beams that spanned the small waterway glowed eerily in the night. Here and there, hot embers sparked in between the heavy timbers.

Could she risk driving over the smoldering bridge? She had to! There wasn't any other way to get to the field station. With this part of the marsh on fire, how many minutes would she have to reach the field station before that, too, became caught in the spreading inferno?

She hesitated for a moment. What if her tires melted? What if the bridge crumbled underneath her? Did she have any choice other than to try and save her research? To save her little home? But would she be able to escape?

A strange buzzing sound filled her ears, growing in intensity as she paused, wavering in her resolve. The frightening noise sounded like a swarm of vindictive bees ready to devour everything in their path. The buzzing grew to a roar and Samantha quaked in fear while panic lodged in her throat. She knew it wasn't a pack of angry insects. The very heart of the blaze burned nearby. When the copse of stunted cedars exploded into a vivid orange firestorm, she screamed in terror.

Mesmerized with fright, she watched the flames from the shrubs tower high up into the night sky. She had to drive past that obstacle, and she had no idea in which direction the fire would move next. What if she did get caught in it? She glanced at the road behind her. There wasn't a sign of anyone. What had happened to her friends?

Had they turned back? After all, it was not their whole life about to turn to ashes. Should she go back?

From some reservoir deep within her, steel determination rose up and forced all her fear aside. She must try, with every last ounce of strength she possessed to snatch whatever she could before it all turned to blackened charcoal. She could not let her work go without a fight. Besides, dear, sweet Cassie and the guinea pigs needed her help to escape as well.

She shifted the car into reverse and backed the car up a few hundred yards. *I need you now, Lord.* She gritted her teeth with renewed spirit. The future lay in His hands.

The image of David and James flashed briefly through her mind and she bit her lip to prevent herself from dissolving into tears. Then, before she could think of them again, she put the transmission into overdrive and plowed ahead. The car neatly sailed over the bridge, landing on the other side with a resounding jolt. She clenched her teeth together and drove onward toward the blazing bushes. She passed them in a blur and never looked back.

Without any warning, the smoke suddenly gathered so thickly about her that it obliterated everything. She choked in the caustic atmosphere. Covering her mouth with the sleeve of her shirt, she gasped for air as she slowed the car and rolled up the window. Flipping on the air conditioning in the car, she continued to creep along.

She blinked furiously when her eyes teared from the sooty fumes. Cold terror gripped her as the lack of oxygen and the noxious fumes began to overcome her. The sweat on her brow turned to ice and her stomach churned. She felt so weak she could barely breathe!

She fumbled to put her foot on the brake and turn off the ignition. Groping for the door handle, she struggled to free herself from the car. Somewhere, in the back of her mind, she remembered something about crawling along the floor. Disorientation fogged her mind. What floor? Where was she?

She tumbled out of the car as the door swung open. Landing on the shell-shrewn road with her face in the dirt, she found air! Breathing in deeply, she shook herself to clear her head. Blessedly, the wind shifted and the heavy cloud of smoke lifted.

Her whole body trembled as she crawled back into the car and started it moving forward again, but this time she did not drive recklessly. She still felt sick and lightheaded from inhaling all the smoke.

Then she glanced ahead toward the field station and felt as if someone had punched her in the stomach. The cottage was totally engulfed in orange walls of fire. Pulling up into the yard, she opened the door of the car. The intense heat of the blaze stunned her as she stepped out. She clawed her way around to the relative safety at the back of her vehicle. A sob caught in her throat as her heart was seared with agony. She had locked the door to the cottage before she left. Her little Cassie had become a prisoner in that incinerator. Her angel. Her sweet, precious pet. Her best friend.

Black emptiness settled deep into her soul. She shook so badly, she could barely stand. With a supreme effort, she turned and stared at the lab. It appeared to be whole and safe. But for how long? She had to save her research.

She started across the yard toward the lab. A dry sob burst past the ache in her throat while tears blurred her vision. She knew she had to hurry. She planned to grab as much as she could, stash it in her car, and then escape from the marsh before she, too, became a victim.

However, the sounds from the blazing cottage caught her attention. She heard something like a whine, a high-pitched squeal, along with hisses and groans that set her teeth on edge. She could not resist another look at the cottage that she had called home and where her sweet Cassie lay trapped.

She swayed unsteadily as the roaring inferno hypnotized her with its deadly beauty. Waves of heat rippled up into the night sky and thousands of dancing sparks shot upward. A blast of red-hot air curled and shriveled the ends of her hair. The smell of her own singed tresses made her stomach heave and she sank down on her knees.

Again, she heard that one sound above the others—almost human, like the note of a violin, piercing and tense.

"Cassie?" Her voice sounded harsh and the pain of calling out burned her throat. She got back on her feet. She was responsible for leaving Cassie all alone. It was her fault that the dog would die.

Strangely enough, it suddenly seemed to her as if the screen door on the front porch opened. She didn't consider how it could be possible for that door, which she had secured herself, to swing wide. In fact, she really didn't reason at all. She wanted only to save her dear Cassie. Surely, the frightened dog would be right inside that door, trying to get out. Or maybe little Cassie had become overcome by smoke as she pawed against that door in a frantic attempt to escape.

"Cassie! Cassie!" It seemed she didn't have enough air in her lungs to shout above the crackling of the fire as it gobbled greedily at the dried wood and cedar shingles of the old building. Without being conscious of the danger to herself, she staggered toward the blazing building, hoping against all odds that she might save her lovable and trusting pet.

* * *

David clutched James against him in an attempt to shield his son from the impact as the truck slammed into another cluster of bushes. Fish had done his best to insure that they would be jostled unmercifully while he drove on with a vengeance.

However, if David had been at the wheel, he probably would have driven even faster. The tension in him spiraled as they drew closer to the burnished haze in the distance. The rank stench in the air grew intolerable, but the only one who seemed unable to deal with it was James.

"It's stinky." He whined and covered his nose with both of his hands.

David handed his son a handkerchief and told him to try keeping out the smell with it.

With his heart pounding heavily, David realized that Samantha had come to mean more to him than he had planned. All along, he had figured that he couldn't develop an attachment for her, since he could not remain in Clam Creek. Now he realized that he felt something stronger for her than he had ever felt before with any woman, including his ex-wife. And if anything happened to Samantha...

He gulped and fought down the sense of panic that threatened him. He rubbed his hand across his face remembering that he hadn't had time to apologize to her. And what could he have said anyway? *I'm sorry for being such a jerk? Excuse me for acting like an idiot?* Words just didn't seem sufficient.

How could he have questioned her motives after all she had done for him and James? How could he have doubted her? Like a ray of sunshine, she had touched him and warmed his cynical heart. She had enveloped him in her own goodness, and he had begun to notice that the world still had a lot of sweetness in it.

...the fruit of the Spirit...

No. He set his mouth grimly. He could not attribute her disposition to any special gifts from above. She was simply Samantha. Because of her attitude, he had come to see that every day had something wonderful about it—even rainy days, even steamy summer nights. No matter how desperate his situation, every day held some special magic. Picking, and eating, blueberries fresh from the bush. Kissing Samantha's soft and yielding lips.

He cleared his throat and swallowed with difficulty. His son had bloomed like a wildflower full of hope and promise with Samantha's guidance. Once nervous and timid, James now looked healthy and he even seemed happy most of the time. He studied his son's face in the uncertain light of the truck cab.

The boy's features bore signs of strain. Not for the first time, David wondered how James would fare after they left Clam Creek, and Samantha, far behind them. David closed his eyes and pictured Samantha with her golden hair trailing down her back and her serene gray gaze staring into his soul. A vise clamped around his heart.

David opened his eyes as he and James were pitched viciously against the door when the truck stopped abruptly, a cedar sapling in its path. Fish shifted the gears and stamped on the accelerator. The truck slammed against the sapling and it snapped like a matchstick.

"We're close to the bridge," Fish announced. The grim set to his mouth, shadowed by the bizarre glow in the sky, lent him a fearsome look.

David knew that Fish would do anything to help Samantha, but what could anyone do if the field station went up in flames? That field station meant everything to her. He had begun to realize that much of her joy came from the fact that she loved her work. Without it, what would be left of her? Would she survive the shock? Would her God get her through that trauma?

How deep did her faith go? And what would he and James do if Samantha....?

No. He couldn't think like that. He wouldn't allow Samantha to get hurt. He would drag her out of danger—research materials or no research materials. He would not let her gamble with her life over a bunch of data on those pesky mosquitoes.

Fish continued to drive the truck hard along the

impossible track, barely big enough for a dirt bike, let alone a full-sized pickup truck. Still, the old fisherman pressed forward, mowing over the tall reeds and short shrubs with the vindictiveness of a Sherman tank. The truck broke through another patch of tall reeds and Fish spun the wheel. David hit the door panel once again, but this time with a resounding thud that took some of the wind out of him. Fortunately, his body cushioned the blow for James.

The truck burst out onto the marsh road.

"Not far now," Fish said.

Dread began to tighten in David's chest. The closer they came, the more the air reeked with the pungent odor of charred wood. Perhaps they were already too late to do anything.

Within moments, the bridge lay ahead of them. On the other side, the dire scene filled David with alarm.

"Everything is on fire! She wouldn't go there!"

"She already has." The gruff tone of Fish's voice held a touch of grief. "Spun her wheels right there." Fish pointed to the churned up earth visible in the headlights.

The blood in David's veins chilled.

"Jesus is with Miss Samantha," James stated softly. "He will watch over her."

"You say a prayer, son. Sammie's gonna need a powerful prayer," Fish said as he ground the gears on the truck. "And we're gonna need one, too."

Obediently, James folded his hands, but David couldn't hear the words his son uttered because Fish threw the truck into high gear and roared over the bridge into the scorched landscape beyond.

Every nerve in David's body tensed when he caught sight of the field station. The scene looked like something out of a nightmare with the entire cottage consumed by flames that sent sparks rocketing high up into the night sky.

Fish pulled the truck up behind Samantha's car just as the roof of the cottage collapsed in a fiery maelstrom.

David spotted Samantha running toward the cottage. At

the same time, he saw the front wall of the cottage beginning to fall forward. Samantha was headed directly into the path of certain death. "Samantha! No!" David yelled as he scrambled out of the truck.

She stopped and turned to look at him, her eyes wide open and dazed. Behind her, an ominous cracking sounded as the last supporting beams of the cottage gave way.

David rushed toward her. The heat from the fire seemed to suck the air right out of his lungs, but adrenaline gushed through his heart. He flew at her, lifted her off her feet, and kept running.

The crashing wall sent glowing embers raining down on them, but David didn't feel the sting of the hot coals. He stumbled away from the perimeter of danger realizing that Samantha had lost consciousness. Carrying her limp body in his arms, he sat down on the bumper of the truck. In the glare of the headlights, he gazed at her pale skin with its ashen hue. The soft pink lips he had kissed now had a blue tinge. Desolation swept through him with such force that he shuddered.

"Miss Samantha? Is she okay, Daddy?"

Fish lifted her wrist. "Pulse's faint. Maybe the smoke got her, or shock. Lay her down in the back of the truck."

"Wake up, Miss Samantha! Wake up!" James shook her shoulder.

David saw the tears start from his son's eyes but his own remained dry. Instead, numb heaviness settled deep into his soul with each step he took to the back of the truck.

Fish spread a blanket on the flatbed. The old fisherman sniffed and wiped away the moisture on his face with the back of his hand.

David gently lay Samantha down upon the frayed khaki wool blanket. Her long tresses spread out in tangled disarray and he ran his fingers through the honey-colored strands in a futile attempt to align the golden mass properly. He had always wanted to touch her beautiful hair, to enjoy the soft gossamer silk against his own skin. It gave him no pleasure now, only pain.

James clung to his leg and sobbed. "Miss Samantha is my friend. Please, Daddy pray for her."

David groaned. A kind and gracious God would never let this happen! Someone as good, smart, and beautiful as Samantha didn't deserve this. He covered his eyes.

"Daddy say a prayer!" James wailed louder.

David gathered his distraught son in his arms.

"God, don't let her die." His muttered plea sounded more like a curse.

Then, above the crackling of the fire and his son's unhappy cries came the pulsing whine of sirens in the distance. He turned toward the sound and saw the wildly swirling lights of firetrucks and ambulances barreling toward them.

James sniffed. "Amen."

Chapter Twelve

Samantha gazed out the window from her hospital bed and noticed that some of the leaves had started to turn. In the two weeks she had spent in the hospital, summer had withered into an early fall. There had been no rain at all and the spacious lawn surrounding the hospital grounds had dried up into matted straw.

This morning, though, gray clouds hung overhead and the threat of a deluge seemed imminent. The bleak sky did nothing to stop the overwhelming sense of despair sweeping through her because today she was supposed to leave. The doctors claimed that she would soon be fine if she just took it easy for a while. Though they considered her healthy enough to go home, she found that the insidious lethargy that had taken hold of her would not let go.

Her heart thudded dully. God had punished her. She suspected that if anyone from Holy Redeemer knew of her conviction, they would assure her that God didn't work that way.

However, she realized now that a stumbling block had been placed in her path and she had tripped over that obstacle. She had been tested and failed.

Idly she glanced at the clock on the wall. David and James should be arriving at any moment. They intended to whisk her off to her new home, a trailer placed at the field station's site. She squeezed her eyes shut. Once, long ago, she had lived in a trailer with her father. She had been terrified of the cockroaches that had seemed to be everywhere.

The lab had been saved from the fire. Everyone proclaimed it a miracle. David had gathered all her research together and sent it off for her. The committee had been delighted with her work and offered her another project. Her thesis advisor had visited her in the hospital with best wishes for her new title as Ph.D.

She put her hand over her eyes and held back her tears, though the fear and loss descended upon her with a vicious impact. She was afraid to go back to the field station. She didn't think she could bear to see the devastation left by the fire. She tried to collect her emotions and sat up. The room tilted a little. She grabbed the rail on the bed to steady herself.

"Your chariot awaits, my mosquito queen!" David's voice called from the door.

"What's a chariot?"

Samantha turned to see James jerking at his father's sweater. The sight of David and his son sent a familiar ache swirling through her heart.

"A chariot is a fancy carriage pulled by lots of horses," David explained. Then he added in a whisper that Samantha had to strain to hear. "I'm just pretending the car is a chariot."

"Oh. I like to pretend. We're pretending we don't have a surprise, right?"

Samantha frowned when she saw David wince at the boy's ingenuous remark. She didn't like surprises. Then she thought of the carefully planned speech she intended to give David. It would be a cruel blow after all he had done for her, but she must not soften in her resolve, though her throat felt tight and raw.

David plopped a shopping bag on the bed. "Winnie said these should fit you, but I guess you'll have to dress yourself. Um—although I could probably tie your shoelaces or something."

Samantha saw his face flush and her heart turned over. She could not deny that she loved him. A sharp pang of regret stabbed at her, but she had made her decision. She would demand that he and James leave Clam Creek, something she should have done in the very beginning.

David pulled the curtain all around the bed. "Take it slow and easy. No fast moves or you might get dizzy. We've got plenty of time."

Her hands shook as she pulled the clothes out of the bag. Hiring him had been wrong. She had been thinking only of her own needs. What she had done had not helped James at all. She had been a facilitator in David's scheme to continue to keep his son away from his mother.

She had made up excuses for herself, convincing herself that she was helping James, but she had plenty of time to mull over the situation in the hospital. She had even reviewed her own traumatic childhood experience. Providing assistance to David and James merely highlighted her selfishness.

Her lip quivered. She felt God's retribution had been just. She had lost the home she had wanted to keep so desperately. She had lost her gentle pet as well.

Samantha struggled against her emotions. She did not want to upset James, but she knew that what she meant to do would hurt him, at least temporarily. Still, it was the right thing and after she paid David for his two weeks of work, there was no reason for the pair to remain.

Taking careful, shallow breaths, so that she would not start coughing, she fought to get her borrowed nightgown over her head. She ran out of breath halfway through and stopped.

"Why don't we count the blue cars that go by?" David's voice drifted through the curtain.

"Okay."

"There's a blue car!" David sounded excited.

"Where?"

"Over there, see?"

"That's green, Daddy."

"It's blue-green. Close enough. It counts."

"That's cheating."

"No, it's not."

Samantha listened to the two chat back and forth—the deep rich timbre of David's voice contrasting with the sweet, high tones of James' childish words. David seemed to have acquired more patience in dealing with his son. Perhaps, their sojourn in Clam Creek hadn't been a total waste.

Nevertheless, she could not condone the abduction any longer.

"Owww." David moaned from the other side of the curtain.

"I'm sorry, Daddy. That's a sore spot, huh?"

"Yeah, sport. Hands off."

"Can I see it?"

"No."

Samantha took some deeper breaths and managed to tug the nightgown off her head.

"You didn't tell me that you had gotten some bad burns," she called out.

"It's nothing."

"He has big bandages," James blurted out. "And medicine that smells bad."

"You missed another blue car, sport."

"Where?"

"It drove away when you weren't looking."

"Oh."

Samantha shuddered at the thought of the burns. She tried to shove away that last vivid image she had of the cottage thoroughly engulfed in flames, but it seemed to haunt her constantly. She couldn't count the times she dreamed of the fire and then woke up screaming. Even here in the hospital, the scent of charred wood seemed to linger in her nostrils.

Most of all, though, she missed Cassie, who had given her unconditional love and affection for nothing more than a pat on the head and regular meals. It felt as though a piece of Samantha's heart had been cut out, leaving the rest of it empty and hollow.

Fish had told her about David's injuries. In his plain and simple way, he had also offered his opinion of David Halpern. Fish said that David was a brave and honorable man, despite the fact that he had abducted his own son. Fish felt absolutely convinced that Samantha should keep an open mind, that there had to be extenuating circumstances forcing

David to try such a drastic option.

"He isn't vindictive, like your father was," Fish said.

She shivered. David *had* saved her life, but he was still living outside the law. She knew she could not count on him staying in Clam Creek. There could never be anything permanent for a man on the run.

She fingered the lacy bra that had been tucked at the bottom of the bag before putting it back. It was miles too big. She glanced down at her ribs. She could see every one.

"There's a blue car, Daddy."

"That's purple."

"Blue-purple. It counts. That's two cars."

"How are you doing in there? Need any help yet?" David asked.

"No!" Samantha started with fright and hurriedly slipped the long-sleeved turtleneck over her head. Next she wrapped herself in a heavy wool cardigan. Fumbling with the buttons took forever.

"There's a light blue car." David's tone sounded soothing.

"That's like the sky."

"I guess we could call it sky blue."

"Does it count?"

"Sure. Any kind of blue counts."

"Heaven is in the sky."

"Is that so?"

"Miss Gregory told me that's where Cassie went. Heaven's blue, too. Right?"

"I really don't know. If it's up in the sky, maybe heaven is gray today."

"No. It's blue. Miss Gregory said the clouds hide the sky but if you get in an airplane, you can fly right through the clouds and the sky will always be blue on top of the clouds."

"So it's not going to rain in heaven today."

"It never rains in heaven, Daddy."

David's indulgent chuckle sounded warm with love, that special kind of simple joy that parents, good parents, usually seemed to possess in abundant quantities.

Samantha had only known that wondrous love for a short time with her mother. She fought against the memory of her desolate childhood as she pulled on the pair of corduroy pants. The exertion of dressing had tired her out to the point of exhaustion. Or perhaps all her strength had been sapped by the emotions she tried so desperately to suppress. Either way, she would have loved to lie down and take a nap.

"Miss Gregory's favorite color is blue."

"So I've heard. Do you have a favorite color?"

"I like red. Red is my favorite. Do you have a favorite color, Daddy?"

"I don't know. Well, maybe gold. Like Miss Samantha's hair. It reminds me of sunshine."

It was the most poetic remark Samantha had ever heard from David and it cut her like a knife. She choked back a sob, determined not to let his words sway her decision. Even if he loved her, it would make no difference.

"Are you ready for help with shoes and socks?"

Samantha lay back on the bed and closed her eyes. "Yes."

She heard the curtain being pulled open.

"Can I put on a sock?" James asked.

"Sure!" David said.

Samantha opened her eyes. "Hey. I think I should get to decide who puts on my socks."

James' face fell. Samantha's heart ached. She had lost so much and now she would lose James and his father, too. But it had to be that way, she reminded herself. It was for James' own benefit. It almost pained her to smile at him.

"James gets to put on both socks," she said.

The boy clambered up onto the bed with delight.

"Now we'll never get out of here." David shook his head, but wore a good-natured grin.

"I know how to do socks, Daddy. Socks are easy."

"Right." David chuckled. He winked at Samantha.

Samantha swallowed hard and turned her head, afraid to meet his eyes, knowing that he could destroy all her determination with a simple look.

"You're going to love your new place," he said quietly, gently folding her hand in his.

The warmth of his hand sent a languid heat radiating up her arm. It was a reaction she could well do without, but she felt loath to pull her hand away.

James bunched up the sock and jammed it over Samantha's toes. She tried not to flinch.

"The trailer has some nifty amenities," David continued.

"It has a dishwasher!" James piped up. "You won't need helpers anymore."

Samantha thought of her charming little cottage and how she had shown David and James to do the dishes on that first fateful day. A crushing weight settled around her heart.

"There's a garbage disposal and a trash compactor, too." David sat down at the edge of the bed. His nearness set her pulse racing. "Today the electrician is supposed to wire up the trailer so we get to see if everything works."

"Daddy, this sock is bumpy."

David laughed, a full rumble that echoed off the solid walls.

"That bump is supposed to cover the heel of her foot."

"Oh."

Samantha glanced at James. He giggled.

"Can you fix it, Daddy?"

"No problem." David squeezed Samantha's hand and then let it go. She shivered.

"I'll give Miss Samantha a hug." James scrambled to the head of the bed.

Samantha prepared for the assault by bracing herself. James threw his arms around her neck and clung to her. Anguish tore at her as she thought of their parting, but she steeled herself to be strong. No matter how negligent the child's mother had been, she deserved to know what had happened to her son. When David had snatched his child away, he had committed a crime. Samantha didn't doubt that James' mother had suffered, just as her own mother had.

Susan Lyons had worried herself into an early grave. Samantha prayed that James' mother would survive the separation.

James ended his stranglehold, but fixed her with the gaze from his wide, blue eyes. "Daddy and me prayed for you."

Samantha blinked in confusion. Had David undergone a change of heart? She studied him as he put on her other sock, but he seemed engrossed in his task with his face a mask of concentration. Or was it deliberate avoidance?

"I wanted you to hurry up and come home, but Daddy said we had to wait. I fed all the guinea pigs every day. Max ran away but Daddy caught him."

Again David let out a warm laugh that seemed to brighten the whole room.

"That crazy guinea pig had plans, big plans." David picked up a shoe and loosened the laces. He still did not turn his head to look at her.

"He knew he had a ticket out of there. No more mosquitoes for him! He scooted under the lab table where you have all those beakers. I swear he knew I didn't want to risk breaking the glass to get him."

"Daddy only broke two jars."

Samantha saw the flush creeping into David's face again.

"Aw, come on, sport. You weren't supposed to tell. Not yet anyway."

He slipped the shoe on her foot, adjusted it and tied the laces snugly.

"There you go, Cinderella, the shoe fits."

The light-hearted banter had chased away some of the gloom that lay so heavily on Samantha's soul, but not all of it. It would be wonderful to be surrounded by David and James everyday, to count on being a part of their life, but it could never be. Forever wasn't part of a wanted man's vocabulary. How could she have been so blind? Her hand trembled as she covered her eyes.

James started bouncing on the bed.

"Hurry up, Daddy. I want to see the surprise."

Samantha stiffened and removed her hand from her face in time to see David roll his eyes.

"What surprise?" she asked James.

"Um. It's a secret, right, Daddy?"

"Right. So not another word, sport."

Samantha pressed her lips together tightly. Sneaky, underhanded surprises annoyed her. She didn't feel up to dealing with any shocks right now. She lifted up the telephone receiver and held it out to David.

"If you've planned a big homecoming party, you can just call everyone up right now and tell them I'm not feeling well and would like some rest."

David walked over, took the receiver out of her hand and placed it back in its cradle.

"There isn't going to be a party."

She didn't believe him. Anxiety tightened in her chest. She couldn't face a mob of people. The hand of God had descended to strike her down, though she had finished her project, gained her title, and remained in Clam Creek, she had paid a price for her greed.

"I'll stay right here," she insisted. "I won't leave."

David only shook his head, turned his back to her and stared out the window. James slid down to the floor and joined his father.

"Did you see another blue car?"

"Nope."

"Then why are you standing here, Daddy?"

David sighed and spoke in a voice barely above a whisper. "You've got to see it, Samantha. Fish had some friends come in with bulldozers. Then everyone raked and smoothed it out. You've got some great people at Holy Redeemer."

"I raked, too," James said. "And I dug a hole and planted a...flower. What was the flower, Daddy?"

"A mum."

"It's yellow! You have to see my flower!"

The exuberance in the young boy's face lit up the room,

but it only seemed to increase Samantha's despondency. She should have guessed that everyone at Holy Redeemer would pitch in and fix up the field station. She didn't feel she deserved such kindness, but she knew that her friends would not agree. They followed the dictates of their faith.

However, she had allowed herself to stray from the path and she couldn't forgive herself when she thought of James' mother waiting endlessly for word of her son.

"We really should get going." David suggested gently. "Before the rain starts."

Taking in a sigh, she nodded. There was no use fighting it. She must go back and face the grim scene. She folded the nightgown and placed it in the bag. From the night table she picked up a brush, a book, and the cards she had received. It didn't take long to gather the rest of her possessions. She thought about all the things she had lost, from irreplaceable photographs, to her fancy bath towels, to personal letters—all of it nothing but ashes now.

For you are dust and to dust you shall return.

The Biblical phrase came to her mind and her shoulders slumped. Just as Adam and Eve had sinned and been expelled from the garden so had her little paradise been taken away from her. Well, not all of it, but the part that had delighted her the most—her home, something she thought was solid and permanent.

"It's raining, Daddy." James had his hand up on the window tracing the first few raindrops as they rolled down the glass.

"I'll pull the car up to the entrance," David said as he picked up Samantha's bag. "The two of you can meet me there. You hold Miss Samantha's hand real tight, James."

"Okay, Daddy." James rushed over and grabbed Samantha's hand. "See, I'm holding tight."

"Good. Tell her to go slow and take it easy."

Then David was gone.

Samantha walked up to the window with James at her side. A cascade of drops splattered against the pane and then trickled downward. Like tears, she thought. She had cried so much for her dear Cassie but not a single salty drop had eased her grief.

Hadn't she learned long ago that tears didn't help and they didn't change anything?

She straightened her shoulders. She still had her work. God had left her that much.

"We're going to take care of you." James smiled up at her. Emptiness clawed at her heart as she stared into his sweet face. She lowered her lashes to hide the pain.

Chapter Thirteen

A knot tightened in David's stomach as they drew closer to the field station. For the past two weeks, David had seen the forlorn look in Samantha's eyes and wished he could make it go away, but her lost expression had only gotten worse. He knew it would take a miracle to bring back the same woman he had kissed in the lab that one night, but he didn't believe miracles happened. Only lucky breaks—and Samantha was lucky enough to be alive.

She seemed to have withdrawn into a private world where he could not follow. Each day she faded further and further away from him. Though her body healed, the joy that used to radiate from her paled into a dim memory, as if the light inside her had turned to ashes along with her cottage and her precious pet. He mourned the loss of her smile but he found it far worse to gaze into her gray eyes and see the awful truth. Once as changeable as the swirling fog, her eyes now appeared flat and lifeless, like slate.

The rain beat down heavily as he drove along, turning the rutted marsh road into one long, muddy quagmire. It was impossible to avoid the puddles. Though David drove as gently as he could, the car sloshed into a number of deep depressions that gave them all a few bone-jarring shocks.

He noticed how Samantha grimaced at every bump, though she made no sound and kept her gaze firmly fixed at some distant point on the horizon. Her fragility made him ache. He would wait on her day and night, if need be, until she was healthy again.

"Daddy, the bridge! We're almost home!"

David glanced at Samantha. Her eyes had closed and her body appeared to be as stiff as a seashell.

James, in his enthusiasm, kicked David's seat repeatedly from behind. A mild reprimand ended the barrage but it didn't stop James' energy.

"It's a new bridge, Miss Samantha. Daddy said it's a big plate of steel but it isn't round, it's a rectangle!"

David couldn't suppress a small glow of pride. He had been telling James about shapes all week. Round wheels were circles, doors were rectangles, a slice of pizza was almost a triangle, and the table in Miss Samantha's new kitchen was a square. James had practiced copying the shapes. There seemed to be some innate, insatiable need within the child for learning that one particular concept.

David found it fun and satisfying teaching James. His only regret was that he hadn't started sooner, but he had plenty of time to make it up to his son now.

Unfortunately, when it came to reading material, David had to rely on the stack of books that Marion Gregory had handed to him which contained nothing but illustrated children's Bible stories. James wanted to hear them over and over. After only a few days, David could practically recite them with his eyes closed.

Oddly enough, there were passages that seemed to speak right to the crux of his personal problems, but he realized that human nature hadn't changed much in two thousand years. Mankind's struggles persisted through the centuries and it didn't seem to matter what God people called upon. For him, the whole concept of God sending His Son to die for man's sins continued to sound like nothing more than a Greek or Roman legend.

Because James loved Jesus—almost as much as he loved Santa Claus and the Easter Bunny—David had relaxed his anti-Christian stance. Soon enough, James would find out that Jesus was nothing more than a myth.

David's throat closed up as he thought about the first few nights in the hospital when the doctors and nurses didn't hold out much hope for Samantha's recovery. James had prayed with such fervor, that David had feared for his son's health. It frightened him to see one so young begging God for Samantha's life.

He shuddered remembering the crisis.

He drove carefully across the crude substitute that had replaced the wooden bridge over the small stream. As soon as he got to the other side, he gave Samantha another sidelong glance and his heart twisted. She had covered her eyes with a shaky hand and it looked as if she would start crying. Staring out at the barren landscape, he could see what had upset her. The whole marsh from that point onward was one level, blackened scene of devastation. The charred stubble of the salt hay made a dreary image with the gray deluge from the sky pouring down upon the scorched earth.

"Now it's time for the surprise, isn't it, Daddy?"

"No."

"But we're almost there."

"We aren't there yet."

"But—"

"Don't spoil the surprise," David warned. He could see James in the rearview mirror. The kid wanted to blurt out the secret. He looked as volatile as a bag of microwave popcorn with all the kernels exploding at once.

"There's the trailer!" James practically screamed out the news.

David stopped the car at the edge of the little enclave. He reached over, and patted Samantha's shoulder.

"Hey. Take a look. It's not bad. We all planted mums and Fish rigged up an awning so you won't get wet at the front door. We put down some patio blocks and somebody found a bench so when the weather's nice you can sit there in the evening."

"It won't be the same." Her voice sounded strained.

"It's only temporary. Your boss is sure they'll get funding to replace the cottage."

He knew nothing he could say would ease her misery, but he took heart in knowing that the surprise might bring a smile to her face. He gave her hand a tender squeeze.

"Where's your car?" she asked.

"It burned up," James replied.

She had a stricken look on her face as she slid down in the seat.

"Hey, that old tin can had 240,000 miles on it." David put the car back into drive and pulled up next to the lab. "Look at the great job the firemen did in saving the lab. We scrubbed the soot off, so it looks better than new."

"Are you going to get another car?"

He heard the note of fear in her voice and watched her twist a button on her sweater round and round.

"I'm staying right here and taking care of you."

"Me, too." James piped up.

Her eyes darkened like the heavy clouds overhead, and tears gathered along her lashes, ready to spill down her cheeks.

"You can count on us. We aren't going to leave you."

She didn't cry, but he could see the fight she had holding back her emotions. She straightened up and knit her hands together so tightly he could see each knuckle turn white.

It tormented him to witness her heroic display of courage. He knew she had every reason not to trust him. He clenched his jaw and vowed that he would prove exactly how reliable he could be. She had done so much for him and James. He wanted to repay her. But he also wanted the old Samantha back.

"When's Fish going to get here?" James whined.

"I guess he'll be here in a few minutes." David grabbed an umbrella, and got out of the car. He held up the umbrella as he opened the door on Samantha's side.

"Why are we stopping here at the lab?" she asked. Then she narrowed her eyes. "You told me there wouldn't be a party!"

"Fish isn't a party. He's going to visit whether we want him to or not."

"Fish is bringing the surprise! Right, Daddy?"

David rolled his eyes. He should never have mentioned it to James. It was a wonder that his son hadn't spoiled the surprise already.

"James, would you please stop mentioning that?"

"Okay, Daddy."

James did not look at all contrite. He looked turbo-charged. This whole surprise idea had fired him up. Of course, serving him a bowl of sugarcoated cereal for breakfast probably hadn't helped the situation.

David cleared his throat and turned to Samantha again. "I—uh—I had something I thought you should see behind the lab. If you want to, that is."

Samantha's eyes filled with dread. Seeing the fright so vivid on her face had David swallowing past the tightness in his own throat. He didn't want to cause her any more distress, but he thought she needed some sort of closure. He took a deep breath.

"I wanted to show you where Cassie is buried. I picked out the spot myself."

"I put a flower there, too!" James jumped up and down in the back seat of the car.

Though James' exuberance was beginning to wear on David's nerves, Samantha turned to give the child a wan smile.

"Thank you. I'd like to see it."

She swung her legs out of the car, and David gave her his hand. The delicate, white fingers in his seemed no wider than the stems of the reeds in the marsh. She had grown so thin that he feared he would bruise her frail bones with his big clumsy paw.

James raced off ahead of them, undaunted by the heavy drizzle. They came upon him at the corner of the building where he had found a puddle filled with the rain that had spilled from the roof and out of the gutter.

"I think this worm drown-ded." James held up the limp body of an earthworm on a thin stick. "I'll bury him." Solemnly, he started to dig a hole with his fingers.

"Good idea." David agreed.

He led Samantha to the spot where he had picked blueberries for her. The berries had all vanished, but the leaves still remained green despite the cooler weather. There, raindrops glistened on a dark granite headstone. It rose only about a foot above the ground, nestled in between the low bushes. David held his breath as Samantha stared at the small memorial with the bright yellow mum in front of it.

For a pet, the headstone had been a ridiculous expense, especially since David had put a rush order on it, requesting it to be finished as quickly as possible so that it would be ready for Samantha's return.

Written in large Gothic letters it read, "Cassie." Under the date of her death, David stared at the inscription, "..every perfect gift is from above...James 1:17."

Time stretched on and Samantha said nothing.

"Marion thought that was an appropriate verse. We all know you loved Cassie. You'll miss her. But we'll be here to help you through your loss."

Her hand trembled so violently, that panic shot through him. He slid his arm around her waist and drew her close.

"I'm sorry if this has upset you. We'll get you into the trailer so you can rest and I'll warm up some soup—"

"Stop it!" She shoved him away and stumbled back beyond the shelter of his umbrella. "You shouldn't have done this! You shouldn't even be here! Why didn't you leave? I want you to go away!"

She spun around and nearly lost her footing in the muddy earth. He caught her elbow.

"Samantha, don't send me away. I love you."

"No!" Her raw, wounded cry echoed eerily in the sodden atmosphere. She viciously wrenched her elbow from his grasp with a strength that amazed him before she hurried off.

The rain turned into a sudden downpour. A gust of wind tore the umbrella out of David's limp hand. He did not go after it. He stood stunned, battered by her words.

"Daddy! Daddy! Fish is here with the surprise!" James appeared out of the gloom and grabbed his hand. "Come on! He took it out of the truck!"

Still in shock, David staggered along after his son. He

didn't know how he managed to put one foot in front of the other. He was beyond pain, a creeping numbness settling on him as his breath grew shallow and his skin cold.

He loved her, but she did not love him. Something inside him died.

Fish stood under the awning of the trailer with a dog on a leash. The animal appeared to be a cross between a Golden Retriever and a collie. The dog barked and wagged its tail joyously. James dropped David's hand and fell onto the dog, burying his face in the dog's fur. The dog licked James' face with its large tongue.

"Sammie went inside. She didn't even say hello. Slammed the door and locked it. Guess she's still sick."

Even though David felt like his stomach had turned to ice water, he could hear the mournful tones in the old fisherman's voice.

"I like this dog!" James tickled the dog beneath her chin. The dog seemed to be smiling with bliss though her whole rear end kept right on swinging back and forth. "What's her name?"

"Goldie." The old fisherman sniffed. "I picked her out 'cause she's got fur the same color as Sammie's hair. The shelter said she was good with kids."

"Hey, Goldie, you're going to be my new friend!" James squealed as the dog showered him with doggy kisses.

"I figured it'd be too soon for her to have another pet." Fish let out a sigh and sat down on the bench. Goldie sat down on the paving stones at his feet. "Needs time to mourn her Cassie."

David tried opening his mouth but no sound came out. Inside him everything felt hollow and the emptiness threatened to take away his sanity.

James plopped down beside Fish and stroked the dog's lustrous coat. "Cassie liked hot dogs. Does Goldie like hot dogs?"

"I don't know, son."

"Dogs like meat."

"That they do."

"Do you have a hot dog?"

"No, I don't."

"What are we going to give Goldie to eat?"

"I brought along some cans of dog food. The shelter lady said Goldie loves dog food."

"Can we give her some now?"

"It's not time for her dinner yet."

David struggled to gather his breath. "Samantha wants us to leave."

Fish slowly turned his grizzled head in David's direction and frowned. "She'll be saying things she doesn't mean 'cause she's feeling real bad."

The old man's words gave David a small measure of comfort.

"You've got to pray for the strength to get through this. The Lord's love is a wonderful thing but you have to be patient," Fish nodded.

David covered his eyes as the grief ripped through him.

"Come on, sit down here with us, we ain't going nowhere. Samantha will come out soon enough."

In the face of disappointment, all of David's hopes washed away as quickly as the thin soil of the field station in the rain. He sat on the bench and James crawled into his lap. He hugged his son as if the boy was his life preserver.

"Tell a story, Fish." James begged, settling against David's chest.

"I don't tell no fairy tales, boy."

"That's okay. Animals don't talk."

The ache in David's heart lessened as Fish told them about Samantha's mother—how she was the most beautiful girl in town and she was sweet on him.

"We were good friends and we could talk half the night about nothing, but I had this terrible longing to see the world. I wanted to leave Clam Creek far behind, but Susan—that was Sammie's mother—she thought this was the best place on earth. I liked her, but I didn't want to be stuck here in this backwater town for the rest of my life. No sir. So I stopped seeing her, broke her heart, I did, and joined the Navy."

Fish heaved a huge sigh and sniffed loudly.

"And he got five tattoos, Daddy! There's the snake, and the spider, and the skull—that's scary—and what's that other one?"

"Doesn't matter, son. Wish I didn't have them now, 'cause you can't wash 'em off."

David leaned back against the side of the trailer. He didn't have tattoos, but that didn't mean there weren't things he would like to erase from his past. Guilt seemed to have imbedded itself in him as permanently as any tattoo. If he could have obliterated the mistakes he had made, life could have been so much sweeter.

As Fish continued his tale, he told them how he had found out that Clam Creek wasn't such a bad place—in fact, he decided that it was closer to paradise than he was ever going get so he returned. Unfortunately, he discovered that the most beautiful girl in town had married, had a child, and then separated from her nasty brute of a husband.

"It hurt me bad. I had been a fool. I didn't know I loved her when I left, but all over the world, her face kept haunting me and I realized that I had thrown something wonderful away. When I came back, it cut me like a knife to know how John Lyons had treated her. When he would swagger into town and buy little Sammie ice cream, I wanted to punch his lights out for what he had done to Susan."

Fish held up a huge fist and stabbed at the air. James imitated the movement with perfect precision. David took in a deep breath and pressed his lips together tightly. He had lived with that kind of hatred for his wife. The idea of forgetting it all seemed impossible to him. Linda had nearly killed James.

David glanced down at the round blue eyes of his son. James smiled up at him and David kissed the boy's forehead. He loved the boy—loved him more than anything, except for

Samantha.

But she didn't love him. For a moment, as he remembered her angry words, David didn't think his heart would beat any more. Then it began pumping again, but with the sad, slow rhythm of loss.

Fish's voice quieted as he told them about Sammie's abduction and the long, long years of hoping she would be returned.

"Susan got sick and I couldn't bear it. Oh, I took care of her, sat at her bedside and nursed her through all the pain, and she was the one who led me along to Jesus. But then I prayed like crazy that Susan would get better and she didn't. I cursed at the Lord when she died. I felt like I had lost everything. I started drinking, even though it didn't take away the hurt. I would drink until I couldn't see no more, but the ache in my heart would always come back."

"What did you drink?" James asked.

"Beer, wine, hard stuff—you best stay away from those, son. Made me so sick, I finally wound up in the Veteran's hospital, all ready to die myself. So I was laying there by myself one night and I heard this voice say, 'Sammie's coming home. You take care of her.'"

David swallowed as he felt an icy shiver work its way down his spine.

"I knew there was no one else in the room with me, and I was scared out of my wits."

"Was it an angel?" James yanked at Fish's overalls.

"I don't know, boy."

David simply assumed that an ailing alcoholic would be delusional—that the "voice" he claimed to hear was simply another manifestation of his delirium. Then David frowned because, of course, Samantha had returned to Clam Creek.

The heavy rain slackened as Fish described his recovery and Samantha's arrival in the sleepy little town. By the time he finished his story, the sky had cleared and James had fallen asleep.

They sat there for a few moments in silence, listening to

water drops run off the canvas awning that had sheltered them from the storm.

Then the dog lifted up its head and perked up its ears.

"Someone's coming." Fish noted gruffly.

David glanced toward the road. He caught a flash of white barreling along the blackened marsh. He didn't feel like welcoming visitors and James' sleeping form had grown heavy in his arms. He stood up slowly.

"I'll put James in for a nap," he kept his voice soft so he wouldn't wake his son. James hadn't been sleeping well since the fire, but a short afternoon snooze seemed to do him some good.

"Sammie'll be all better soon and spreading her sunshine on us." Fish patted Goldie on the head.

David nodded. He sure hoped that Fish was right.

David carried his slight burden across the yard, stepping carefully so that James would not be jostled from his dreams.

When he reached the door of the lab, he saw a white sedan pull into the field station. However, a gray one that nearly matched the charred remains of the salt hay in the marsh pulled up right behind the first vehicle as well.

A sudden spurt of anxiety had David tightening his grip on James. They rarely had that much company out here in the marsh. He swallowed hard, unexpectedly rooted to the spot as the car doors opened.

The moment the men stepped out, he knew the nightmare had started. His heart froze in his chest.

Chapter Fourteen

Screams roused Samantha from her troubled sleep, rending the curtain of slumber with such violence that she woke up shaking with panic. For a few moments, she had no idea where she was, what time of day it was, or even whether the shrill cries had come from her own throat. Pushing the hair back from her forehead, she sat up on the bed, glanced around her and remembered. When she had first rushed into the trailer, she had thrown herself across the bed and wept until she found herself in a place where vague terrors and menacing images threatened her. She realized now that it had been a dream.

She heard another shriek and her heart lurched. That was not a murky fantasy, it was James. His frightened cry alarmed her and she jumped to her feet. Swaying dizzily, she stumbled through the trailer, grabbing handholds on the furniture as the sound of another desperate wail reached her ears.

Opening the door, she looked out at the scene and gasped. The police had come to take David and James away. Somehow they had been discovered.

"Nothing we can do, Sammie, except make it worse." Great tears rolled down into the creases of Fish's lined face as he sat on the bench beside the door holding onto Goldie's leash. The dog whined and paced.

A police officer shoved David, with his hands cuffed behind his back, into a gray sedan. Two other men struggled with James. The distraught boy fought and kicked, shattering the calm of the sodden marsh with his piercing pleas. Then he saw Samantha and his howling grew more intense. He begged her in his most pitiful tear-laden voice.

"Miss Samantha! Help me!"

All the life in her seemed to be swallowed up as her heart bled with pain. She sank down to the floor, knowing she could not intervene. She could not prevent herself from thinking that perhaps witnessing David's arrest and James' ordeal was part of a punishment she deserved. After all, isn't this what should have happened in the first place? Isn't this what she should have initiated before she fell in love?

She covered a sob with her hand and tried to remind herself that now James' mother would know what had happened to her son. She prayed that James' suffering would be brief and that, with luck, he would soon be leading a normal life—going to school and meeting friends his own age.

Still, each one of James' terrorized screams chilled Samantha to the bone. She knew exactly how he felt. Once she, too, had been ripped from her father's arms and though John Lyons had not been a good parent, he was all she had at the time, all she truly remembered. She had never forgotten the sheer black fright of that moment.

She closed her eyes, wishing to block out the tragedy, but she couldn't shut out the sound of James' bawling. His voice faded as his energy waned and his valiant, but doomed battle came closer to surrender. He would soon be back with his mother. Perhaps, by now, his mother would be better able to handle the child. Surely, his mother would love him. Or would she?

Had James' mother abused and neglected him? Would the boy be safe in her care? Would James, who Samantha loved as if he were her own child, be victimized? She opened her eyes and wrung her hands with worry. Did she believe David?

Samantha, don't send me away. I love you.

David's words sliced straight through her. He had said he loved her, and she did believe that. She didn't doubt that he meant completely, totally, and without any reservations. After all, he had saved her life, gathered up her research, and promised to take care of her. That one magical kiss they had shared felt like a pledge of devotion. All her life, she had wanted to be loved and when she finally found the one special person who would give her his heart, she could not accept it.

Anguish shattered her fragile emotions into wretched torment. She loved him, too. She would always love him, but it was so hopeless. Her hands went to her throat at the thought of the dark and lonely future awaiting her.

The men stepped into the car with the spent, but still sobbing boy and the door slammed shut. The engines revved up.

Without thinking, Samantha stumbled out of the trailer and staggered across the yard. Fish called after her, but she couldn't stop. She wanted one last look, one last touch, one last promise that maybe someday they would meet again.

However, the sedans pulled away quickly as the rain began to fall once more. She caught a glimpse of David through the window, his face twisted into a mask of agony, and from the second car she could hear a muffled sound as James repeatedly called out her name.

She collapsed down into a heap of misery in the mud as the cars disappeared from view. She had no tears left, and it seemed to her that even heaven joined her in her sorrow as the cold drops of water splattered around her.

It never rains in heaven, Daddy.

A bleak heaviness settled in Samantha's chest as she recalled James' words, spoken such a short time ago. She lay weighted down upon the morass of brown slime in the yard until Fish came over and lifted her up to carry her back into the trailer.

"The Lord will bring them back, Sammie. He brought you back."

She didn't believe him. No. She would never see them again. She would never taste the wonders of David's kiss or listen to the sweet joy of James' laughter again. What little energy she had left drained out of her as the cold rain pelted her face. She had been tested and failed. Her punishment would be a lifetime without love. "I want to die." She moaned.

"I won't let you." Violence rumbled deep in his chest,

startling Samantha out of her grief. She cringed in fear until she saw the tears in his eyes and realized that his pain mirrored hers. "God willing, they'll be back, Sammie." He softened his oath.

Chapter Fifteen

Samantha sat at the table in the trailer warming her hands with a mug of coffee. Outside the window, Thanksgiving Day had dawned cold and blustery with heavy clouds on the horizon that threatened to deliver the first snow. Tucking her feet beneath her as a draught swirled across the floor, she put the mug down and rubbed her arms to ward off the chill.

Despair rose up so bitter in her throat that it nearly choked her. Everyone in Clam Creek had asked her to share in their festivities, but she had declined each invitation. Instead, she thought she would try to forget the holiday by working, a strategy that might have succeeded if she could have gotten David and James out of her thoughts as well, but she had not. For the brief span of time when they had all been together, it had almost felt as if she had achieved the one thing she had always longed for—a real family. It was wrong, of course, for her to think that way, but the feeling persisted.

As a child she had dreamed of having a mother and a father who loved her unconditionally, but that wish had been denied. She realized that she had replaced her fantasy with her cottage, but she had learned a very hard lesson when it burned. It had only been a building, a place, a spot on a map, a simple shelter of wood and mortar.

She glanced around at the trailer with its bland furnishings and knew that if James and David could share it with her, she would consider it a palace. She had tried to be thankful for the trailer, for her job, and the people of Holy Redeemer, but the losses she had suffered continued to weigh heavily on her. She lived under a cloud of grief that never left her. No matter what the weather was like outside, her soul lay shadowed and barely alive.

It occurred to her that if she found out what had

happened to David and James, she could gain some solace. Being assured that they were both okay would guarantee her peace of mind, if nothing else, but she had searched endlessly for news of the pair and found none. They had simply vanished. While the time had flown by, the awful ache inside her had not left and today it seemed more acute than ever.

Would James be celebrating this wonderful feast with the warm love of his family surrounding him? Or could he have retreated once again into his own world, where his imaginary friend, Kyle, was all he had for company? Samantha shivered as the image of the innocent young face with the startlingly blue eyes filled her mind. She could almost hear his sweet voice talking.

Heaven's blue.

She gazed upon the dismal skies outside her window and the gloomy weight of sorrow pressed down on her once more. For months now, there had been no sunshine in her heart. Still, she hoped that James had found his blue skies and a happy home life.

And what about David? Where was he tonight? Alone? In prison? Vivid memories stabbed her as keenly as a knife twisting inside her chest. Over and over again, she saw David's tortured features staring at her as he had been driven away. With the desolate nights of fall growing longer, she kept the anguish away during the day with her work, but at night those last horrid images returned to haunt her, disturbing her dreams.

She picked up the phone bill on the table and pressed her fingernail under the number that must belong to David's lawyer. She had considered calling at least a hundred times, but until now she had always changed her mind. However, today she decided she must know what had happened to them. She could not stand the agony of wondering anymore.

Her finger trembled as she punched in the numbers. The answering machine in the lawyer's office picked up almost immediately. She panicked as she tried to think of something to say.

"Um. Uh. This is Samantha Lyons from Clam Creek. One of your clients worked for me and I—um—I have been concerned about how he and his son are doing. H-he was really such a good father to the child, but then the police took them away—"

She had to stop for a moment to control her emotions. Then taking a deep breath, she finished off the call by rattling her number into the receiver before she hung up.

Her head seemed too heavy to hold up, so she cradled it in her hands. Keeping her gaze on the phone, she waited for it to ring, but as the seconds ticked away and nothing happened, she considered the possibility that the lawyer would probably not return her call and she would never, ever hear from David and James again. She knew she had to get on with her life, and she had tried to do so for months. However, in that hollow empty space where her heart used to be, the wound never healed.

She closed her eyes and tried to conjure up a vision of one of the happy moments they had shared, but the sound of grinding gears and squealing brakes shattered her concentration. She opened her eyes and turned to the window, watching as Fish climbed out of his ancient pickup. She did not want to see him—she did not want to see anybody at all. She had done her best to avoid the people of Clam Creek but they were a stubborn lot and had refused to pay any attention to her wish to be left alone.

Fish's heavy fist on the door shook the trailer. Samantha took a deep breath and gathered her strength. Sighing with resignation, she got up to answer his knock. The fact that he walked in smelling of spicy cologne unsettled her slightly. Not only that, but he looked scrubbed, right down to the fingernails. He wore neatly pressed slacks, a crisp white shirt, and a bow tie under his trimmed beard.

What had happened to her simple fisherman? This man could pass as the captain of a cruise liner.

"You're coming to the deacon's house with me."

Samantha set her mouth in a stubborn line. "I called

Winnie last night with my regrets. I have to go through several applications—"

Fish crossed his arms over his chest. "I am not leaving here without you."

"It doesn't matter if I don't show up—"

"It matters to me."

She turned her back to him. "I have work to do."

"It can wait."

Picking up a sponge in the sink, she started wiping off the counter.

"Right now, I don't have anyone to help me take care of the lab, but I've received several applications, so I have to read through them and see if there's a suitable candidate for the job."

"It's Thanksgiving."

Samantha swallowed hard as her throat tightened. She didn't feel like celebrating, that was the problem. So she decided to try another excuse.

"I can't find Goldie again. She's run off for the umpteenth time."

Fish chuckled. "Should have named her Houdini."

Samantha didn't think that was funny. She set the sponge back beside the sink and took in a ragged breath. She had never wanted to hurt Fish's feelings but Goldie had been more trouble than she was worth.

"I know you had nothing but the best intentions when you gave me that dog—"

"She's just young and foolish. Gone off to sow her wild oats. Everybody gets that way now and again, but she'll come back, like she always does."

"But what about the snow we're supposed to get. What if Goldie winds up out there in a blizzard?"

"She's got a fur coat."

Fish went to the closet and pulled Samantha's coat off the hanger.

"The young ones were all hoping you'd do one of your little science experiments for them."

Samantha glanced at the phone bill on the table.

"But I'm—I'm expecting a phone call."

"You've got an answering machine."

Samantha bit her lip before it started to tremble.

"Ah, Sammie." Fish slipped the coat over her shoulders and gave her a comforting pat. "We've all been praying hard for you. But sometimes it takes a while for the good Lord to get things done. One of His days is like a thousand of ours. Seemed like it took forever for you to make your way back to Clam Creek. Might take David and James a little longer than you'd like, but God will be watching over them all the same."

Samantha's shoulders slumped. If only she had told David that she loved him. Now she would be trapped with the truth of her own feelings through eternity.

She still didn't know if she could bear to resign herself to a cheerless future. She continued to go on, but it took all her energy to get through a single day. Nevertheless, she sniffed, straightened up, and put her arms into the sleeves of the coat. Fish wouldn't put up with more excuses. She might as well go and get Thanksgiving over with.

*   *   *

When they reached the deacon's house, Fish parked the truck behind an unfamiliar, bright yellow car.

"Did the deacon get a new car?"

"Nope. That's Marion's. I helped her pick it out and taught her to drive it, too. She almost didn't pass the driving test. For a little lady, she's got a heavy foot." He gave a deep, full laugh that shook the cab of the truck.

Samantha frowned at Fish. She had never heard him sounding so jolly.

"But I thought she was too nervous to learn to drive."

"Marion?" Fish turned off the engine and flashed a smile that wrinkled up his face. "Why that woman's fearless. She drove all through Philadelphia last week. We stopped at that big art museum and then we saw the Liberty Bell. Did you ever see the Liberty Bell?"

Samantha shook her head numbly. She felt as if somebody had pulled the rug out from under her. "Did you and Marion go on a date?"

Fish let out a whoop of merriment. Samantha felt the blood drain from her face.

"Nah." He chuckled some more and wiped away some moisture from the corner of his eyes. "We're just good friends. Since her mother died, she's been needing some company."

It was a date. Not only that, but Samantha would place a bet that Fish and Marion were in love! Even though they could be grandparents! What had happened to all the undying devotion Fish had claimed to have for her own mother?

Samantha found her hand shaking as she reached for the handle on the door of the truck cab. How could she hold herself together when her friend and neighbor had betrayed the sacred bond of love he had professed for her mother? How could Fish be so fickle in his emotions?

The bitter wind seemed to slice right through her coat as she stepped out of the truck. The cry of seagulls overhead caught her attention. The birds careened crazily in the sky, heading away from the coast, seeking shelter from the coming storm. Had David's love for her flown away, too? Could any man be trusted?

Feeling betrayed, with her heart raw and bruised, Samantha walked into the deacon's house. She was surprised when Winnie and Marion welcomed her with warm hugs. She had not gone to the funeral of Marion's mother, Agnes, who had died suddenly of a stroke about a month ago. Guilt had gnawed at her, but Marion didn't act at all upset with her. However, Samantha's nose twitched when she realized that the overbearing odor of sweet lilacs usually clinging to Marion had been replaced by the heavier aura of a musky perfume.

"I'm really sorry about your mother—"

"Mother lived a long life with many blessings," Marion interrupted. As soon as Fish walked in, she immediately latched onto him. With her hands resting on his massive forearms, Marion gazed up into his face, her eyes as bright as neon emeralds.

Samantha struggled not to gasp in surprise. Marion had to be wearing colored contact lenses! And her nervous tic seemed to have disappeared altogether. Wearing a fluffy chenille sweater and neat slacks, she had the look of a very sophisticated lady.

Samantha glanced at her own jeans and worn flannel shirt as her cheeks grew hot with shame. She should have dressed up for the occasion. Uncomfortable, she made a quick foray into the kitchen where she found Deacon Bob wearing an apron and attempting to mash up a batch of rutabagas.

He turned a wan smile at her. "These things are tough. I've been attacking them for a while now and they're still lumpy."

Samantha peered at the deacon's handiwork. "I think they're done. Rutabagas aren't like potatoes. You can't get them to be real smooth."

"Oh." The deacon sighed. "I never cooked them before. Winnie insisted that we had to cook fresh vegetables. Otherwise, she said it wouldn't be a proper Thanksgiving." He pointed to the counter at a jumbled pile of assorted produce.

Staring at the counter, Samantha realized that aside from the rutabagas and the turkey roasting in the oven, nothing else had been prepared yet!

"When did you intend to serve dinner?"

The deacon gave a careless shrug. "I'll get it all done eventually." The glint of amusement sparked in his eyes. "Have no anxiety at all, but in everything, by prayers and petition, with thanksgiving, make your requests known to God." The deacon brightly quoted the scripture verse.

God helps those who help themselves. Samantha bit her lip

before voicing her thoughts. If she wanted to get back to the field station at a reasonable hour, obviously she would have to pitch in. She rolled up her sleeves. She peeled potatoes, whipped up cream sauce, chopped up broccoli, and cauliflower. The deacon boiled water for instant stuffing and popped some refrigerated biscuits into the oven. His kids set the table and located a few extra folding chairs.

Meanwhile, Winnie breezed in and out of the kitchen, seemingly unconcerned about the chaos. When Samantha carried the covered dish of rutabagas to the dining room table, she saw Winnie sprinkling gobs of metallic confetti on the tablecloth next to tented placecards. She pointed at the one with her own name on it.

"Aren't these lovely? I stamped and embossed them myself with gold. Now everyone will know where to sit at the table."

Samantha nodded while trying to feign interest in Winnie's handiwork. It didn't take a research scientist to figure out that Marion would be sitting next to Fish and that Samantha would most likely be relegated to a spot right in the middle of the kids—her function being to separate the combatants.

Winnie nearly knocked over the large centerpiece as she reached across the table to dump another handful of glittery confetti in a strategic position. Samantha caught the centerpiece, a replica of the Mayflower sailing atop a cornucopia. However, though she tried to right the Mayflower, the ship which had already been sailing at a drunken angle on top of the cornucopia now listed threateningly to the starboard side.

"This boat won't stay in place."

"Oh, my. I'll get Marion. She put it together." Winnie dashed off while Samantha stood there, holding the vessel upright and preventing a shipwreck. The tinkle of Marion's laughter floated into the dining room and grated on Samantha's nerves.

Marion sailed into the dining room with Fish in her

wake.

"Dear me, the Mayflower is being swamped by a squall!" Marion giggled.

If Samantha didn't know better, she would have sworn that Marion had been drinking.

"Winnie bumped into it."

"We'll have to make her walk the plank for treason." Fish remarked in a jovial manner.

"I didn't know you liked to do craft projects." Samantha relinquished her hold on the ship as Marion gently lifted it from the table.

"Taking care of Mother never left me any time, but I've joined the Christmas decorating committee at Holy Redeemer and some of the women are so clever that I've learned a lot from them. You should join us on Thursday night. We have lots of laughs."

Samantha frowned. She used to laugh so much, but she seemed to have forgotten how. She hurried back into the kitchen where Winnie stood on a stepladder reaching up into a cabinet.

"Everyone must have a nice stemware glass for the toast and I know we have them here somewhere. They don't match, but that doesn't matter."

Despite the warmth of the kitchen, an icy shiver slid up Samantha's spine. Why would they all need a special glass? Would some important announcement be made? Would Fish marry Marion?

Would Fish forget all about Samantha's mother? Would he abandon Samantha, too? True, she knew she hadn't been very good company lately, but nevertheless, she looked forward to his visits.

An ache swelled in her throat and she knew she couldn't speak. She felt once again like that lonely, cast off child, the one nobody really wanted.

Jesus loves you. The words echoed inside her head. Hadn't she explained it all to James? Why couldn't she believe it herself? Just because she had fallen in love with the wrong man—or because she didn't really believe in God's promises.

Her head started to throb.

Finally, they all sat down at the table and the deacon said a brief blessing over the food before they dug in. The toast was brief and ambiguous. Winnie recorded the event with her camera. The bright flashes of light popping repeatedly in front of Samantha's eyes made her headache intensify. She did not feel hungry.

However, since Winnie hadn't had a hand in any of the actual cooking, the food tasted okay. Fish and Marion raved about how delicious it was. The deacon grinned broadly and had at least three helpings of everything.

"Does your dad always eat like that?" Samantha nudged one of the kids next to her.

"Oh yeah. Mom says he eats like a horse. She says she wished she had his met—metab—"

"Metabolism?"

"Yeah. He burns it all up, she said."

As they finished up, Samantha showed the kids how to make different sounds with the stemware glasses and eventually they played "Mary Had A Little Lamb" using all the stemware filled with varying levels of water.

"Can you play 'Jesus Loves Me?'" Marion's enthusiasm for Fish hadn't waned at all during the meal. They had progressed to holding hands.

Still, their familiarity wasn't what made Samantha's throat close up. The mere mention of the song she had taught to James had her eyes misting. She shook her head.

After that, Fish herded the youngsters into the living room and regaled them and Marion with his tales of the sea, but Samantha had heard them all before so she wandered back into the kitchen where Winnie and her husband were cleaning up. Winnie shooed her away.

"You are not getting your hands wet! You're a guest, remember?"

Samantha would have liked to point out the fact that she had already baptized her hands by washing the broccoli, but she thought better of it and clamped her mouth shut. The fireplace in the den beckoned her and she sat down on the floor in front of it by herself, gradually becoming more morose as she stared into the flames.

… in everything, by prayers and petition, with thanksgiving, make your requests known to God.

The scripture the deacon had recited came back to her. She had prayed, over and over, but she didn't believe God had listened to her at all. She drew her brows down. What did she really expect from God? What did she really want Him to do for her?

Please forgive me, Lord. She barely moved her lips with the soundless words. She took in a quivery breath and waited. If the Lord had truly forgiven her, wouldn't she know? Wouldn't her heart heal? Wouldn't there be some other sign, a clear indication that His love for her remained? Could her guilt ever be purged?

No, she decided. Besides, what had she done to deserve forgiveness?

* * *

"I haven't had such fun in a long, long time." Fish smiled as he drove Samantha back to the field station later that evening. "Did you know that her great-great grandmother on her mother's side was a duchess? Real royalty, right here in Clam Creek. Don't that take the cake?"

"Princess Marion." Samantha couldn't help the hint of sarcasm in her tone, but it didn't seem to bother Fish at all.

"Yeah."

Even in the dim light of the truck cab, she could see the goofy grin on his face. *He's in love.* She stared at him as her heart sank lower. How could Fish be so smitten? He had loved her mother, he had told her so himself. Were all men like that?

By now, David must have forgotten her, too. After all, he

was handsome. He could convince any woman that he loved her, and she would believe him. Well, maybe not any woman—only the gullible ones, and obviously, she had been more naive than most.

She closed her eyes and tried to keep back the pain. She still loved him. She would love him for the rest of her life. She would love him in prison garb or if he worked some menial job and got paid minimum wage.

She sighed deeply and opened her eyes to study the scene outside the window as the truck rumbled along the marsh road. The expected snowstorm had arrived. In the headlights, she saw the fine flakes blowing across the landscape in a horizontal line. Dusted with a thin layer of white, the marsh had an ethereal quality to it. The salt hay, frozen together in clumps and covered with snow, gave the illusion of foaming white caps on the sea while the *Phragmites,* draped in gossamer chiffon, reminded her of sails fluttering in the wind.

An involuntary shiver whipped through her as she thought of her mother, her father, the foster families she had lived with, her little Cassie, David, and James; all the souls who had breezed into her life and then left her in their wake. She lived in a cycle of loss—it was all she had ever known.

She realized that just simply living in Clam Creek would never satisfy the deep yearning in her soul. What she truly longed for was a family of her own, one where the strong bond of love would never be severed.

For one wretched moment she considered whether she could stop loving David in order to find someone else, someone who could give her the happiness she so longed to have. The bleak chill in her heart told her that would be foolish. She would never stop loving him.

"Starting to pile up out there. You got enough food?" Fish's question startled her.

"I-I ought to." She stared down at the three containers of leftovers in her lap and knew she didn't need to worry about being snowbound. "But I hope Goldie's back."

When they reached the trailer, Samantha got out of the

truck and called out the dog's name, but the gale tore her words away as she shouted into the storm. The fast-driven snow stung her cheeks. Pulling up the collar of her coat, she scanned the area, but the visibility had narrowed to little more than a few yards.

Fish got out of the truck and shouted for Goldie, too, but not even an echo came back to him.

Samantha stamped toward the trailer. "If she survives this storm, I'm taking her back to the animal shelter."

"You can't do that, Sammie. You've got to love her no matter what. Just like the Lord loves all of us, not that we deserve it, but He keeps right on loving us and forgiving us and sooner or later most of us wise up to His incredible kindness. Goldie'll be a devoted dog one of these days, you'll see."

"Goldie might be an icicle by tomorrow morning."

Fish scratched his beard. "I got one of those special dog whistles in the truck. It's the kind you blow in and you can't hear a thing. But the dogs can hear it clear as a bell." He went to the back of the pickup and dug into a tackle box.

Samantha wasn't surprised that he had a dog whistle in his truck. Whatever she needed, he always seemed to have it handy.

"Here you go." He handed her the small cylindrical whistle. "Can't remember where I picked it up exactly, but it should work like a charm."

Samantha turned the whistle over in her hand.

"Did you keep this next to some decaying squid?"

Fish's roar of laughter drowned out the sound of the wind for a few moments.

"Maybe I should have used it for a lure!"

Samantha sighed but she decided to hold onto it. She could sterilize it in the autoclave.

Fish rubbed his hands together.

"Might make me a little extra cash doing some plowing tomorrow if this keeps up."

Samantha had never seen him so deliriously happy, and

her throat ached. He had been her best friend and it would hurt if he forgot that she existed.

"Maybe I'll take Marion somewhere fancy. You know anyplace fancy?"

Samantha could only shake her head.

"I know! I'll ask Dr. Peller. He's been everywhere." Moving with a definite bounce in his step, he swung easily back into his truck and ground the gears. Within moments, his truck had faded into the storm and Samantha felt more alone than ever out on the marsh.

Just like the Lord loves all of us, not that we deserve it, but He keeps right on loving us and forgiving us and sooner or later most of us wise up to His incredible kindness.

Fish's words kept repeating in Samantha's head as she puttered about the lab. With the wind gusting up to sixty miles an hour, she feared whether the trailer would stay on its foundation. Besides, in the lab she had the guinea pigs for company. They had happily greeted her with their squeaks and she rewarded them by digging into the bag of carrots in the lab refrigerator and pulling out four baby carrots for each guinea pig. The furry creatures stuck their noses out of the cage bars as she handed each one a fair share.

"It's Thanksgiving, piggies. *Bon appetite!*"

He keeps right on loving us and forgiving us...

Samantha froze. She kept right on loving David. He had done a terrible thing in abducting his own child, but she still loved him. She could forgive him.

Forgive and you will be forgiven.

Samantha frowned as she remembered the words from Luke's gospel. She reached into the autoclave and pulled out the dog whistle, hoping that all the microbes had been obliterated.

…you will be forgiven. She gulped hard. Was it really that easy?

She went outside and stood in the yard. Already, four inches of snow lay on the ground, and drifts had begun to form. She blew into the whistle until her cheeks hurt. Then she waited, but nothing happened. Goldie did not materialize. All she could hear was the screaming wind making an eerie sound as it swirled around the trailer and the lab.

Clenching her teeth in anger, she went back into the lab and pitched the whistle into the trashcan. How stupid she had been! Believing in dog whistles! She had as much sophistication as her own mosquito larvae.

Believing that God would forgive her was just as ridiculous. Why should He bother with her? Who was she? Just another obsessive scientist stuck out in the middle of nowhere with a herd of guinea pigs, an autoclave, and a microscope. In all the billions of people in the world, what did one scientist matter—especially a scientist who hires a man on the run with a child in tow who has been abducted from his mother's arms. Especially a scientist who falls in love with both the man and his son.

How could she have done it?

Because she so desperately wanted to be loved? Memories swirled around her while the wind whistled around the corners of the lab. She thought of all those years when she had been a foster child, and all the times she had misbehaved only to wind up in a different home. The agony of those times sent a cold shaft of fear piercing straight to her heart. She winced with the pain.

"Why couldn't I have had what everyone else has, Lord? A family, a home. People who will always love me—no matter what."

At that moment, the lights went out and Samantha screamed.

With her hands shaking, she felt her way around the lab. She found the matches first. She struck one and felt relief flood through her with the cheerful glow of light.

God is light. She recalled the line from John, if her memory served her correctly. She furrowed her brow and stared at the flame as it burned lower. There was something else in John, something else about forgiveness.

She opened a drawer and found a whole box of candles. After she had placed one candle in each of six beakers, she went searching for the little Bible she had dumped in the bottom drawer of her desk.

Leafing through it rapidly, she found what she hoped was there.

"...and will forgive our sins and cleanse us from every wrongdoing."

In the flickering glow of the candles, she paused uncertainly as something shifted inside her. Until she had hired David, she realized that she truly had not considered herself as a sinner. She had always felt herself a victim who needed to forgive others, but not a sinner. A strange, new kind of warmth washed through Samantha as she read those words. It was that simple and that wondrous. She had sinned, but it didn't matter. Jesus still loved her. Peace settled deep upon her as love poured into her starved soul. *Yes, Jesus loves me.*

The line from the little song she had taught to James had a far, far greater meaning for her now. She felt a hot tear slide down her cheek.

Suddenly something scratched at the door, and Samantha jumped as her pulse raced. Next came a mournful whine, followed by a hoarse bark. Evidently, the dog whistle actually had worked.

Breathing a sigh of relief, she went to open the door. Goldie lumbered in, looking more bedraggled than usual.

"Oh you crazy dog!" Grabbing an old towel, Samantha knelt down beside the dog to wipe off the snow. Goldie licked half of her face.

"You shouldn't go running off like you do. Especially on a night like this. Look at you, you're half frozen."

Goldie shivered and sank down on the floor. Samantha sensed that something was terribly wrong. Goldie quivered and an overwhelming flood of anxiety had Samantha running for the phone.

When she picked up the receiver, she did not hear a dial

tone. Evidently, along with the power line, the phone line had gone down. Totally isolated out on the marsh, she gulped back her panic, and slowly turned to glance again at Goldie in the wavering light of the candles. The dog trembled.

Samantha lifted an extra lab coat from the peg and settled it carefully down upon the dog's suffering form.

"I don't know how to help you, Goldie." She gingerly patted the dog's head. "Please don't die."

She could do nothing else but pray and so she did. With her eyes tightly shut against the menacing shadow of death, she begged for Goldie's life, for electricity, and phone service. She thanked the Lord for all she had and for His never ending love. She knew that His will must prevail and if Goldie should die, then she had to accept His decision, but she admitted her dread and asked the Lord for guidance. Surely, she could do something to alleviate the poor dog's suffering.

When she heard Goldie move, she warily opened her eyes and realized that Goldie was licking at something small and wet.

A shiver of disgust mingled with alarm had Samantha fighting down a touch of nausea. Blinking in the dim glow of the candlelight, she thought that perhaps her eyes had been mistaken. Reaching for the rest of the candles, she quickly lit one after another, using up all her clean beakers and heedless of conserving her only source of light even though she knew that the power would probably not be going back on for some time.

The smell of simmering wax filled the lab as the bright glow of a dozen candles chased the shadows to the farthest corners. Samantha held one candle in her hand and stared at Goldie who had started licking at a second slimy little bundle.

Trying to quell the icy flutter in her stomach, Samantha brought the candle even closer. The small shape under Goldie's tongue stirred to life as miniature paws clawed uselessly at the air. It was a puppy, a pink-faced dwarfish version of its mother.

"You gave birth?" Stunned, Samantha watched as Goldie

finished cleaning up her baby and then went on to competently handle—all by herself—the birth of four more tiny blessings. With the miracle of life going on, Samantha forgot all about the snow and her precarious situation on the edge of civilization.

Much later, when several candles had sputtered out and the blizzard had died down, she crossed the hall into the room that David and James had shared. Grabbing all the blankets and pillows, she dragged them into the lab. There didn't seem to be any point in going out into the snow just to sleep in her cold bed in the trailer. Besides, Goldie might need her.

She set up a quadrant of boxes around Goldie so that the puppies wouldn't wander off. The new mother lay spent and exhausted with her six squirming puppies nuzzling against her warmth.

After offering Goldie some water in a pan, and a bit of leftover Thanksgiving turkey, Samantha extinguished all but one candle. She smiled. She had wanted a family and now she had one—sort of. She decided that perhaps God had a sense of humor because for the first time in months, she felt a spark of joy in her heart.

True, none of those six little puppies could ever replace Cassie, but they were each a blessing nonetheless. She gently stroked the tiny babies with the tips of her fingers. One had a dark spot near his nose, so she thought she would name him, Spot. Not very original, but descriptive. Another seemed to cry more than the others, so she thought she would name her Singer. She dubbed the rest Butch, Angel, Prince, and Honey.

Though they still had their eyes closed and they were only minutes old, the puppies all had very different personalities. Samantha adored them. She still loved Cassie, but she knew now that she had plenty of love to give.

Samantha sat down on the floor in the middle of her makeshift bed and stared at the flame of the lone candle she had left burning. Fish could continue to love her mother and still have plenty of affection for Marion as well. Everyone is born with an inexhaustible supply of love.

Jesus loves everybody. There's no end to His love.

Samantha leaned over to give Goldie one more pat. "You did an awesome job. Thanks."

Goldie sighed.

Finally, Samantha crawled beneath the blankets and put her head down on a pillow. David's cologne teased her nostrils and the sad little ache that had darkened the preceding months threatened to return. She thought of his incredible kiss and knew she would never, ever find anyone like him. Then weariness overtook her and she slept.

Chapter Sixteen

The bright sun in the clear sky did nothing to chase away the frigid temperature in the cemetery but Alan Nugent did not pull up the collar of his coat. It didn't matter. He doubted that he would ever be warm again. Shock held him in a glacial grip that left him numb.

However, for a moment, as the minister intoned a long prayer, Alan let himself slip back to those few weeks in Clam Creek when he had called himself David Halpern and had been warmed by the sunshine of Samantha's smile in the cottage on the marsh. The happy image vanished as he stared at the lush collection of flowers heaped about the grave. The memory of those precious magical days faded, leaving behind an ache that felt as merciless as the point of an icicle at his heart. It all seemed a lifetime ago even though it had been little more than three months.

He stared at the fake grass carpet and tried to ignore the faint whir and click of the cameras in the background. Though there seemed to be fewer reporters assigned to record this particular occasion, he suspected that the reason wasn't because the media had become more discreet. Perhaps they had simply become weary of the storyline, or maybe they had found something far more titillating. Or, most likely of all, they found the arctic weather in a Connecticut graveyard to be only for the most rugged and determined journalists.

Tuning out the intrusive sounds, he found himself wondering why he had spent so much time hating Linda. That caustic anger had hurt him and Foster more than he cared to admit and for his son, the damage might never be undone now that his former wife lay cold and still in the most expensive mahogany coffin money could buy.

Alan glanced up at the red roses in the bouquet atop the gleaming dark wood. The crimson petals had shriveled in the freezing temperature, exactly like the heated wrath in his heart. Still, the color reminded him of his last meeting with Linda. She had come to court in a red dress more suited for a nightclub act, but her outrageous outfit hadn't shocked him as much as her pasty skin and emaciated figure. She had looked wasted.

He drew in a gulp of air and felt the frosty jolt in his lungs. Could he have done more to help her? Probably not. Whenever he had broached the subject of her dependency, she had flown into a rage. Nevertheless, only now did he realize that he shouldn't have given up trying to get her into a detox program.

Still, how could he have known she would wind up killing herself? He could not understand why someone who had everything money could buy wanted to spend her life in a dream world.

She hadn't seemed to care at all as the sordid details of her lifestyle had been revealed in open court and a guardian had been appointed for their son. She had wobbled out of the courtroom on her stiletto heels, a pathetic figure anxious to get back to her fog of fantasy. Pity replaced Alan's former hostility, and something more—something like a dark chill that had run through him like a premonition.

When he heard Linda had died, the shock of it sickened him. She had drowned in the hot tub after a night spent in a drugged haze accompanied by a male companion. Alan had been grateful that Foster wasn't there.

"Jesus still loves Mommy," Foster said. His budding spirituality grew stronger every day. He liked his court-appointed guardian. She was a devout Christian and delighted in teaching the boy anything he wanted to know about the Bible. Today, though, the guardian had refused to allow the child to attend the burial. He had been running a fever and was scheduled to see the doctor.

Alan wished his son could be with him now, holding his hand. Foster radiated a gentle peace that never failed to calm him. While much of that tranquility came from his unfailing

trust in Jesus, his faith had helped him through so many
upheavals in the past three months, that Alan had to be
grateful that the child had something to lean on—even if later
he realized the uselessness of it all.

Alan had nothing to bear him up through his never-
ending nightmare except brief remembrances of the magical
days on the marsh and Samantha. Though he knew she didn't
love him, the memory of her serene gray eyes, her sunlit hair,
and warmth of her tender lips buoyed him through many
dreary days. Otherwise, it seemed that all he had left inside
him was the icy frost that had crept into his soul. Guilt had
become his frequent companion. His stomach churned
whenever he remembered the results of Linda's autopsy. His
former wife had weighed ninety-two pounds when she died.
His gut tensed in a painful spasm. Again, he wondered if he
should have tried harder to get her into some kind of program
to cure her dependency.

The bright sunlight bounced off the snow-covered
ground and stung his eyes.

To his left, he heard Linda's mother whisper loudly.

"When is this going to be over?"

Linda's father tried to cover up his wife's impatience by
clearing his throat.

Though Alan had not seen the pair since the day he had
married Linda, he was not surprised to see them at the
funeral. The reading of Linda's will would take place
immediately after the burial, and he knew that Linda had
assigned her parents custody of Foster. Her malice continued
beyond her death.

From somewhere far off in the background he heard
light laughter and a pleasant image came mercifully upon
him. Once again, he recalled Samantha telling the story of the
Three Bears while his son listened in mesmerized awe. A
touch of warmth graced his heart, endeavoring to melt the
permafrost that now encased it like a sarcophagus.

His lawyer nudged him sharply as the minister finished
the prayers. Alan blinked before he snapped back to the sharp

reality of the scene before him. Clenching his teeth until his jaw hurt, he fingered the white rose in his hand. A thorn pricked his thumb but he welcomed the distraction. He started forward before tripping awkwardly on the fake grass carpet. Catching himself, he tossed the rose toward the coffin. He did not wait to see where it landed. He spun around and with his head down, walked rapidly away while the reporters hurried after him.

He slid into the waiting limousine. His lawyer jumped in right behind him and they sped off.

"If I hadn't been in jail, I probably would have been accused of murdering her." Alan closed his eyes and shuddered.

"Your one lucky break."

Alan opened his eyes and studied Chuck Richards' face. He could never read the emotions in the lawyer's face, and that worried him.

"If Linda's parents want to raise Foster, we've got a real conflict on our hands." Chuck flipped open the case of his PDA and turned it on.

Alan's throat ached. Until now, Linda's parents hadn't shown any interest in Foster. In fact, they hadn't even been around for their own daughter. Maybe their lack of love helped to explain why Linda had chosen to become a strung-out druggie, though Alan knew he could have acted more responsibly. If he had helped her instead of hating her, maybe she wouldn't have died.

Tormented by guilt, regrets weighed him down, feeling as heavy as the marble slab that would soon grace Linda's final resting place. His marriage had started off happily enough, but had turned overnight into a battleground. Originally, he blamed only Linda, but now he realized that he had been at fault, too.

Chuck broke into his miserable musing.

"Before I agree to take you on as a client for the custody battle with your former in-laws, there's something we have to clear up first, or any efforts on my part will be wasted."

The portly lawyer scribbled hasty notes on the glowing screen he held in his hand.

Alan sat up straighter. "I don't have anything to hide. I'll do anything to get Foster back and you know it. Anything." "Were you and Samantha Lyons lovers?"

The question had the impact of a slap in the face. Alan could feel the sweat beading up on his brow. Why was Chuck asking him this now? Had somebody told Chuck some bald-faced lies? And who could have done that?

"No. I told you that before. Nothing happened in Clam Creek."

Chuck snapped the PDA case closed and stared at Alan. "You're lying."

Alan swallowed hard.

"I won't deny that I fell for her. Hard. But you can be sure that the feeling wasn't mutual. Besides, we had plenty of distractions, even a chaperone—"

Chuck flipped open the PDA case again. "Name?"

"Marion Gregory. And Samantha's neighbor, Fish, was always coming around, too."

Chuck's massive bulk increased as he took in a deep breath and then exhaled slowly.

"Fish. That's real helpful."

"Nobody ever mentioned his last name. I wasn't there long enough to think of asking about it."

"You were there long enough to play the hero."

Alan narrowed his eyes. "Who told you that?"

Chuck put his hand into his coat pocket, pulled out a newspaper clipping, and thrust it at Alan.

His hands shook as he unfolded the yellowed paper. He found that he held page three of the October edition of the *Creek Reporter,* Clam Creek's monthly newspaper. A photo of Samantha transfixed him and he found himself momentarily speechless while his heart pounded so loudly that he was sure Chuck could hear it.

Samantha's silver eyes faded into the gray tones of the photograph, lending her the appearance of some ethereal being—like the angel he and Foster believed her to be. She was beautiful, though seeing her face so somber nearly broke his heart. In the picture, she sat propped up against the pillows in the hospital bed where she had spent so much time recuperating.

The strength of his affection for her hadn't diminished at all and it stunned him. The embers of his love glowed deep within, banked against every chill, dark night that had passed since they had last seen each other.

He loosened his necktie and glared at the byline. Marion Gregory had written the piece.

"How did you get this?"

"I have my sources."

Chuck's cryptic reply sent a disturbing rush of alarm surging through Alan. Had somebody from Clam Creek sent this to Chuck? But nobody in Clam Creek knew Alan's proper identity. Or did they?

Alan loosened his tie, then pulled it off and jammed it into the pocket of his coat. He hesitated before reading the article. He tried to remember all the things he had done in Clam Creek. Though he had been surly at first, he had changed for the better, but he couldn't claim to be perfect.

He found Marion Gregory had spun a yarn that reminded him of something out of an old western. She envisioned him as a legendary hero, who just happened to wander into town to save the beautiful, though beleagued, female mosquito research scientist.

Marion left off all references to his ride into the sunset in a police vehicle. She also did not mention his, or Foster's, real names.

The vise that seemed to be clamped around Alan's temples unwound slightly. He sighed and handed the article back to Chuck.

"Anybody would have done the same thing. Samantha would have been burned alive if I hadn't grabbed her."

"You were badly burned yourself." Chuck carefully folded the clipping and tucked it into his breast pocket.

Alan shrugged. "I healed."

"You saved her life, injuring yourself in the process, fixed up the grounds of the field station after the fire, sent off her research, and bought an expensive headstone for her deceased pet."

"I was her employee, after all."

"It would seem that you went above and beyond the call of duty."

Alan narrowed his eyes at the implication he heard in Chuck's tone. "I had no place else to go at the time."

"Can you say in all honesty, that despite appearances, your son was, in no way, harmed by this supposedly innocent relationship?"

Alan felt the blood rush to his face.

"You know yourself the damage that Linda did!"

"Linda's dead."

Alan's throat grew tight and it hurt to speak.

"If you react that way in court, this isn't going to turn out well."

Alan's shoulders sagged. Chuck had deliberately baited him and he had attacked. He swallowed, despite the ache it caused, and tried to compose himself. "Samantha is a good woman. She was wonderful to Foster and he adores her."

"Think about the judge. What will he make of your story?"

Alan froze. If he behaved in an angry manner, he might never get his son back. A wave of despair crashed down on him. He leaned back against the smooth leather seat of the limousine and closed his eyes.

The Lord's love is a wonderful thing but you have to be patient.

Fish's philosophy had often haunted Alan in the past few months. When Fish had told him the simple tale of his lost love and Samantha's miraculous return, Alan had believed most of it to be a coincidence. Nevertheless, he could not get the story out of his mind. As time went by and Alan's troubles escalated, he would often picture that last calm moment in his life when Fish's words soothed him like a balm. He silently repeated Fish's words to himself as the limousine wound smoothly through traffic and out of the city.

He still could not believe in the existence of a Supreme Being, but he had learned a lot about patience.

"Ms. Lyons left a message on my answering machine. She wanted to know how you and your son are doing. Sounded very emotional. Practically in tears."

Alan's eyes opened and he bolted upright.

"Samantha called?"

"On Thanksgiving Day."

"That was over a month ago!"

"You were still in jail."

"Was she okay? Was she sick? Why was she in tears—"

"You do love her," Chuck interrupted.

A crushing emptiness sank against Alan's chest. He crossed his arms over the anguish and turned to stare out the window at the passing scenery. He felt himself pressed into the seat as the chauffeur jammed his foot down on the accelerator to gather momentum on the incline as they headed toward Talcott Mountain. Heublein Tower rose up on his left against a sky so blue, it nearly blinded him.

"Yes. But she doesn't love me. She made that quite clear."

He heard Chuck clear his throat, but then the lawyer lapsed into silence.

They reached the summit and the limousine headed down the other side of the mountain. Alan spotted a flash of color and watched in amazement as a lone hang glider launched off from the mountain's edge and sailed out over the valley below. For a moment, Alan suspected he saw only a mirage. After all, with the frigid temperatures a hang glider pilot would risk hypothermia, at the very least. However, the valiant craft left a shadow on the crusted snow far beneath it, something an illusion couldn't do.

Mesmerized by the sight, Alan held his breath as cross

winds buffeted the hang glider and sent the craft careening wildly from side to side.

"Crazy fool," Chuck muttered.

Alan would never try the stunt himself, but he felt admiration for someone willing to cast off all his fears and plunge out into the clear void where he had no visible support.

The hang glider struggled for control and ultimately won. The delicate contraption gained altitude, soaring above the shadow of Heublein Tower.

The sight inspired Alan. He felt a kinship with the hang glider for he, too, had been battered and thrashed by the winds of life. Taking his son and running had been very much like jumping off a cliff. Watching the hang glider soar gracefully upward somehow diminished the yawning emptiness at his center.

He frowned as he recalled part of the song played at Linda's funeral—something about eagle's wings and how God holds you in the palm of his hand. Alan watched the hang glider slowly circle toward the empty field below. Did that man have faith? Did he believe in God's promises? Had God protected him?

What about Alan's own family—his father, mother, sister, and grandmother? They had been believers, but maybe they weren't good enough believers.

Had God protected Samantha because her faith was stronger? She nearly died. Had God saved her due to her powerful trust in Him? Would Alan's heroics alone have saved her?

He remembered his prayer in the marsh as Samantha lay unconscious in the back of Fish's truck. He had only said it for Foster's sake, yet help had arrived immediately afterward.

"Do you think Samantha Lyons would be a good witness?"

Chuck's voice shattered the silence and Alan's troubled thoughts.

"I don't know. She changed after the cottage burned. She

was still ill and weak—"

"What about Marion Gregory and that Fish person?"

"Maybe if Fish had a good suit. Marion is old-fashioned, but she enjoys being with Foster." His son made friends wherever he went. Nobody seemed immune to the child's innocent joy, except his own mother.

Alan sighed and rubbed his hand over his face. He could almost forgive Linda, but he found it most difficult of all to forgive himself for the mistakes he had made. All his incredibly successful managerial coups at work hadn't helped him to deal with real life. What truly mattered had nothing to do with fame, fortune, or being vice president of a powerful corporation.

"If Linda's parents are granted custody of Foster, you are going to need a good job to try and get him back. Plus you'll have to come up with a plan for his care while you're at work."

"I thought I'd set up my own business and work at home."

"Doing what?"

"I am an actuary."

"Who's going to trust you?"

Alan glared at Chuck.

"You've got a record now." Chuck shrugged.

"So you don't think I can get him back."

"We'll appeal."

"You're going to get rich fighting my battle for me."

"We could win. Stranger things have happened." The lawyer didn't crack a smile. That didn't give Alan much comfort.

He glanced at his watch and pulled out his cell phone. Foster should be back from the doctor's appointment by now. He punched in the numbers for the guardian's house. However, nobody answered the phone.

Slightly annoyed, Alan punched in the numbers for the pediatrician's office. He was put on hold as the limousine cruised into Simsbury.

Finally, he was put through to the doctor, and explained who he was.

"Your son has an ear infection, Mr. Nugent. We prescribed antibiotics. He'll be fine."

"But an ear infection! Isn't that painful?"

"He's taking a pain reliever, too."

"Are you sure he'll be okay? Won't that affect his hearing?"

"We caught it early. Don't worry, Mr. Nugent."

Then the doctor hung up. Alan stared at the phone for a few seconds feeling bereft. If he could just see Foster himself right now—but he couldn't. He couldn't see him until Saturday. Frustration churned inside him.

"Kids get those infections all the time. My kids are always sick," Chuck commented.

The limousine pulled up into a parking lot and Alan clamped his hands into fists when he saw Linda's parents step out of another car. Linda's mother wore a scowl on her face as she directed a sharp remark at her husband. Her shrill voice could be heard easily right through the limousine's closed windows.

"Don't tell *me* what to do!"

"I can see where Linda acquired her temper." Chuck lifted his attaché case from the floor of the limousine.

"Would you want that pair raising your kids?" Alan could feel his blood pressure soaring.

"Nope. But the state might think they'll do fine."

"But where have they been for the past four years? They didn't come to visit at all, not even when Foster was born!"

"And where were you that day? Where were you for most of the first three years of Foster's life?"

All of Alan's fury withered away. He was guilty as charged. It had taken him a long time to realize what really mattered in life, and he could lose his greatest treasure in just a few minutes.

"Try to be charming," Chuck warned. "Maybe they don't really want Foster. Maybe they came because they hoped it would be a profitable day for them."

Alan closed his eyes. He wished he believed in God. He wished God could help him get his son back. He needed a miracle. Samantha's words floated into his mind. *I know that the Lord brought you here. God is watching over your son, and Jesus is healing him. Right now.* Alan lowered his head. He wished it was all that easy.

Chapter Seventeen

Samantha held Honey in her arms and nuzzled the soft fur on the puppy's coat. The puppy rewarded her with a lick from its little pink tongue, and Samantha's heart warmed. Since the puppies had been born, life at Field Station Number Thirty-Seven had become more chaotic, but she didn't mind one bit. Goldie and her brood livened up the remote outpost with their antics and somehow made the sting of grief easier to bear, especially as winter dragged on and the days continued to be short, dark, and cold.

Samantha had not forgotten David or James, but the puppies provided her with a considerable amount of distraction. Their arrival had been her one beacon of hope in an otherwise bleak future. To her it had been a sign, assuring her that God hadn't ignored her prayers. A little over a month had passed since the surprising birth, but day by day, Samantha had felt herself climbing out of the gloom where the misery of heartache had left her. She could almost feel the sun shining on her face, just like the words from Aaron's blessing.

The Lord bless you and keep you!
The Lord let his face shine upon you, and be gracious to you!
The Lord look upon you kindly and give you peace!

She had found some peace, and with it, a quiet understanding. She no longer doubted that the Lord still loved her, that He had forgiven her sins. and that He would always be there for her. She had briefly lost her way, but her own sad experience had helped her to grow in her faith.

Nothing goes to waste in His creation.

Fish had said that so often, and now she knew he was right. Her trials had changed her. She had been tested, but through the Lord's grace, she had survived. Obviously, the Lord had more work for her to do.

She sighed and put Honey back down on the floor as the rumble of Fish's truck announced his arrival with the day's catch. He met her at the door of the lab with a net bag full of clams.

Samantha went to reach for it, but Fish held onto it.

"I'll put this in the trailer for you. These shells are heavy. Don't want you straining yourself."

Samantha studied him. He walked stiffly and his skin was reddened and chafed. "Why did you go out with the clammers? Raking up shells is the hardest work of all."

"'Cause they were short one man."

A chilly tingle of fear crept up Samantha's spine. She worried about Fish. Ever since he started going out with Marion, he seemed to take more chances, as if he were a much younger man.

"You shouldn't be doing anything so demanding."

"And why not?" He glared at her. "I ain't dead yet!"

The irritation in his gruff retort wounded her. In an effort to smooth over the troubled waters of their friendship, she fumbled through an apology of sorts. "I'm sorry. I didn't mean it that way." She gave him a smile and he seemed to soften. "But—but clamming is dangerous."

Fish shrugged. "Nah. Only if the wind comes up. Anyway, the clammers are always looking out for each other."

The thought of losing Fish sent a host of anxieties swirling through Samantha. He had remained her stable anchor through everything. While she did trust in the Lord, she just couldn't stop worrying about Fish, no matter how hard she tried.

She leaned back against the countertop and tried to remain calm, even though her insides felt unsettled. "I guess I'll be having clam chowder tonight. Would you like some?"

"Nah. I told Marion I'd stop by and try her pot pie. She's says it'll stick to my ribs." He chuckled and a dreamy glow lit up his eyes. "She's a great cook. I haven't eaten this good in a long time."

"Is that why you have so much energy lately?"

He nodded as a wide grin split his face. "Probably. Well, that and the fact that I seem to have found myself. At last."

Samantha frowned. Her confusion must have shown on her face, because Fish let out a roar of laughter.

"It ain't no secret. First off, I'm going to become a member of Holy Redeemer. I thought you should know so when the roof falls in, you won't be surprised." He winked at her and chuckled.

Samantha sighed with relief. She never knew what to expect from him anymore. "That's nice news. I'm really glad." She almost expected him to announce that he would be taking up skydiving. The reliable, predictable Fish she had known had become a completely different person.

"I'll be sitting right up front in the first pew with Marion every week."

Warmth flowed through Samantha's heart. "You'll be tasting some of Marion's doughnuts afterwards, too."

"Yep. Already sampled those. Convinced me that Holy Redeemer is where I belong." A bemused smile touched his face. "Funny, ain't it."

Samantha shrugged. It amazed her how Fish and Marion had "found" each other despite living in the same town all those years. Their lives seemed to include some strange twists and turns.

"And my other plan is to open up the fish factory again."

Her disbelief came out as a gasp of astonishment. Fish was full of surprises today, and she could do without them.

"But that place is a wreck! Everything is rusty and disintegrating. It looks like it's ready to fall down."

Fish shrugged. "Yep. I'll probably have to bulldoze most of it and rebuild. We'll have to start small, of course. Thought a depuration plant might be the way to begin." He patted the bag of clams. "I watched how they do it, pumping fresh seawater in to clean out the clams."

"But-but you should be retiring. You should be taking it easy at this time of your life. You could have a heart attack or something!" She blurted out the words without even considering the fact that she might be insulting him.

Fish scowled and set the bag of clams down on the counter. "I spent a lot of years drifting about aimlessly, like a tiny boat caught in the current without a rudder or an oar to steer it. I thought I knew a lot about the way God works, but I hadn't opened a Bible in years. Marion got me to do that, to really study what the Lord has to say."

Samantha twisted her hands together. "There aren't any verses in the Bible about building a fish factory."

"'The thief must no longer steal, but rather labor, doing honest work with his own hands, so that he may have something to share with one in need.' That's from Ephesians."

"You've never been a thief!"

"I was plain old lazy, Sammie, and wallowing in self-pity. There's some days I don't feel one hundred percent, but there's lots of people have it worse. Sloth is a sin. God needs people with some gumption. I can make a difference in the lives of a lot of people."

Enthusiasm vibrated in every one of his words and for a moment all she could do was stare at him. He sounded like an idealistic youth ready to march off to save the world. She believed he would have more luck building a castle in the clouds.

"It will take years to get that plant back into operation. Where will you get the money?"

"First off, I'll sell some of the property. I don't need all of it. I've got two people interested in one parcel already. It's right on the waterfront, after all."

Fish bent down to pick up one of the puppies that had been sniffing at his feet.

"Hey Butch, you're gonna be my dog. Don't forget that."

Samantha rubbed at her temple. She could feel a migraine coming on. She really did not believe that Fish had thought this all through.

"Who is going to work for you? There are no young

people in town."

"I'll put an ad in the paper—same as anybody else. They need a job, they can come and look around. Clam Creek's a nice place to live. Lots of fresh air, good for little ones. Quiet."

"There aren't many houses! Where would they live? There is only one very small restaurant and there are no theaters or—"

"Bars?" Fish chuckled and put Butch back down on the floor. "We don't need bars, but we could use some nicer shops, and once this thing gets going, people will start thinking that maybe Clam Creek would be the perfect place to sell things. You just wait and see."

"But there's a million details involved with such a gigantic undertaking. You can't possibly succeed!" Samantha put her hand over her eyes as the pain in her head throbbed. "You aren't supposed to build on the wetlands. Have you checked out the EPA's rules?"

Fish just shook his head. "You're so full of questions today. I didn't plan to be interrogated—just wanted to give you those clams. And I've got to get over to Marion's house before that pot pie is burnt."

"This is a serious matter!"

"Exactly." He hoisted the clams into his arms. "So I'm leaving all the big troubles with the Lord. You know worries and doubts are one of the ways the devil gets to us. Can't let the devil win, Sammie."

Samantha leaned her forehead against the storm door and watched him walk across the yard to the trailer. The icy glass window numbed the pulsating agony in her head. She knew he was right, of course. The devil sure got to her easily enough when she worried about him. However, if Fish did get the old factory back in operation, Clam Creek might avoid becoming a ghost town. As it was now, if all the residents died off, there would be nobody left.

The phone rang and Samantha leaned over her workstation to pick it up.

David's voice on the line had the impact of a collision. All her carefully constructed tranquillity and renewed faith disintegrated into a massive mound of rubble. She groped for the chair and sat down quickly, finding herself too weak to stand on her rubbery legs.

"My son ran away!" His voice was thick with emotion.

Chapter Eighteen

Samantha nearly dropped the receiver as her breath caught in her throat.

"He slipped out sometime early this morning and it's twelve degrees outside!"

Samantha couldn't speak at all. Her hand went to her heart, certain that it had stopped beating.

"He might call you. He had your phone number inside his backpack. He's got a cellphone with him."

Almost dizzy with shock, she fought for control.

"D-david—I—I—where are you?" All she could manage was a raspy croak.

"In Simsbury, Connecticut. Near Hartford. Please call me back right away if he calls you!"

She heard the anguish in his strained tone, and she felt it, too. Her heart thudded dully as she remembered the sweet child looking up at her with his sky blue eyes. The thought of such an innocent child, all alone in sub-freezing weather had her sick with fear.

"I've been trying to call him but he hasn't answered. I'm afraid...that he's hurt...or worse."

Her hand shook as she lifted it to stifle the cry that welled up inside her.

"He packed a few peanut butter and jelly sandwiches, but that's not much and there's coyotes in the woods—"

"I-I'll pray," she stammered, though the moment she said it she knew David would consider her offer useless. But what else could she do? She was helpless. Hartford must be at least four hours away. However, her words seemed to calm him down. He quieted and she heard him draw in a deep breath. The memories of David and James rushed back at her and a scorching ache seared her heart, an agony that burned far, far worse than seeing her cottage go up in flames. She blinked, and a few salty tears eked out, stinging her cheeks.

"I had hoped that you would still care about him—" His voice broke and Samantha felt her world shatter. If only she could tell him that she loved him as well as James. She closed her eyes and tried to forget everything about their time together, but that was impossible. Nothing about their sunlit summer days had left her, those magical weeks always lingered in the back of her mind, and time hadn't softened the pain at all. Every moment of every day for the rest of her life would be saddened by the fact that she had to spend it apart from him. "The police are looking for him, too, and we've got volunteers signing up to comb the woods. But there's a lot of territory here—"

She valiantly tried to get a grip on herself. Straightening her shoulders, she vowed to be strong. She dashed away her tears with the back of her hand before grabbing a pen and asking him to give her his phone number.

He rattled off a string of numbers. "That's my cellphone, but use the pager number if the cellphone is busy. And-um- by the way, my name isn't David, it's Alan—Alan Nugent. And James is Foster. He-he's done nothing but talk about you and Clam Creek and how he wants to go back there —"

He paused again and drew in a deep breath. "I'm going to do a videotaped segment for the television news and hope that somebody has seen him."

Please, Lord, find him soon! She prayed deeply, from the depth of her soul. She twisted her hair around her finger. She wanted to go there, she wanted to help somehow. No! It would be foolish to see David—Alan. She covered her mouth before a moan could escape. She couldn't see him again! The temptation would be too great, and that would be wrong for James—Foster. The child needed to be found and returned to a stable home life. Samantha should stay away.

But what if Foster never did return home?

The sinking sensation in her stomach felt like the floor had given way. She closed her eyes once more and thought of the young boy with his dimpled cheeks and tender smile. She could remember exactly how he sang in his sweet, high voice. "Jesus loves me, this I know, for the Bible tells me so." The memory felt like a keen knife cutting through her, but the thought of how his faith had shone out with such radiance for one so young gave her a measure of hope. How he had loved learning about Jesus! He would call upon the Savior in his time of need. If only Dav—Alan had faith. If only he could believe.

"You must not give up," she told him in a soft tone.

"I know. There's still a chance—but I am afraid. Oh, God—I'm so afraid for him.

It was almost a prayer, she decided. If his son returned, perhaps there was a chance that he could acquire a deep and lasting faith.

Then fear edged into her once more and the numbness seeped back into her bones. Would Jesus protect the child from the bitter cold? From the coyotes? What if that wasn't part of God's plan?

Suddenly Alan's husky voice came over the wire again, startling her.

"It's good to talk with you again. It helps."

He sounded weary. He had sounded exactly the same when she had sat on the porch of the cottage in the heat of the summer and explained to him how to catch mosquitoes. It seemed a century ago, so much had happened since then.

"You're still special to us, Samantha. You always will be."

Samantha nearly broke down again. They were both so special to her, too. "I won't stop praying."

"I'll let you know if he's found..."

The "if" got to her. That single word jabbed straight at her heart like the tip of a fine blade. Still, she remembered that there was someone else who could be going through far greater torment.

"How is Foster's mother taking this?" She could not prevent the tremor in her voice when she asked the question.

The silence on the line grew tense, Samantha could feel the chill through the miles.

"She passed away…recently."

Samantha's world seemed to tilt on its axis. She clutched at the edge of the desk to steady herself. How the poor woman must have suffered! And it was Alan's fault! He had stolen her innocent child and her health had failed from the stress of not knowing what had happened to him. Just like her own mother's fate!

However, as Alan went on to detail the sordid details of his former wife's death, Samantha shook her head. She couldn't believe it. She couldn't imagine a mother who would behave so recklessly, a mother who really did not care at all for her own life, much less her child's.

"I should have gotten her into a treatment program. The last time I saw her, she looked horrible. I didn't realize how bad it had gotten until then.

"She wanted her parents to have custody of Foster, but he never met them until the day after Linda's funeral. He was supposed to fly back to Arizona with them today, but he didn't want to go."

I don't know what I'll do if I lose him—" The line hummed with strained silence. "—nothing would matter anymore—"

The way he said it frightened her, the utter desolation and hopelessness in his voice chilled her to the core. She lost control. "No! Don't talk like that." She shouted into the phone. "You'll find him!"

"If he is out in this weather, there isn't much time left to find him alive."

The firm resolve she had held together so carefully simply crumbled. She could not wait idly by the phone while the young boy she loved froze to death in the Connecticut woods or worse…

"I'll help! I'll be there as soon as I can."

"There's no point in you driving all the way up here."

"I'm coming!"

"Samantha—"

"Give me your address," she demanded. "I'll ask Marion

to sit here by the phone."

"By the time you get here—"

"Don't say anything more!" She interrupted. "I will be there. Nothing is going to stop me!"

She loved him and he had saved her life. She owed him everything.

*   *   *

Surprisingly, she made good time keeping up with the traffic, even though she had decided to risk taking I95 through the heart of New York City. I95 was the most direct route, but gridlock often went with it. However, her fears of getting stuck in a massive tie-up never materialized. Everything kept moving. She took a break only once at a rest stop. She couldn't eat, but she needed a hot cup of coffee along with a few moments to clear her head and stretch her cramped legs. She called Marion from a payphone. Both Marion and Fish had agreed to sit at the field station and wait for word, but no one had contacted the quiet outpost on the marsh. They promised to keep praying, and Fish intended to sleep at the lab building that night to take care of the puppies and the guinea pigs.

Samantha paced around the perimeter of the parking lot with her head down and her collar pulled up. The bitter wind pushed her along and the sting of the frigid cold on her skin reminded her of the evening's forecast predicting single digit readings for the tri-state area. Foster didn't have a chance if he did not find shelter.

Deep in thought, she nearly crashed into a huge mountain of snow when she came to the end of the lot. The mound, created by the plows, had an accumulation of black soot all over its surface from the filthy exhaust of all the cars, trucks, and buses racing by on the busy interstate highway. The grimy covering almost gave it the appearance of granite. Jesus talked about mountains. He said mountains could be moved with faith. *Whatever you ask for in prayer with faith, you will receive.*

Samantha closed her eyes and offered up another prayer for Foster. She opened her eyes and her gaze slid upward. The sheer size of the man-made pinnacle made her feel small. She kicked at it with the toe of her hiking boots. It was packed solid, so if she wanted to, she could easily climb up to the top. If Foster was with her now, she would grab his hand and scramble up the giant snow mound—just for fun. She had wanted him to have a wonderful life, a happy childhood, and to know all the simple pleasures that she felt she had missed. If only he could have stayed in Clam Creek with her. Desolation swept through her and an ache rose up in her throat that nearly choked her. She remembered the beautiful picture that Foster had made of her as an angel. Though she had done so little to help him, she had led him to the Savior. One especially comforting verse came to her mind. "...it is not the will of your heavenly Father that one of these little ones be lost."

Please, Lord, please take care of Foster. Struggling for control, she reminded herself that the Lord loved little children most of all, and everything was in His hands. Then she hurried back to her car.

*   *   *

The sky had grown dark by the time she reached the town of Simsbury. Passing a church, she had a strong compulsion to go inside. She had prayed all along the way in the car, but her desperate petitions had done nothing to calm her. Every nerve in her body had wound itself into a tight spring. In the quiet hush of the sanctuary, she knew she could center her thoughts and find the gentle peace she needed for her meeting with Alan. She might find him in complete despair, and she didn't know if she could handle that.

She glanced at the time on the dashboard and sighed,

deciding that it would be best to find Alan's house first. She cruised slowly along the road, peering at the street signs until she found the right one.

Driving further along, Samantha stared in wonder at the huge houses along the road. When she finally found the correct address, she could hardly believe it. How could the man who didn't have enough change for an ice cream cone live here?

Lights blazed in every one of the many enormous windows, spilling a bright glow onto the trampled snow of the large yard. She switched on the interior light in the car and checked the number she had written down. Then she stared at the mailbox. This had to be the right place. She stared up at the height of the steeply pitched, gabled roof. How much did a house like that cost? A half million? More?

Who was Alan Nugent? Blinking in disbelief and swallowing hard, she parked along the curb. On the driveway, a group of people huddled together near a news van, distinguishable by its tall antenna and the brightly emblazoned letters on its side. At the door of the house, a uniformed officer stood guard.

Weary from the hours of driving and weak from hunger, she hesitated before getting out of the car. She did not wish to appear on the local news and she most certainly did not want to be interrogated by a policeman. What if the search for Foster had been called off? What if Foster's body had been discovered? Would she be able to keep her composure? Would she be any help at all to Alan?

She straightened her tired shoulders. *Lord, please help me to be strong, to bring peace, comfort, and—and faith to Alan.*

That last part of her prayer was a very tall order, but she had no doubt that the Lord could handle it. She had journeyed all this way and she would do what she could, but she needed help. It looked like she might have to run a gauntlet to bring solace to the man who had saved her life and her job. She stepped out of her car and kept her eyes focused on the crusted snow as she walked straight across the yard toward the front door. She hoped that if she acted as if she belonged at the house, she could avoid attracting the attention of the media people. Unfortunately, her appearance started a stampede. Nothing could have prepared her for the assault as the video cameras turned on her and several microphones were thrust in her face. They behaved like a pack of coyotes moving in for the kill.

"Who are you?"

"Why are you here?"

"Are you a friend of the family?"

"A relative?"

"His girlfriend?"

"Did his wife know about you?"

That question shook her composure.

She tried to back away from the intimidating horde, but they pressed forward. She felt smothered while a cold sweat beaded up on her forehead. "I-I came to help," she stammered.

The reporters crowded up against her. "Are you the psychic?"

"Can you tell us where his body is?"

"Are your visions always accurate?" Her empty stomach churned ominously. She knew from their questions that Foster had not been found.

"Did you know the boy or do you have to use some article of clothing to find him?"

"Can you use a photograph?"

"What's your name?"

Her hands shook as she held them up to fend off her attackers and keep the light from blinding her. Fear, combined with the effects of a long drive filled with hours of tension, had her feeling light-headed. "I'm just a friend!"

"Did you break up the marriage?"

"No! Please leave me alone!" She turned, but crashed into another camera right behind her.

"Hey lady, watch out for the equipment."

"Get out of my way!" In a panic, her voice rose.

"Why don't you tell us who you are?"

"You hiding something?"

"You know where the kid is, don't you?"

"No! Now move away from me!"

"Samantha!" Alan's deep voice called out from the doorway.

Instantly, the cameras panned toward him, opening up a direct path for her that led to the porch. After the treatment she had received from the probing reporters, she had every inclination to throw herself into Alan's arms until her head stopped spinning. She stiffened as she realized that sort of behavior would be exactly what the hungry news hounds wanted. She had not broken up Alan's marriage. She was not his girlfriend and she did not want to be branded a harlot by the obnoxious reporters. She stepped forward cautiously, trying to rub the escalating pain out of her temple as she went. Then her foot caught on a cable from one of the cameras and she stumbled. She didn't lose her balance completely, but at her small cry of alarm, Alan rushed from the house. The cameras zoomed in as he caught her elbow.

"You shouldn't have come," he growled. Nevertheless, he led her into the house. He closed the door against the prying media and Samantha sank down on a chair in the foyer. Exhausted, she shut her eyes and leaned back. "It was pointless for you to come here. I tried to warn you. Those guys out there would make a flock of vultures look like amateurs."

She could hear his footsteps pacing back and forth on the floor.

"I was worried about you and what you would do if Foster isn't found."

She heard his restless feet still. In the silence that followed, she could hear her own heart ticking off the seconds. She held her breath waiting for some response, but none came, and she couldn't stand the quiet hush a moment more.

"Do they have any leads?" Her voice wavered, but she

didn't know what else to say, only that she had to say
something. She heard Alan take in a deep breath. Cautiously,
she opened her eyes. He had focused his gaze on the floor, but
she could see every line in his face, and each one bore the
strain of his anguish.

He shook his head.

"Did they stop searching?"

He turned away and stared up the long, winding
stairway.

Samantha looked up and saw the row of large, framed
photographs—all of a beautiful blond woman in an
assortment of sensuous poses showing off indecent amounts
of skin. Samantha's heart twisted as an ache squeezed it. She
recognized the face that had graced many fashion magazines.
So that was Linda. Not a single flaw marred the perfect
proportions of the woman's finely chiseled features. A sudden
cloud of inadequacy settled upon her.

"They called in the helicopters, though there's an army
of volunteers still out there on foot with flashlights. But it's
cold, Samantha. By now, he—"

She saw him clench his fists. Then he swung around to
face her. The pain that had creased his face now turned into a
mask of anger.

"You wasted your time coming here! Go back to your
mosquitoes! There's nothing you can do!"

Each one of his words cut into her, slicing her heart until
it bled. She gripped her hands together to stop them from
trembling. "I'm going to get myself a cup of tea. Would you
like one, too?" Forcing herself out of the chair, she headed
toward the back of the house.

Chapter Nineteen

Alan stared at her hands as she spread mayonnaise on the bread for sandwiches. He had almost convinced himself that he had been hallucinating, that she wasn't really here, but there were scratches marring her smooth skin, and he decided that if he had conjured up an image of her, it would have been perfect.

"What happened?" He reached out to trace one of the deep abrasions.

Her hand drew back from his touch. "Oh nothing. Goldie had puppies and one of them—Butch—got a little rambunctious."

He had fantasized for a moment that he might save himself if he reached for her, but she had pulled away from him. As he felt himself slide further into the dark pit of grief, he hardened his voice.

"You should put something on it."

"It's a week old and just about healed."

"Are you staying here tonight?" He asked the question with steel in his tone, though the ache inside him grew.

"I'll stay in a hotel in town."

He ground out his words. "Because of those reporters? Don't pay any attention to them. Who cares what they think?"

"Me."

He swore, spewing out a whole string of obscenities. It didn't help. It didn't get rid of the black void inside him. She stood very still while he lashed out in his agony.

He ran out of expletives and banged his fist on the kitchen island.

He couldn't stand the silence. He picked up the remote and switched on a small television that sat on the counter. He flipped through the channels until he found one with the news. A short segment concerning Foster ran, taking up only a minute's time. He turned the power off and threw the remote into the next room. It smashed against the fireplace mantel.

Samantha didn't flinch. She continued to put the sandwiches together, adding a few slices of turkey, some cheese, lettuce and tomato. She sliced each one neatly in two, then slid one across the kitchen island to him.

"You need to eat."

He grimaced at the food she set before him. He couldn't remember when he had eaten last, but he did not want to try putting down a sandwich. A sharp cramp seized at his stomach and he clutched the countertop for support. He felt worse than sick, as if something had siphoned out everything inside him and all that was left was a shell—a shell that might shatter at any moment.

"I've lost him. I've lost everything." He had to face the fact. Nothing but emptiness lay ahead for him.

"You have a friend."

The spasm eased and he took a deep breath. Narrowing his eyes, he glared at her. He had done nothing but think of her for months. What had happened since he left Clam Creek? What did she want now? Why had she driven so far?

"Who called the cops on me?"

He waited for an answer, but she only lifted her eyes to his. Her glance held the softness of fog, like the mist rolling in off the ocean, and it touched him—like a balm upon his soul. He remembered that the last time he had looked into her eyes, they had reminded him of slate, hard and brittle. He heard her gentle sigh in the stillness.

"Both Fish and I tried to figure that out, but we didn't have much luck. Though we are fairly sure that nobody in Clam Creek reported you."

Could he believe her? He turned away from her calm and tender gaze. With his back to her, the torment of loss returned.

"You wanted me to leave! I would have taken care of

you. I would have done anything for you!"

"I know."

He whirled around with his heart thundering. "Why did you push me away?"

She shook her head, picked up the plates with the sandwiches and carried them to the table. "Let's sit down so you can tell me who you are, Alan Nugent."

*   *   *

Samantha knew the cameras hovered just beyond the circle of light that spilled from the windows of the breakfast nook. She could feel their electronic eyes trained on her and Alan as they sat across from each other, separated by the round, glass tabletop. Shivers ran along her shoulders whenever she caught a movement on the edge of her peripheral vision. Nevertheless, she had convinced herself that it was better to have all those digital chaperones recording their every move, because without them she would have been tempted to surround Alan with her arms, a move almost guaranteed to lead to indiscretion.

She had not forgotten the wonder of his kiss. It haunted her as she listened to the anguish in his heart and knew that it echoed her own. She loved Foster as much as he did and thinking of the young child's suffering was unbearable. She prayed for strength as Alan talked. She reminded herself that she had come as a friend—and nothing more. She realized now that with his wife gone, she probably appeared to be an opportunist at the very least, but she also knew she didn't want Alan to hurt himself in his grief.

Her sandwich became a welcome prop—something she could hold onto—something to keep her hands busy as she forced down small bites with mechanical precision—something to help ease the tight ache in her throat when her strength waned and Alan's words nearly overwhelmed her.

Alan didn't eat or drink anything. He shoved the sandwich aside and in a low voice, he told her of the death of his family while he had been away at college. He admitted that he didn't realize how seriously the shock of losing them all at the same time had affected him because, despite their deaths, he had gone on to finish up his degree. In looking back, he knew his scarred emotional state was a factor in the way he had fallen head over heels for Linda when he met her at a fashionable club in New York City. A few friends warned him about Linda, but he refused to heed their advice. He threw caution to the wind and married her after a very short engagement. Almost immediately, he feared he had made an incredibly bad decision.

"I found out that she didn't just smoke a little weed now and then, she had a serious problem."

He told her about his goofy dog, Blarney, about Foster's birth, and about the failure of the marriage.

"By the time we split, I didn't care about anything other than getting away from her. I gave her everything; the house, the car, the *au pair,* and Foster. I didn't think about what would happen if the *au pair* left." He gave a bitter laugh.

"I threw myself into the job and made a meteoric rise to the vice-presidency. I thought I could fill up all the emptiness in my life by working non-stop."

Haltingly, he explained how he found out that Linda had abused and neglected their son. "It was the doctor's bill for the broken arm. I hadn't seen Foster in months and then the bill showed up. I felt guilty and realized that I should be spending more time with him. When I visited, he barely remembered who I was, but I could see then that he was afraid of Linda." He hung his head with the weight of his sorrow.

Samantha's shoulders sagged as his grief wrapped itself around her, too. The agony of hearing of the brief, unhappy life that Foster had led had her stoically holding back tears. She knew that talking about it would help Alan, but it ripped her soul into pieces.

"I was as guilty as Linda. I should have been there for Foster and I wasn't." He lifted his head and twisted his mouth into a cynical smile. "I even prayed. I was like a drowning man reaching for a life preserver. And, of course, it didn't work."

Samantha fingered the crucifix at her neck. Could she help him with faith? Jesus taught with parables. She had only her own story to tell, but it would be like opening an old wound. "After you were taken away, I told Fish that I wanted to die. I felt God had justly punished me. After all, I had been abducted by my own father and yet I fell in love with you."

"Love...?" The single word came out garbled, a harsh croak in the hushed room.

She could only nod her head while she fought against the well of emotion. She took a deep breath and sat up ramrod straight in the chair. "I figured that God had put you in my path as a trial—as my own personal stumbling block, and I failed the test."

His hand reached across the table to hers.

She held on and felt the warmth flowing through her.

"But you told me—"

"I told you to leave." She closed her eyes and savored the strength she found in his touch. "I didn't say I didn't love you. You couldn't go on living a lie."

"I went to prison."

She opened her eyes and saw the dark desolation sweep over his expression. Her already bruised heart ached, but she knew she had to go on. "I decided that God had taken away my cottage, my dog, you and your son because I had sought only my own ends by giving you shelter when you should have been reported. Originally, I had tried to justify everything by telling myself that I was helping Foster, but afterwards I felt certain that God hadn't seen it that way."

He spat out angrily, "That's the problem with religion—all that moral judgement—"

"Morality is a good thing," she interrupted. "But forgiveness is even better. I assumed I had committed an unforgivable sin—"

"You didn't commit any sin!"

She squeezed his hand. "We all sin. Every one of us, but God is perfect and forgives us all perfectly—if we want to be forgiven."

"God didn't burn your cottage or kill your dog. He didn't kill my family or Foster. There is no God!" His thundered oath ricocheted through the spacious house.

"God gives us enough rope to hang ourselves, but He doesn't want us to. He wants us to walk with Him. He wants to show us a better way, He gave us His son to teach us that way. Ask for His forgiveness, read his Word, follow his Way, believe in Him and the gates of heaven will open for you—"

"You are so helplessly brainwashed."

His pitying glance did not surprise or disappoint her. She expected it. "The point is that I have peace. You don't."

"What good is peace? I've lost everything."

"No you haven't. Not yet, anyway."

His dark eyes sharpened. "Will you stay here?"

"I'm staying at the hotel, but I'll come back tomorrow morning."

"I'm paying the hotel bill and don't argue with me."

"I'm not the one who's shouting."

He lowered his head. "Sorry."

"It's okay. But I'm tired now and I'd like to get some rest."

"I'll lead you there."

"I'd appreciate that."

* * *

Alan felt lightheaded as he drove the BMW along the winding road to town. Getting his own car out of the driveway had been a major feat of logistics with all the media vehicles in the way.

He wanted to outlaw journalists! Put them behind bars

for causing untold additional suffering. He glanced out his rearview mirror and saw the huge van with the ridiculous antenna tailing Samantha's car.

Samantha. Thinking about her could almost make him forget about the video jockeys. She loved him—had loved him all this time! Did he believe her? Or had she been motivated by her Christian principles to say that so she could prevent him from killing himself? He gripped the wheel tighter as his stomach went into another paroxysm. Icy sweat covered his brow. Briefly, he wondered what was the matter with him. Then he decided that he would welcome death if it came, but he had to get Samantha to the hotel first.

He clenched his teeth against the sickness that threatened to overwhelm him. He knew that tomorrow Samantha might say she loved him as Jesus loved her, as God loves all of us. She might even tell him that she held for him a spiritual love that transcends passion.

He pressed his lips together as a wave of nausea shuddered through him. Samantha hadn't changed. Her Christian babble went on and on, but it didn't alter a thing.

While the misery settled on his shoulders, he thought of her voice which still had all the softness of the breeze rippling over the marsh grass. Her hair still smelled of sunshine and summer days. Her eyes could quietly mesmerize him.

He decided that she was an angel sent to torture him.

He recalled the crayon drawing that his son had made. How he wished he had a copy of it now. He remembered the tin can that had started a ridiculous argument. He would be glad to carry that tin can around with him if he could have his son back.

He forgot about the road. He saw in his mind the big blue eyes of his son. His throat ached as he tried not to think about where Foster's body might lay. He had stopped hoping. In fact, the moment he learned that Foster had run off, he had known that the child would never come back. Alone in his car, he allowed himself to grieve. One choked sob and then another rocked him. Life, for him, had been completely pointless—one long nightmare. He wished he had never had to go through it all. What little joy he found had been taken away from him. He had no control over anything! The endless striving to make things work out had drained dry the last of his dreams.

He didn't care anymore. He cursed at everyone and everything that had brought him to this point in time. What had he gained in his journey? Nothing but continual heartache! He found his virulent oaths didn't ease any of his pain.

I have peace.

Samantha's words whispered in his ear. Peace. Yes, one of the fruits of the Spirit. *... love, joy, peace, patience, kindness, generosity, faithfulness, gentleness, self-control.*

The smallest doubt edged into Alan's thoughts. Could he have denied God all these years because he had blinders on? Were the fruits of the Spirit truly gifts from above? Foster certainly had seemed to possess all nine of those personality markers. Samantha did, too. The moment he saw her, he felt like a man parched from struggling through the desert who had finally come upon a stream of cool water. Her life had not been easy. She had suffered one hardship on top of another, but she did not seem bitter about any of it. The memory of her gentle laughter brought with it a touch of warmth to his heart.

She had peace.

Fish had it, and the road his life had taken had been a torturous one. Still, he believed.

The Lord's love is a wonderful thing but you have to be patient.

Patience. Another fruit of the Spirit. Marion Gregory had it. Foster's guardian had it. The cleaning lady, and his lawyer. They had all gone through some terrible times, but they had survived. They all seemed to possess a core of stamina that he didn't have.

From a deep memory imbedded in his mind, he recalled something from scripture that claimed it was possible to do anything because the Lord would give you strength. He couldn't quite remember the exact phrase, but the idea now made perfect sense to him. Bad things happened to everybody, even good people, but the believers were never defeated by their misfortunes. They had obviously received an abundant supply of tenacity from the source of all power.

With a flash of clarity, he suddenly knew that their strength came from the sum total of the fruits of the Spirit. Those nine gifts bestowed a resiliency upon them that defied the cruel blows of life. They could not be crushed. A strange sensation came over him and he knew he could not deny the evidence—the truth—any longer. God was real.

A cold sweat beaded up on his brow. After all these years of his rejection of the Lord, could he now ask for the Lord to help him? He tapped the steering wheel. He had to get through tonight. He had to find out if Samantha really did love him. He clamped his jaw together. He wanted to get through tomorrow, even if it hurt. He had to turn to God. What other options did he have? He was powerless.

He cleared his throat. "Lord, I want...um...please Lord, forgive me and help me to be a believer again. I'd like to have Foster back...but... um...well...help me. Help me get through tonight...um..."

From the past, the memory of his son's words haunted him. He had almost forgotten how to end his prayer.

"Amen."

He took a deep breath and glanced in his rearview mirror. He realized that Samantha's car wasn't behind him anymore, neither was the huge media van. Panic gripped him and he slammed on the brakes. The road behind him didn't have a single car on it!

He spun the wheel and turned around. Now what? An accident? Had she slid off the road on a patch of ice and landed in a ditch? He had been so caught up in his wretched despair. He should have been paying attention. He had promised that he would lead her to the hotel and he hadn't managed to do it!

If anything happened to Samantha, he didn't doubt he would turn into a madman, a demented maniac capable of anything! Gunning the motor, he retraced his route. He spotted the media van first, parked in front of St. Mary's church where all the lights blazed brightly out into the frigid winter night. Next to the van, Samantha's car sat—without any visible dents or damage. He pulled into the church lot and got out of his car. He had to hold onto the door for a moment until the dizziness passed. The bracing onslaught of the glacial air helped to steady him. The video jockeys were hoisting their cameras onto their shoulders.

"What's going on?" he asked them. His heart hammered in his chest, and his hands shook.

"She stopped here. Maybe she's gonna pray, huh? Make a nice shot. Touching."

"You okay? You don't look so good." One of the other journalists asked Alan. He didn't bother answering. Muttering to himself that he wished she had told him of her intentions, he grabbed the handrail to get up the steps as an odd weakness turned his knees rubbery.

"Hey, the front door's locked, she went in the side. Some kind of meeting going on there tonight, so it's open," one of the crew called out.

Biting back a retort, he began to turn on his heels as the world tilted at a peculiar angle. He heard a loud click. Frowning, he glanced back at the door. The edges of his vision seemed to be fading into a dark haze. The heavy door opened slowly, blinding him with the dazzling glare of the interior. He shaded his eyes as a silhouette appeared—a woman carrying a child in her arms. She had hair that shone like the sun while the little boy's black bangs just touched eyes as blue as the sky on a cloudless day.

The boy reached out toward him. "Daddy!"

The light faded completely and Alan sank into the blackness as it swallowed everything.

Chapter Twenty

Samantha sang softly as she loaded the dishwasher in Alan's kitchen. "Little ones to him belong, they are weak, but he is strong."

She smiled as joy surged through her. Alan and Foster would both be fine. She hadn't slept, aside from a few light naps in the hospital waiting room, but it didn't matter. Foster was safe and Alan would recover quickly if he could remember to feed himself.

She glanced off into the family room where Alan had fallen asleep on the sofa. After she had brought him home from the hospital, she had gone into the kitchen to make some soup. By the time she finished heating it, he lay so soundly asleep that she hated to wake him. Now that she had finished her solitary lunch and cleaned up a bit, she must return home.

She gathered up her coat and handbag, and walked into the family room. She knelt down on the thick Oriental rug and patted Alan's shoulder. "Hey, sleepy head. I've got to go now."

He didn't move. Her finger traced the neat row of stitches on his forehead. When he passed out, he hit the granite steps. Not only had he scared the wits out of her and Foster, but also several people in the media crew turned hysterical at the sight of blood. At that point, Foster had grabbed his cell phone. "I'll call 911." He had punched in the numbers and then told the dispatcher where he was and the problem at hand. By then, the cameras were rolling. Samantha hadn't gone near a television set. She didn't want to relive the incident. Thinking about it gave her the chills. However, the police had arrived quickly and had whisked Foster off to his guardian's house.

She followed the ambulance to the hospital and waited

through all those long dreary hours in the early morning until the doctor decided that the dehydrated Alan had been sufficiently rehydrated. He had passed out from a lack of food and water. The doctor allowed him to go home, but he stipulated that Alan would need to be watched in case he had a concussion. "Alan, come on. Wake up. I called your lawyer and he said he would send somebody here to keep an eye on you."

Alan groaned.

"I have to leave, Alan. My mosquitoes are getting hungry."

"No!" He rumbled. "No!"

She watched the rapid movement of his eyes beneath the lids and sighed. It must be some nightmare. "Alan, it's only a dream." She shook his shoulder. "Wake up."

"No! I told you—" His eyes flew open. With a wild look, he cast his glance all around the room. Then he turned to peer at her, his dark gaze still in the grip of his imagined fears. "What did I say?"

"Mostly, 'No!'"

"I was dreaming."

"About what?"

"About—about—who else is here?"

"Nobody. But your lawyer said he'll send somebody over to keep an eye on you."

Alan groaned again and put his hand over his eyes. "It'll be Gretchen. I know it. She thinks she's still fighting the Gulf War. She stamps around in her combat boots destroying the enemy—disinfecting imaginary germs. The whole house will smell like bleach."

Samantha laughed.

"Do that again."

"What?"

"Laugh."

The eager, boyish look in his expression touched her, but she only gave him a gentle smile while she brushed back his rumpled hair.

"I have to go."

"You would leave me at the mercy of Gretchen?"

She stifled a giggle. "You can cal. me."

"I want you to stay."

The seriousness in his eyes nearly took her breath away. "B-but I can't."

He sat up, wincing as he placed a hand over the stitches. "Tell me what happened last night—again. I know you went over it all in the car when you drove me back here, but my mind was fuzzy."

Despite his weakened condition, the intensity of his dark gaze reached out and held her captive. She lowered her eyes to break the power of that tie. "I wanted to stop in the church and just meditate for a while. I knew it would help me sleep. I figured you would notice that I turned off, but you didn't."

"I thought you slid on an ice patch and crashed into a ditch."

She cringed inwardly. "Sorry."

He reached out and clasped her hand in his. His touch warmed her heart. "It's okay. I should have been paying attention."

"I went into the church, walked up to the first pew, knelt there—and then—then I started crying." She had to stop for a minute, because she felt the tears prick at the back of her eyes.

Alan leaned forward and kissed her forehead. That tender contact brought back all the beautiful summer days they had shared on the marsh.

"I still love you," he whispered into her hair.

"I know." She could barely speak. Her voice came out high and squeaky.

"You sound like a guinea pig." His low, throaty chuckle coaxed a ripple of humor from her.

She took a deep breath and went on. "Suddenly, I felt a tug on my coat and Foster was beside me telling me not to cry, that he had just come to church to talk to Jesus and tell Him to fix things because he didn't want to go far, far away

with his grandmother and grandfather since they were
strangers to him."

"I remember you said something about him hiding out
in the choir loft."

"Yes, evidently he was quite cozy up there."

"But how did he get to the church?"

"A delivery van from the cleaners. He hid behind some
clothes. He knew about the truck and that it also stopped in
town."

Alan shook his head. "He could have been Federal
Expressed to Siberia."

They shared a laugh on that remark. Her heart lifted.
Now that the terrible crisis had passed, the relief left her
giddy.

A clock on the mantle chimed the hour. Her shoulders
sagged. "I really must get on the road. You take care of
yourself and keep in touch."

He reached out and gripped her shoulders. "Samantha,
something happened to me, but I don't think it was a dream.
I mean, I said that…but…"

"You hit your head rather hard. I'm sure it was a terrible
nightmare."

"No!" He raked his hands through his hair and winced as
he pulled at the stitches. "Sorry. I didn't mean to shout. I
think…I hope…I'm a believer again."

The shock of his words took her breath away. This was
all she had hoped for, but had hardly expected. Could it be
true?

He bowed his head and went on. "I realized that I was
completely powerless. God was the only option and…and I
prayed. Then…"

She clasped her hands together as a sudden gust of joy
surged through her. Though she had always trusted that the
Lord's grace could soften even the hardest heart, until now
she hadn't imagined the wonder of it. Almost immediately,
doubts darkened the bright hope that warmed her. What
would have happened if Foster had not been found? What if

Alan had prayed but had gotten no results? She forced her reservations to the back of her mind and closed her eyes to offer up her silent thanks.

She had to believe that this was a miracle. She had to accept that this was God's plan to win Alan back to his faith.

When she heard Alan take a deep breath, she opened her eyes. She found Alan staring at her in an almost frenetic way. She could almost touch the tension that suddenly filled the atmosphere, replacing the pure elation of the previous moment. His hands clutched hers fiercely.

"I want you to stay, Samantha. Please, don't leave me. Especially now. I need you."

She could not mistake the desperation in his voice. She felt the blood drain from her face. Her heart thudded dully as she pulled away from him. "You know that would be impossible."

"Look, I'm sorry about criticizing you when you tried to teach Foster about Jesus. I was wrong. I'm not working right now, but I do have a modest income from some lucky investments I made, so you won't have to work. You know I love you and I'll always take care of you—"

"You want me to live with you." A hollow note crept into her voice as dread stole back into her soul, and any semblance of joy faded.

"We could be so happy together. We get along well and though the custody battle may take a while to be resolved—" His brow darkened. "A marriage certificate is only a piece of paper. It has nothing to do with love! I don't ever want to go through a miserable divorce again."

His rough voice cut her with the cold edge of his words. It took all her strength to reply with a measure of quiet dignity. "You told me that you're a believer again. How can you make an offer like that in good conscience?" She watched him press his lips together grimly.

"All I have to do is have my lawyer draw up an agreement. You would have an income, and medical benefits—it's the same thing."

"No, it isn't." Her hands felt like ice as she clutched at her handbag and coat. She stood up and put a hand to her heart. How could it possibly be broken again?

"Clam Creek is my home. I'm not leaving it just to live with you, Alan. Not now, not ever.

He called after her, sounding frantic. She didn't answer. She slammed the heavy front door behind her, and hurried to her car before the bitter torment crushed her soul.

Chapter Twenty-One

The crocuses bloomed early, vivid purple and yellow flowers that clustered about Susan Mallory Lyons' headstone in cheerful defiance of the weatherman's prediction for more snow. Samantha had walked outside to the cemetery as soon as the Sunday service ended, foregoing the doughnuts and coffee in the basement of Holy Redeemer. She bent down and picked one of the yellow flowers. It was like holding sunshine in her hand, but it didn't cheer her.

"For see, the winter is past, the rains are over and gone. The flowers appear on the earth…" The calm voice of Deacon Bob disturbed her unhappy thoughts as he came up behind her.

"Winter isn't over yet."

"That doesn't matter. You did the right thing."

"What? Picking a crocus?"

"Planting them."

She turned to see him still robed in his deacon's garb—the saintly robe and sash. She decided he appeared even more pious in the apron he donned at Thanksgiving when she helped him cook all those vegetables. "Last summer, when I thought I would lose everything, planting those bulbs became my ultimate goal." She tossed the little yellow flower away. "I thought if I could just hang on until the fall, and plant the bulbs, I would be so happy."

"Do you know how many times Jesus talked about planting things?"

"No."

"There's a bunch of them—many, many passages all about planting and seeds—something everybody can understand." The trace of a smile crossed over his thin face. He leaned over, selected a purple crocus, and lifted it out of the ground. "What a beautiful miracle this is." He fingered the tender petals.

"I'm lucky the bulbs came up. I'm much better at propagating mosquitoes than I am at growing flowers."

"It all depends where you plant the bulbs. It has to be the right environment. 'But as for the seed that fell on rich soil, they are the ones who, when they have heard the word, embrace it with a generous and good heart, and bear fruit through perseverance.'"

"I know that—the Parable of the Sower." A small glow of warmth chased away some of the chill in her heart.

"Look at this perfect flower, you must have put it in the right place." He handed the delicate bloom to her.

"I guess so." The petals had the touch of the softest silk— such fragile things and so easily bruised. She regretted tossing the yellow one aside with such little regard. "It really is quite amazing. Isn't it? I dug a hole and dropped it in the ground, but God did all the rest."

"Indeed He did." The deacon beamed.

At that point Winnie rushed up to them. "Oh my goodness! What are you doing out here? Hurry up, we've got to get over to the fish factory soon. I just found out that the governor is coming to the groundbreaking ceremony, too. Can you believe it?"

"Since there haven't been any groundbreaking ceremonies in Clam Creek for at least the last fifty years, I think the governor has made a wise choice."

Samantha thought she detected a touch of sarcasm in the deacon's voice.

"They'll probably have reporters and photographers!" Winnie bubbled with enthusiasm. She patted her husband's shoulder. "I do think you should put on your suit, dear. Yes, a suit would be perfect, with that nice topcoat, and that wonderful felt hat."

The deacon's brows drew down in a frown. "I don't much care for hats."

"I don't much care for reporters and photographers." A tingle of apprehension shimmied up Samantha's spine as she remembered her last run-in with the media. "I think I'll stay home."

"No! No, you've got to be there!" Winnie glared at her husband. "Didn't you tell her?"

"Tell me what?" Samantha tensed.

"I was getting to it." The deacon tapped his chin with his finger. "Yes, yes. Now I recall. I think you're supposed to cut a ribbon or something."

Winnie rolled her eyes.

Samantha gaped in complete surprise. "This is the first I've heard of it."

"Well, Fish has been busy, but he never doubted that you—of all people—would show up."

That stung and Samantha winced. What a terrific friend she had been!

"Hmmm." Winnie peered at her thoughtfully. "I believe if I put that flower in your hair..." She stuck her hand in her coat pocket. "Look at that, I've got three hairpins. We'll add more flowers." She stooped down and snatched up two more crocuses. "Now hold still. This will only take a second."

Samantha restrained an impulse to protest while Winnie pinned the flowers in a clump near her right ear. When she finished, Winnie stepped back and admired her handiwork. "You'll look so much fancier in the newspaper."

Samantha stiffened. "Which newspaper?"

"Whichever ones show up. Why, there should be video cameras, too, what with the governor coming! I just can't get over it. Right here in Clam Creek!" Winnie hurried her husband out of the cemetery.

Samantha fingered the little nosegay of flowers in her hair.

...the winter is past, the rains are over and gone...

The deacon's verse came back to her mind. She couldn't recall where that particular one came from, but it sounded light and happy—like spring. Like she should be right now. She sighed and gazed at her mother's headstone.

"Mom, I miss Alan and Foster. It's like being homesick,

even though I'm home. I think it's because my heart is with them. Does that make sense?" She lifted her face up to the sky. Surveying it she found patches of blue peeking through the threatening clouds. *Heaven's blue.* Remembering Foster's words made her throat ache.

"I know you're watching out for me, Mom, but keep an eye on Foster and Alan, too, if you can. Thanks." She sniffed and turned her gaze back to the cheerful row of flowers. Her spirits lifted slightly. "Bye for now, Mom. I have to go and cut a ribbon. Honestly. Why can't the governor do that? He's the VIP, not me."

* * *

Alan and Foster walked away from the gathering crowd at the site that would soon be Fish's new depuration plant. Neither the governor nor Samantha had arrived yet and Foster could not stand still another moment. Alan spotted a sandy path through the grass that led to the beach and set out with Foster in tow to explore the shoreline. Spring had barely touched Clam Creek. Alan narrowed his eyes as a fierce wind blasted across the bay, whipping up foamy white caps and briny spray. He turned up the collar of his coat and squeezed Foster's small hand.

The miracle of being able to hold his son's hand in his was a blessing he would never again take for granted and he offered up a silent prayer of thanks. The darkness in Alan's soul had been conquered by Foster's unswerving faith. No doubt, the Lord had a major part in helping Alan to win custody. Through Foster, he had come to know Christ once more, and found far more than the strength he needed to turn his life around.

He now realized the great debt he owed to Samantha who had instilled the love of Jesus in his young son. He needed to thank her, but he couldn't help feeling anxious about seeing her again. They had spoken on the phone only once since their last meeting. He had called to let her know that he had been awarded custody of Foster. The conversation, full of awkward pauses, had been brief and painfully stilted. He winced at the memory of it. He had caused most of the uncomfortable silences because he simply didn't know what to say. Hopefully, this time would be better. Then again, it could turn out far, far worse.

Foster tugged at his hand and brought him back to the present. "Where are the hermit crabs, Daddy?"

"They only come here in the summertime."

"Where are they now?"

"I don't know."

"Maybe Fish would know."

"We'll ask him later. He's very busy right now."

"He looks funny."

"He's wearing a suit because it's a special occasion."

"He doesn't look like Santa Claus anymore."

"He trimmed his beard and got a haircut."

"I like the old Fish."

Alan sighed. "I guess you're going to have to get used to the new Fish."

"He and Miss Gregory are getting married."

"He told you that?"

"He said it ain't no secret."

"Don't say 'ain't.' Say isn't. Isn't a secret."

Foster's eyes clouded with confusion. He asked softly, "Is 'ain't' a bad word."

"No, it isn't proper English."

"Like lello?"

"Right. We say 'yellow' not 'lello' and we are supposed to say 'isn't' instead of 'ain't.'"

"Okay. I'll tell Fish."

"Why don't we look for driftwood?"

"Can I keep some?"

"Whatever you can carry." Foster smiled with delight and set off to search along the high tide mark, running gleefully into the wind. Alan lagged behind. He slipped his hand into his pocket and felt for the velvet box. He stroked the warm, soft nap. He knew he had to start off with an apology. He had not treated Samantha with the respect she deserved—ever. Though he had been ill and distraught during their last encounter, he should have realized what her reaction would be to his crass offer.

His mistake made the risk bigger this time. It might not be as dangerous as jumping off Talcott Mountain in a hang glider, but he knew if she refused him this time, it wouldn't feel much different than crashing beneath the shadow of Heublein Tower.

"Miss Samantha!" The sound of Foster's squeal brought Alan's head up sharply. He felt a steel band clamp around his chest at the sight of her. Alone, she stood on the beach facing the water in a trim woolen coat which only served to emphasize her slender figure. Her long, golden hair danced in the wind behind her. He squinted and thought he saw a bunch of bright flowers near her ear.

She turned at Foster's shouts as he ran toward her. In seconds, he reached her and she bent down to gather him into her arms. Alan's throat tightened at the tender sight. His grip strangled the small box in his pocket.

He hurried forward and nearly tripped over his own feet. Embarrassed by his own clumsiness, he felt the blood pounding in his temples.

"Why do you have flowers growing in your ear?" Foster's fingers bruised the delicate blooms. Samantha's light laugh tingled along every one of Alan's vertebrae. The magical tune sounded like a symphony to him.

"Mrs. Dale stuck them in my hair. Mrs. Dale is always decorating something. Today, I guess it was me."

"Daddy said we're going to live here! We're going to go to Holy Redeemer every Sunday and I'm going to go to kindergarten! And Daddy's going to work for Fish."

She cast a questioning glance at Alan. He found himself momentarily tongue-tied. He should have known Foster would blurt out everything. Well, not everything... He cleared his throat. "I bought one of Fish's waterfront lots. Foster loves this place and we hoped we could leave the bad memories behind us."

For a moment, she stared at him in stunned silence before speaking. "W-what a surprise." Beneath her tight smile, he saw the unmistakable signs of panic.

"I asked Fish not to tell you about it. I mean—I knew you might get upset...after..."

The tense lines in her face deepened. She stood up and took Foster's hand. "Why would I be upset? It will be wonderful to have another neighbor!"

She made an obvious attempt to sound cheerful, but Alan caught the brittle note of alarm in her voice. His own breath seemed to freeze up inside him.

"Daddy said I could keep all the driftwood I can carry." Foster's words brought a warm gentleness into her features that nearly melted Alan on the spot.

"Are you going to make a house out of driftwood?"

Foster laughed. "No! Daddy said we're going to build a barn for all my collections."

"Are you going to live in a barn?" Though she teased Foster with her question, the sadness that lingered around her eyes sent apprehension spiraling through Alan.

"No, we're going to live in a cottage."

Her gaze caught Alan's once more and fear spread through him like the chill wind screaming across the bay. He had made such meticulous plans, but every one of those details unraveled as he found himself lost in the mist of her eyes.

His mind went blank. His lips moved, but no sound came out of them. He tried to swallow.

Lord, help me.

In desperation, he drew out the box in his pocket. His fingers fumbled with the lid.

Foster tugged at his coat.

"Daddy, you have to put one knee on the ground."

Alan took a deep breath and nodded. Okay. He had practiced this whole scenario several times with Foster. He dropped one knee onto the sandy beach and continued to struggle with the velvet-covered box. The sweat on his palms stained the smooth fabric.

"Press the little gold button." Foster pointed to the tiny catch on the rim.

Alan's hands shook. He had never been so terrified in all his life. This was worse than jumping off Talcott Mountain.

The lid popped open. Inside, nestled in satin, lay the diamond ring that Alan's father had given to his mother. A fire of rainbow-colored sparks leaped from the gem and danced on Samantha's dark coat.

Alan stared at the dazzling lights and then focused on the ring. It had to be well over thirty years old and though he had it cleaned and polished, it had come from a less stylish era.

"Say 'Would you marry me?'" Foster coached in Alan's ear.

Alan moved his lips, but his dry, raspy words didn't carry over the sound of the gusts.

"Louder, Daddy."

Alan mustered his strength.

"M-marry me?"

"Say 'Please.'" Foster nudged him.

Alan lowered his head as the uncertainty clawed at him. From the distance, he heard the sounds of the crowd rise above the wind. The governor must have arrived which meant he had only a minute to finish his proposal.

...the fruit of the Spirit is love...

He loved Samantha. Completely. He had to try his best to convince her of his devotion. *Lord, please help me say the right words.*

A touch of warmth settled upon him and the pent-up words tumbled out. "Samantha, I'm sorry for hurting you and I hope you'll forgive me. I never thanked you for teaching Foster about Jesus, but I am grateful that you did. His faith pulled me through our trials, and brought me back to the Lord. I don't know how I would have survived without that." He didn't look up. He hesitated a moment, waiting for her to say something, but he only heard the rumble of the people in the background. Samantha's silence tormented him. Feeling dismal, he sought to finish quickly. "I love you and I always will, but I'm staying here in Clam Creek whether you marry me or not. But I hope you will. I'll try to make you happy. And so will Foster."

Foster giggled.

Steeling himself for the worst, Alan dared to glance up at Samantha. His heart nearly stopped as he saw the tears running down her cheeks. He felt as if a knife had pierced him. Still, he got to his feet, pulled out his handkerchief, and pressed the cloth against her damp face. "I'm sorry. Please, don't cry! I didn't mean to upset you!"

"I'm not upset."

He frowned as he watched her try to cover up another sob. "Then what are the tears for?"

"I'm happy."

Bewildered, he stared at her. "That doesn't make any sense."

"Yes, it does. They are tears of joy." She let out a sob and threw her arms around his neck.

Alan managed not to drop the box and the ring. He hugged her close and buried his face in her hair, but he still felt confused.

"Well, if you're happy, does that mean you'll marry me?" She nodded.

"She said, 'Yes!'" Foster called out.

A loud chorus of voices cheered. Alan felt the blood drain from his face. He turned to see that the crowd now stood less than twenty feet from him. Nearly the entire population of Clam Creek, plus the governor and his entourage, had witnessed his inept proposal.

Samantha's face lifted to his. Right through all her tears she started to laugh. "I think this means you can't ever back out of this."

Alan gazed down into the depths of her misty eyes. "I never want to."

Epilogue

Foster lay safely tucked in his own bed for the night with Goldie and Honey guarding him while Samantha and Alan sat on the couch in the family room of the new cottage. The cheerful blaze on the hearth easily conquered November's chill. Nevertheless, Samantha snuggled closer to Alan on the couch as she stared into the flames. Her husband talked of the progress at Fish's depuration plant and the plans for the modern fish factory that would be built in the spring.

Samantha loved the sound of his voice. They had been married for one month and sometimes the contentment she felt almost frightened her. She couldn't stop fearing that it would all vanish, like a dream, and she would be returned to her lonely life on the marsh.

Alan's arm tightened around her and chased away some of her anxiety, but not all.

Unexpectedly, he stopped talking and lifted up her left hand to stare at the engagement ring he had given her that magical day on the beach. The facets of the diamond caught the light from the fire and flung brilliant bursts of radiance about the room. Not a single corner could hide from the glimmery sparks. Samantha marveled at the dancing rays. Those flashing sparks were like their love. It was everywhere in the snug cottage, so tangible that it almost blinded her. But how long would it last?

"I was so amazed when I slipped this on your finger, and it fit perfectly. Do you really like my mother's old ring?" he asked.

"Of course I do. It's unique. Like you." Her heart stirred as she looked up into his dark eyes. How could he become more handsome each day, she wondered?

"I never did tell you about my dream." She felt him sigh deeply and saw the flickering glow from the hearth cast harsh shadows along the creases in his face. "Remember when you brought me home from the hospital after I had passed out and hit my head?"

Samantha nodded as a chill swept over her. It was a day she would like to forget since the agony of it still shook her. The memory could stab at her with an intensity that took her breath away. She might never have seen Alan or Foster again. She might never have known the joy she knew now. She cuddled even closer to her husband. She listened to the steady cadence of his heart. In him, she had found everything she could ever have wanted in a spouse. She thanked the Lord for him at least ten times a day, but she prayed just as hard that she would never lose him. Her trust in the Lord seemed to go only so far, but she kept working at gaining more of it.

"In my dream, I was sitting in the kitchen of the house where I had grown up when my family walked in the door and joined me at the table. The dream was so realistic. My father, my mother, my sister, and my grandmother all smiled and chatted—like we used to do, not about anything important and I was happy to see them. They all looked so good and I felt reassured that they were all right."

Samantha frowned and lifted her fingers to touch the scar on his forehead. It had become barely noticeable, a thin white line against his tanned face.

Alan took her hand in his again and kissed it. "As we sat there at the table, my mother took off her diamond ring and put it in front of me. She told me that I should give it to my wife. I explained that my wife was dead, but my mother didn't say anything else, she just sort of smiled one of her very gentle smiles. Then I woke up."

Staring at the ring, Samantha felt a funny tingle shiver up her spine. "But—you asked me to live with you."

"I'm still sorry about that. I was confused. Linda had died. I carried around all this guilt after her death and then I wondered after that dream if maybe I should have buried her with the ring—even though she had never wanted it. Our marriage had been a nightmare, and I didn't want to go through something like that again. But I did love you. And I didn't want to let you go.

"After you stormed out the door that day, I went looking for the ring. I practically tore the house apart. I couldn't remember where I had placed it. Finally, I went to the bank and found it in my safe deposit box. Alone in the bank's cubicle, I reached in and took out the ring. When I held it in my hand, I felt this incredible peace wash over me—and this *knowing*—it's hard to describe, but I knew the ring was for you."

Joy, wonder, and glorious hope surged through her. The Lord had wrought a miracle in Alan's heart, and in hers as well. Her fears faded with the truth of it. The Lord had brought them together. They were His and had only to believe in his awesome goodness. She lifted her lips to his and kissed him before settling once more in Alan's arms, content.

"However," he continued, "proposing to you scared the life out of me."

The idea that she frightened him amused her. "Am I still terrifying you?"

"Yes."

His smile warmed her right down to her toes.

"Fortunately, the Lord helps me out with some bravery now and then."

"How courageous are you feeling right now?" She grinned back at him.

"As if I could conquer the world."

He drew her into his arms and Samantha offered up one quick prayer of thanks before their lips met again.

~ The End ~

About the Author

Penelope Marzec started reading romances as a teenager and fell in love with happy endings. A genuine New Jerseyan, she is a member of the New Jersey Romance Writers, FHL, and EPIC. Her book, *Sea Of Hope*, won the EPPIE Award for Best Inspirational Novel of 2002. *Heaven's Blue* is her second inspirational novel.

Made in the USA